MURDER
AT THE
MANOR
HOUSE

An absolutely gripping cozy murder mystery full of twists

JEAN G. GOODHIND

A Honey Driver Murder Mystery Book 9

Originally published as
Death of a Diva

JOFFE
BOOKS

Revised edition 2022
Joffe Books, London
www.joffebooks.com

First published by Accent Press Ltd
in Great Britain and the USA as *Death of a Diva* in 2014

This paperback edition was first published
in Great Britain in 2022

Cover art by Dee Dee Book Covers

ISBN: 978-1-80405-598-4

CHAPTER ONE

Honey Driver, Bath hotelier and the Hotels Association's Crime Liaison Officer, was naked and wrapped in a sheet when Detective Inspector Steve Doherty, he of the three-day stubble and iron-hard abs asked her a pertinent question.

'Are you coming to watch me train or what? You'll enjoy the view. I'll be wearing shorts.'

Although the thought of Steve Doherty wearing shorts was an obvious attraction, Honey was as keen on sport as she was on Brussels sprouts, herbal tea, and early-morning jogs.

She wrapped her arms more tightly around the sheet. It was Doherty's sheet. Doherty's bed.

'Ah! There could be a problem with that,' she said while her mind searched frantically for a suitable problem on which to base the excuse.

He fixed her with the kind of look that stripped off her clothes. The problem with that look was that it was kind of like an X-ray, it saw what lay beneath — and not just physically. Mentally too.

'I thought you said things were quiet at the Green River Hotel.'

'Ah, yes, but when business is quiet, I can do stock takes — count bedding, count toilet rolls . . . That sort of thing.'

'So not interesting things.'

'No, but hey, how about I meet you at the Zodiac afterwards – once you've finished running around a muddy rugby ground?'

The Zodiac was their favourite bar. It was situated in an old cellar beneath North Parade, and was dark, atmospheric and rich with the smells of sizzling steak and garlic prawns. OK, so there was the risk of coming out smelling of grilled steak and fried onions, but the ambience was worth it. The smell made you think you had eaten; saved a lot of calories that way.

'I've just told you, I'm in training for the police rugby team. No drinking — well, only within reason and only after the game.'

'The *second* team. You're playing for the second team.'

'OK, the second team,' he said, gently prodding the dip between her breasts with the tip of his finger. 'But we're keen.'

Bless, she thought, her eyes all soft and gentle as she took in the apparent keenness on his face. What was it about team sports and big boys who should know better?

'I have to admit, the thought of all those hard naked thighs is pretty tempting. But the game itself? Hmmm . . . I'm not keen on ball games.'

Her reference to ball games brought a grin to his face that had nothing to do with rugby.

'I might have one drink with you afterwards.'

She grinned. 'If you've got any energy left.'

'Honey, you know better than that. I'm an energetic guy.'

Then it came to her. The mother of all excuses, one she'd totally overlooked. Smack went her palm on her forehead.

'I totally forgot. I've got an invitation to the Roman Baths. Cocktails by torchlight thanks to that estate agent I've been talking to.'

'On account of this country hotel idea? They must think you're loaded.'

'I wish. Dependent on the sale of the Green River, I've got enough to buy something. And I think it's a good idea. Don't you?'

The truth was that up until now her enthusiasm for attending the Bath Property event had been muted. She consoled herself now that there were free drinks on offer and no freezing her rear off watching men bash into each other in a muddy field.

The idea of moving to the country had been mooching around in her head for some time. She'd made enquiries of local agents, had brochures sent to her, spoken to builders and her bank manager, and asked her daughter Lindsey for her opinion. Lindsey had looked at her blankly, possibly because she'd been in the throes of polishing a Roman helmet at the time. The helmet belonged to Emmett, her latest boyfriend. Emmett belonged to a group who dressed up in Roman uniforms at weekends and reenacted ancient battles at agricultural shows. Despite the risks, he occasionally did a stint as tour guide at the Roman Baths. The risks came from older women who couldn't resist men in leather skirts. Emmett blamed Russell Crowe in *Gladiator*.

'You're dead set on this country house hotel idea then?' said Doherty.

'I think so.'

He looked at her. 'You don't sound too sure.'

'Well, yes and no.'

'That's indecisive.'

'I'm taking a leaf out of Mary Jane's book. I'm waiting for a sign.'

Should she stay, or should she go, assuming that Steve would go with her that is? Honey considered the alternative. The Green River Hotel had been hers for a while; the staff were loyal and never took anything that they didn't think was their due. Today being Monday, the laundry man would arrive to collect the soiled linen and leave the freshly laundered. The binmen would also clatter and bang their way among the rubbish, and it was Smudger the chef's day off.

Rooms and restaurant would be fairly quiet, Anna was manning reception, and Lindsey was in charge. What could go wrong?

'Uh-huh!' He nodded sagely, though a smile lifted one side of his mouth. 'Do what you have to,' he said, kissing her on the forehead. 'In the meantime, how about a little encouragement for the prop forward?'

His sexy look was all-consuming — and his reference to 'the prop forward' could be taken two ways.

'I take it the prop forward has finished sitting on the sidelines and is ready to rejoin the game,' she said, head held to one side.

Doherty smiled and hooked his fingers around the sheet. It fell off her in folds. 'Correct.'

CHAPTER TWO

There was something deliciously decadent about sipping cocktails by torchlight, doubly so when the venue was the Roman Baths.

The combination of flaming torches and the sulphurous miasma suited the occasion. Tonight this place, where top totty Romans had once been plucked, pummelled, and pomaded (and a few other things besides), was hosting a party. High-class local estate agents were footing the bill. Not just any old high-class estate agents, mark you, but topnotch estate agents, gold plated with knobs on.

These purveyors of property and land deals in and around the famous World Heritage Site that was the City of Bath were top-drawer. Rarely did they sink so low as to offer anything for sale below the half a million mark, and then only if the vendor was trading up to something more sumptuous, or had bought it for a student son or daughter who had since gone on to a trading job in London.

Prime properties were the name of the game; stately homes complete with helicopter pads, tennis courts, and stables were top of the tree. So too were properties where the air conditioning and heating could be controlled by a flick of a switch on the owner's Mediterranean super-yacht.

Honey wasn't looking for something quite that grand. For a start, she couldn't afford the price tag, and secondly she'd only just mastered the TV remote control, so any kind of complicated satellite-fed device was best avoided.

No. What she was looking for was a stately pile suitable for turning into a country house hotel. Due to financial constraints, it needed to be ripe for conversion. An established hotel would cost too much.

Basically, she was flirting with change, at the same time as doing a lot more than flirting with Doherty. Oh, and sometimes she flirted with John Rees, late of Los Angeles and currently Bath second-hand bookshop owner, too.

Tonight she'd turned up without a male escort; Doherty was off to rugby training. She smiled at the thought of it, wondering how he had the energy left for playing games with the boys after the time spent playing with her.

'Who'll be there?' asked her mother when she found out where she was going.

'A lot of people sipping Champagne.'

'Any names?'

Her mother, Gloria Cross, was all attention, her sharp eyes as blue as the business suit she wore. She had taken to wearing a business suit just after buying herself a laptop computer. The laptop itself nestled in a Louis Vuitton carrying case and she took it everywhere.

Her mother's views and use of technology had soared since launching her online dating website for the over-sixties. The site was called Snow on the Roof. Gloria Cross had declared her intention to stoke up a few old boilers when contacting the *Bath Chronicle*, insisting they write a feature-length article on her endeavours.

'People need something to do when they retire,' she'd declared to the baby-faced reporter who'd shown up armed with a voice recorder and preconceived ideas about the over-sixties. Her mother had strutted around like a media mogul — until she saw the headline: NEW FOR OLD.

The fresh-faced reporter had taken the angle of 'new venture for old lady'. Her mother had not been impressed — in fact she'd been furious, marching round to the *Chronicle* and leaving the editor in no doubt about how she felt, and insisting on a dressing-down for the reporter. The latter was nowhere to be seen, quite possibly hiding out until the coast was clear.

'Make sure you take your mobile phone and get a picture of everyone who's famous. Only the most famous, mind you. No minor celebrities from local radio stations and such like.'

'I don't think I should . . .'

'Oh my!' cried her mother, her excitement sparkling like chipped diamonds in her eyes. 'I wonder who'll be there. Are you sure you can't get me a ticket?'

Honey assured her that she could not. In all honesty, she didn't know for sure if she couldn't, but she was going to treat this seriously.

'Mother, you know I'm not into the cult of celebrity. I won't be taking photos. I don't *want* to take photos.'

So here she was. Not taking photos, but she was looking around, alighting on faces she knew. The result was quite surprising. Everyone who was anyone in Bath was there plus a few gate-crashers who knew someone already there who could get them in. She found herself smiling at people she'd only seen photographs of in celebrity magazines, in film or on television, or, wonder of wonders, one of the lesser royals.

A well-known Hollywood actor nodded in her direction as though presuming that he knew her. His smile was familiar. Then, evidently deciding he'd made a mistake, he looked away.

She tried to place where she'd seen him before. Didn't he used to be Captain Corelli (real name Nicolas Cage)? Didn't he live in a mock castle somewhere near Bath? On second thoughts, she decided she might have seen him at the Zodiac Club, whose secretive ambience and dark corners appealed to a wide cross-section of people, judging by how many tried to get in and how many were refused admission.

Yes, she mused, even a Hollywood star would want to gain entry.

Another American actor with a warm smile and a lot less of the blond hair that he used to have sauntered by.

Honey recognised him as one half of the seventies hit cop show, *Starsky and Hutch*.

'Hi,' he said, and raised his hand.

Honey responded with a handful of wiggly fingers. 'Hi to you too.'

He was saying 'hi' to everyone, and people were smiling.

The famous women in attendance seemed less sociable. Some were from old money and old families. This lot wore blank looks, as if not quite sure what they were doing there mixing with show business types.

Honey recognised one or two as having come into the hotel to dine. She knew their circumstances, Bath was like that when it came to gossip. The fact was that, thanks to taxes and family commitments, estates that had passed from father to son since Henry VIII was a boy were now up for sale, along with the history, the rising damp, and the dry rot.

There was a marked division between the two types of women attending. Newer money was blatantly brasher, the women sporting fixed Botoxed smiles, their firm boobs spilling from plunging necklines — the firmness no doubt thanks to silicone technology, all at a price. Never mind diamonds, firm boobs were the way to go. It helped if a girl married a plastic surgeon, as some there evidently had.

Honey weighed up the cost of the designer clothes they were wearing and decided she would still plump for a new bathroom suite for the coach house over fancy clothes. That's if the hotel didn't sell. She couldn't buy a country house hotel unless she sold the Green River. Still, it was early days. She still had doubts, but after her run-in with the man who kept model trains in his attic at one property she'd viewed, they were melting away. A certain agent had advised her that he had just the right place.

'The right place and the right price, though bits of it need a little tender loving care.'

She had a limited budget and so as long as the place he was offering had four walls and a roof, she had to take a look.

'So time is on our side,' she'd said to Lindsey, her daughter.

Lindsey had been pretty non-committal. 'Your life. Your choice.'

'Excuse me, I'm Clarissa Crump. Who are you?'

Honey knew Clarissa Crump was famous for having been married to a very rich man from whom she'd received a very generous divorce settlement. He'd been her third husband, if Honey remembered rightly, and before that there had already been two very nice settlements. They'd all lived and met in Bath. When it came to relationships, Bath was like one of those old-fashioned dances with an inner ring and an outer ring. One ring goes one way, one the other, and when the music stops — bingo, you've acquired a new partner.

She eyed the woman's stick-thin frame, bejewelled fingers, and bullet-firm boobs. Definitely the product of a surgeon's knife and very little food.

Not for me, thought Honey, shivering at the thought of it. I love food and I'm terrified of knives.

The woman's features tightened as she waited for an answer. Tighten a bit more and her carefully sculpted face would give.

'I don't think I can give you my name. It's top secret. Let's just say I'm on familiar terms with some *royal people*,' said Honey, lowering her voice.

It was a lie, but it struck her as amusing. If she didn't have some fun here, she might as well be watching Doherty running around a rugby pitch.

'Oh, really?' Clarissa lowered her voice to match Honey's. 'Tell me, my dear; is it true they inspect the muscles of their bodyguards before hiring them?'

'Personal inspections.' Honey nodded. 'In their underwear.'

'Oh my!' The face of the skinny woman with big boobs lit up like a Christmas tree. 'Oh, really. Darling, I wonder . . . I'm having a little gathering shortly . . . for charity . . . . I wonder if you could introduce me to one of these royal acquaintances of yours. I would be so grateful.'

It was no more than Honey had expected and made her feel deliciously naughty. No matter how high up the social scale and drowning in money, mention of a royal changed people's attitude; wealth and celebrity could be achieved, but royalty was something you were born into.

Honey shook her head. 'I don't think so. I don't think they could spare the time.'

If she had slapped the woman's cheeks with a pair of kippers, her look of sheer surprise, almost outright desolation, wouldn't have been anything as dire as it was now.

'Oh, my dear!' she cried, almost desperately. 'If you could bring pressure to bear, I would be eternally grateful.'

Honey shook her head again. 'No can do, I'm afraid.'

'Oh!' The woman looked totally dejected. One red-painted nail gleamed against her lips.

'Tell me, do you ever come up to town? Perhaps we could do lunch?' she asked, the skin around her eyes taut with interest — though it could have been an effect of the plastic surgery.

Honey had made up her mind that the last thing she wanted to do was dine with somebody who looked as though they ate just one tomato a day. Worse still, Clarissa probably sliced it into quarters.

Honey grinned. 'I'm pulling your leg.'

'What?'

'I'm pulling your leg about knowing royals. Nearest I've got to knowing anyone with royal connections were the people who ran the Royal Hotel before they raided their nest egg and moved to Malaga.'

She might just as well have said that she had bubonic plague. The woman's chin dropped to basement level before she turned tail and marched away, her tight little buttocks rolling beneath a sheath skirt designed and made for someone half her age.

It was no big deal to be left standing alone. The venue was great, the cocktails excellent, and the nibbles quite delicious. She spotted Casper St John Gervais, chairman of Bath Hotels Association who saw her and nodded briefly in her direction before positively fawning over an actor dressed in black leather trousers and a pure silk shirt.

'Come here often?' said a voice behind her.

The voice was immediately familiar. John Rees. This was the guy she sometimes fantasised about. Their relationship was that of mild flirtation. The serious stuff was reserved for DCI Doherty, though they still gave each other space. He had his career and she had her business. They hadn't needed to discuss the matter in great depth, just laid it out and took it as read. Even if she did go for the country house hotel, he would continue with his career. That was the way they were easy with each other.

She smiled and turned to face John.

'That's an old chat-up line.'

He shrugged, smiling. 'It's the only one I know, but I figured there was only one gal in the whole place who I fancied, so one old line would be enough. Do I stand a chance?'

Honey made the pretence of looking around too. 'There are a lot of good-looking guys here. You may have to join the queue.'

John looked around about and over her head. 'No sign of your policeman lover. Does he know you're out and weighing up the beef on offer?'

Honey grinned. 'Steve is on duty, and just because I'm on a diet doesn't mean I can't still study the menu.'

'I'm glad to hear it. If I stick around long enough, maybe you'll give in to temptation and gorge yourself.'

'Perhaps.' The possibilities were the stuff of fantasy, though so far she'd resisted temptation. They were friends for now, pure and simple. Sometimes she dropped into his bookshop, sometimes she just waved as she passed by. The shop windows were curved and glossy and through them she could see John Rees and his customers moving against a backdrop of book-filled shelves and old maps in ebony frames.

The shop was situated in a narrow alley connecting Upper Borough Walls to Milsom Street. The alley had an air of mystery about it — just like John himself. Rumour had it that John Rees was ex-military. He certainly looked as though he could look after himself — or anyone connected with him. He looked good and he smelled good, a kind of fir tree freshness and not a whiff of musty books.

There had been a time when John Rees could well have been on the menu. Instead she'd fallen for Doherty's edgier sex appeal. And all thanks to becoming Crime Liaison Officer for Bath Hotels Association. From the very start, Steve had been her liaison on the police side of things.

'Can I get you a drink?' John asked now.

She hid her half full glass behind her back. 'You certainly can.'

With nifty sleight of hand, she edged the hidden wineglass onto a handy table while John selected a bluish cocktail that had to contain Curacao; she guessed it had to contain vodka too.

'A Blue Lagoon,' she gushed cupping the glass with both hands. 'My favourite. I'd come here more often for one of these.'

She took a sip. The taste was sweet on her tongue and sent a nice fuzzy tingle to her brain.

On her list of desirable traits in a man, John Rees ticked all the right boxes. He was tall and athletic rather than muscular. Perhaps his face was a tad too long, something to do with his beard, but in a positive way, giving him a wise, bookish look. The twinkle in his eyes seemed to be a permanent fixture.

'Gee. I was hoping you were going to say you'd come here more often if I was here,' he said.

'That would be another reason,' she conceded.

'Nice.'

'You haven't been around much lately?'

He shook his head. 'I've been travelling all over the place, buying rare books and maps, and even paintings.'

'Branching out?'

He shrugged. 'Just interested.'

John had the independent look of a man who worked for himself. Even tonight, when most of the men present were dressed in a tuxedo or a lounge suit, John had managed to get in wearing dark blue corduroys and a denim shirt. Both were old, a bit like his books, and just like his books, they had character.

She dived straight in and asked him. 'So how come you got invited to this? I wouldn't have thought it was your kind of thing.'

'One of those things.'

There was something in his tone and something in the way that he looked abruptly away that made her think there was more to it.

'Another drink?' he asked, changing the subject.

She looked down into her empty glass. 'My God, am I that bored? Not with you, John,' she said quickly on seeing his raised eyebrows. Heaven forbid. 'It's just that when someone here does speak to me only to find I'm not famous, they wander off to pastures new'

'They don't know what they're missing.'

His voice was deep. His hand was gentle as he tucked a stray strand of hair behind her ear. It felt good and she felt mushy as she watched him ease through the crowds to fetch another drink. Out of the corner of her eye she saw another woman watching him; a blonde who seemed vaguely familiar. On seeing that she in turn was being watched, the woman glared at her briefly then looked away. Honey was intrigued.

John came back and pressed another Blue Lagoon into her hand.

Honey thanked him, smiled and persisted with her previous question. 'So how come you're here?'

He nodded to where the same blonde she'd seen eyeing him was holding court.

'I'm a friend of her husband. He used to be a property developer.'

It seemed an odd reason for being invited. This gathering was about people who could afford sprawling piles and had the material trimmings to go with it. On reflection, she didn't quite fit the profile herself, John certainly didn't.

'And you? How come you're here?' he asked.

'Town mouse is thinking of becoming country mouse. I'm considering escaping the city and developing an old mansion into a country hotel – away from the maddening crowd.'

'*Madding* crowd if you're referring to Thomas Hardy.'

'No. Maddening. Hardy never had to deal with a one-way traffic system and droves of shoppers intent on spending their plastic. She looks expensive,' she added, jerking her chin in the direction of the pink-and-white-clad woman. 'A definite designer diva.'

The woman was dressed in a slinky white dress with buttons up the sleeves all the way to the elbows. From there the sleeve split showing tanned upper arms. Her looped earrings looked to be very high carat and her beige blonde bob was held back by a pink Alice band that matched a pair of mules with five-inch heels. Honey thought the night was a bit warm for the pink chiffon scarf around her neck, but then again there was no accounting for personal taste.

She trawled through the mental files of people she knew — some only very vaguely. People came in and out of the Green River Hotel all the time: guests, diners and staff. It was a shifting scene.

'Do I know her from somewhere?'

'I expect so. Arabella Rolfe? You may remember her as Arabella Neville. She used to be a television presenter.'

'Oh! Her!'

Laughter lines fanned out from the corners of John's eyes when he grinned.

'Most women say that when her name is mentioned.'

'Only most women? How about men? At one point I thought she was trapped inside my TV. She used to present just about everything.'

'Until . . .'

Honey's eyes met his. Now she had it. '. . . Until she came between a man, his wife, and his family. A very public affair, if I remember rightly.'

'Full marks for recollection,' said John his glass meeting hers in a toast. 'She had a very public affair with a married man. His ex-wife paraded their kids and his shabby treatment in front of the media. The public were turned off and their TV sets got turned off too. The ratings for her show plummeted to earth like an express lift.'

'So where is her husband now?' Honey asked.

'Adam Rolfe? Oh, I would say that they're going through a bad patch. They've had quite a few.' He sighed. 'Knowing poor Adam, he's keeping out of her way.'

'Any particular reason for that?'

'They've just moved from a big house to a smaller place and she's not happy about it. She doesn't do small and inconspicuous.'

'Well, it's a stressful time – moving house.'

She glanced around contentedly. The savoury smell of food, the tinkling of wine glasses and fiery torches set against the ancient stones, the statues and the rectangle of overhead sky, plus John Rees — what more could she want?

She told herself that the cocktails were the reason that their hands kept brushing, but deep down knew it wasn't strictly true.

The lovely evening couldn't go on, and it didn't. Her phone rang.

'The hotel,' she said apologetically as she flicked her phone open.

Any problems, ring me immediately. Those were her instructions though she'd stressed emergencies only. Hopefully the hotel hadn't burned down and the chef hadn't murdered a diner who had requested a bottle of ketchup with his meal.

Keen to keep John Rees in her sights, she answered automatically without checking who was calling — then wished she'd checked.

'Hannah.' Her mother's voice snapped in her ear. 'I've decided I wouldn't be able to visit if you move to the country. You know I'm a martyr to hay fever. And I hate the smell of cow muck. It steams in the heat. And it attracts *flies*. And I hate wasps. You know I'm allergic to wasps, don't you? And what will Lindsey do in the country? They don't have Starbucks. They don't have nightclubs either.'

Honey rolled her eyes. 'Mother. Nothing's set in stone. Can we speak about this later?'

'I think we should speak now. What if I pop round and gatecrash this little party? I could say I was with you and you've got my ticket?'

The thought of her mother arriving and cramping her style was far from welcome.

'I'm with someone.'

'The policeman?'

'No.'

'That's good news! Who are you with? Tell me and I'll tell you if I approve. In fact, I can do better than that. Mavis has taken to the Tarot cards. Mary Jane showed her how. She can read them for you and let you know might happen.'

'I know what might happen.' Of course she did. It was a mild flirtation. That's all. Well, perhaps not too mild. 'I'll get back to you.'

She quickly terminated the conversation citing a need to visit the bathroom and adding the lie that her phone needed charging.

Teetering on high heels over paving slabs dating back nearly two thousand years was not easy. The bathroom came as something of a relief in more ways than one, being of modern design and having a flat floor. Gratefully she incarcerated herself in a cubicle and sat there, head in hands, eyes closed.

She might have dozed if it hadn't been for the sudden slamming of the main door two or three times. The slamming was followed by raised female voices.

'Arabella Neville! Or should I say Rolfe! Darling, how is the sugar plum fairy? Still trying to get her career back on track and finding she's gone a bit past her sell-by date?'

There was no doubting the acrimony in that voice. Honey's eyes blinked open. The woman in the pink Alice band was outside.

'Quality and sheer professionalism will win through. The less gifted never stand the course.'

The answering voice was equally acrimonious and it was easy to imagine the painted fingernails of the pair of them curling like claws.

'Well, there's new blood on the block, baby. I've stolen your thunder. In fact your thunder's clapped out — just like you!'

'You flatter yourself.'

'And you're kidding yourself. You're through, Arabella. As they say, darling, every dog has its day. And you're one hell of a dog. I'd have you put down if you were mine.'

The woman addressed as Arabella responded quickly. 'If I'm a dog, then you're a bitch on heat!'

'That's rich coming from you, darling. Still paying that gallery manager to hang those atrocious paintings? I hear that in return you massage his ego — and other things. Does Adam know? Do you think I should give him a call, darling? Perhaps even give him a little sympathy — and anything else he might care to have.'

The chirp of a cell phone being engaged was followed by a clattering sound.

Honey guessed someone's phone had been snatched and sent skimming across the quarry tiled floor. She was all ears. This was real life drama, far more fun than a soap opera.

'I'm going to kill you, Arabella!' The voice was a screech.

'You haven't got the guts.' This one was a growl.

'But I do have the money to get the job done. I can pay. You know I can pay!' A more focused screech, an octave lower and charged with menace.

This, Honey decided, is the moment to butt in. 'Nobody's going to be murdered tonight,' she declared loudly.

Whatever else might have occurred was terminated the moment she pulled the flush.

The main door exiting on to the stone walkway back to the party slammed behind the pair of them. Neither woman wanted to be identified, though one was definitely Arabella Rolfe. The other just wanted her dead.

CHAPTER THREE

Coffee untouched, Adam Rolfe looked across at his eldest child, Dominic, and felt instant regret.

'I'm sorry I haven't been there for you . . .'

'You don't say.'

Dominic's tone dripped like acid. He tossed his overlong hair back from his face, his fringe, long, silky, and flicking up at the edges, failed to hide the look of contempt in his eyes.

Adam was unnerved. He stared down into his now cold coffee and uneaten meal; the noise of Café Rouge in Milsom Street all around them, people chatting over chilled wine, hot meals or steaming coffee; waiters darting between tables, scribbling on little pads, smiling and being pleasant.

Despite being surrounded by this bustle, all these people and all this noise, Adam Rolfe felt terribly alone and guilty as hell.

His eldest son was eighteen and had possibly been hit the hardest by Adam leaving his mother for the glitzy, glamorous Arabella.

His guilt had grown of late, possibly because the flames of passion between him and his second wife weren't quite what they had been. And he'd realised that basically, she was a selfish bitch.

Deep down he loved his son and felt compelled to try again to win him round in any way he could. He adopted a bright smile. 'But I can visit you at uni — if you want me to.'

Even to his own ears the offer sounded weak and dependent on how much force Arabella applied when she learned of his offer. She hated him going anywhere without her, especially family things, events she usually persuaded him to steer clear of. If she couldn't or wouldn't go, then he didn't get to go either.

Dominic looked at him, eyes dark with accusation and a maturity Adam had never noticed before.

'If *she* allows it. Let's face it, Dad, she's the one wearing the trousers in your relationship. She can't stand having us around. On the rare occasions *Her Majesty* does allow us to visit it's by appointment only and booked three weeks in advance. Can you even remember the last time we spent Christmas together?'

Adam flinched. The dark eyes in a pale face reminded him of the look Susan had given him when he'd told her he was leaving her and the kids for television's golden girl.

Arabella was warned that her career could be affected, her sugary, girl-next-door image tarnished for ever. But Arabella would have none of it, convinced that she could have it all — anything she wanted — and that included him. At the time he'd been flattered to think that she was risking everything for love — for him.

When the affair became public knowledge, the television company told her to end it, pronto. Full of her own self-importance, Arabella had refused to listen, citing her viewing figures and the tons of fan mail she received each week.

Hopelessly beguiled, Adam had deserted his children and divorced his wife. The wedding photographs had spread over two full pages of a celebrity magazine for which a hefty fee had been paid, both by the magazine and the purveyors of an upmarket ice cream brand.

That centre spread had been the height of their relationship, though neither of them had grasped that at the time.

They should have seen the warning signs, the vitriolic letters from outraged viewers calling her a marriage-wrecker, a slut with no scruples and no heart.

The 'have it all' couple had experienced the big wedding, the big publicity bash, and a tasty cheque to match. After that it was downhill all the way. The television company dropped her. Her career suffered and so had their relationship. Arabella insisted that the children make an appointment to visit: '*In case their presence clashes with my career and our personal arrangements.*'

Even now he found himself making excuses for her.

'She gets very nervous around children . . .'

Dominic's jaw stiffened. 'Dad, it may have slipped your notice, but I'm three inches taller than you and am not a child. She wants to keep us apart. The selfish cow wants you to forget we exist.'

'Perhaps once we're settled at the new place . . .'

'Get real!'

A woman at the next table turned her head at the sound of Dominic's raised voice.

Adam slumped in his chair feeling as though the stuffing had been knocked out of him along with the last lingering belief that Arabella was the love of his life.

He'd come in here with a spring in his step, nervously looking forward to sharing Dominic's excitement before he set off for Leicester. Instead, Dominic had pointed out what he knew deep down to be the truth about himself and his marriage. His son had made him feel weak and ineffective, and he hadn't finished talking yet.

Half rising up from his chair, Dominic leaned forward.

'And don't bother to lecture me about putting booze and birds before my studies. Let's face it, Dad, you've got no right to lecture me on that score. Anyway, I'm far more responsible than that.'

Adam watched his son stalk off down Milsom Street, feeling oddly grateful that he'd at least been allowed to pay the bill; a little gratifying, feeling he was giving his son something, though very little. Too little too late.

Arriving home, he closed the front door with Dominic's stirring outburst still ringing in his ears.

The eighteenth-century mansion echoed more loudly than usual to the fall of his footsteps over the marble floor. Most of the furniture was already moved out. What remained was in boxes ready for the removal men to take it to their new place, a second-floor apartment in the Royal Crescent. The place sounded empty. He felt pretty much the same way.

Due to the cost of maintaining the mansion, his idea had been to downsize financially as well as moving to a smaller place.

'*We only need an apartment*,' he'd said to her. That was after he'd told her that his property development company had gone belly up. The bank had repossessed the mansion, hence the true reason they had to move out, and not because they wanted a slice of city culture, the excuse Arabella trotted out as being the reason for their move. Not that it was a big secret. News travelled fast in the small but perfectly formed city of Bath.

Arabella had insisted that if they were to live in a rabbit hutch it had to be an upmarket rabbit hutch, the Royal Crescent no less.

He'd saved little financially from the intended move, though he'd badly needed to. But Arabella would have her own way. She had no intention of downsizing her inflated ego and upmarket status. And so, under pressure and prolonged silence on her part, he'd caved in.

Wandering from room to room, intrigued that the house that had once been home echoed with the silence of emptiness. He'd expected her to be here, but she wasn't.

In the kitchen he found a box containing a few bottles; all that remained of their impressively stocked cellar. There was just one bottle of cold white wine amongst the red.

He poured himself a large measure and knocked it back. His meeting with Dominic had stirred something buried deep inside him. It was the look in his son's eyes, the hurt he'd always denied existed for her sake — because it would upset Arabella and he loved Arabella, or at least he used to.

Within minutes one glass followed another and soon there was only a third left in the bottle.

'Oh well,' he murmured with a sigh of resignation. 'Mustn't let it go off.'

He poured another glass, gulped, and gulped again. He didn't usually drink so quickly but he had to face his wife when she got home. He was going to tell her about meeting Dominic today, and that he would be visiting him at university no matter what she said.

He paced the kitchen as he thought it through. Yes. That's what he would say first. After that . . .

His courage began to melt like cold ice cream on a hot day. This wouldn't do. It wouldn't do at all.

Pausing before a white-throated cymbidium that had grown too big for its pot, he took a series of deep breaths.

'Now look here, Arabella,' he said, addressing the profusion of cerise coloured flowers. 'They're my children and I insist they come to visit me at our new address. You can always go out if you don't want to see them.'

His voice was strong. But then, he was there all alone and the orchid he was staring down wasn't likely to retaliate.

Well, you could invite them without her knowing,' he said out loud. 'How about sending her away for the weekend? Somewhere luxurious and suitably expensive. A health spa or something?'

He sighed. 'Shame it would only be temporary, Adam old chap.'

The sound of the front door slamming caused him to jump. Wine slopped from his glass.

'Adam?'

Her voice rose like a perennial question mark at the end of his name. It made him feel as though a cheese grater was being dragged down his spine.

'I'm in here,' he called back.

Steeled to what he had to do, he walked out of the kitchen door, the last of the wine crystal clear in his glass.

Her eyes went straight to it.

'You're drunk.'

'I'm celebrating. Dominic's got a place at Leicester University. Did I tell you that?'

His courage began to waver but he managed a weak smile.

Her eyes narrowed and the corners of her mouth turned downwards. Deep lines appeared from jowls to chin. Like a puppet mouth, hinged on rivets, he thought and almost dared voice what he was thinking. He gulped more wine, his double agent antidote to fear and loathing.

'I saw him today. We went for lunch.'

Her eyes flashed accusingly. 'You didn't tell me you were seeing him.'

He blinked nervously. He'd never been much of a rebel — at least not with her. In an alter life, Arabella would have made a good dominatrix; she had the right manner for it. A leather bustier and high-heeled boots, and hey presto . . . a vision of her wielding a bull whip popped into his mind.

The bubble burst quickly. She looked aghast, as though he'd slapped her.

'You didn't tell me.'

'I didn't think you'd be interested.'

'Of course I am. I'm your wife. I expect you to tell me things first.'

His throat went dry and his palms were moist, but somehow he found the words, words he should have voiced years ago.

'Dominic is my son. You just have to accept that. It's certainly time you did.'

'I'll do no such thing!' She had a face like thunder.

He careered on like a horseless cart heading downhill without the benefit of a brake.

'I'm going to invite my children around to the new place for a housewarming.'

'Like hell you are!'

'Why not? They're my children.'

'It's my home. Not theirs.' Her voice was cold, her jaw stiff as steel.

'It's mine too, just like they are.'

Her bottom lip curled outwards. Her eyes seemed to sink back into their sockets like torpedoes getting ready to fire.

Adam felt the knot of fear in his stomach tighten some more.

'If you insist on this, Adam, then I will leave. Take your choice. Me or your brats!'

It seemed as though all his bravado drained down to his toes. Suddenly he wanted to compromise, make her happy again, and assure her that everything was as she wanted it.

'Arabella, darling . . .'

She shook off the reassuring hand that he placed on her arm.

'Get your grubby paw off me.'

He withdrew like a man with burned fingertips. 'You never used to say that.'

'Well, I'm saying it now,' she growled, an ugly redness creeping up her neck and over her face. 'I have no desire to welcome your disgusting whelps into our new home. And if you know what's good for you . . .'

Disgusting whelps . . .?

The words burned into his brain. The years of verbal lashings, the trailing along in the wake of a woman growing more selfish with the years, were finally too much to bear. He barely heard what came after because something had snapped deep inside him.

Suddenly Arabella was spluttering and gasping. He saw his hands wrapped around her throat, her bulging eyes, the flashing rings on her fingers as she fought to loosen his grip.

The next thing he knew was that he was banging on the door of a good friend, one to whom he could confess his terrible sin.

CHAPTER FOUR

Honey Driver blinked her eyes open and looked up at the ceiling. A moth, or was it a butterfly, was fluttering about the ceiling before making a dive for the window and daylight.

Her phone rang, she checked the number, saw it was Doherty and answered.

'Honey,' he said.

'Stevie. Any bumps and bruises?'

'Here and there and in very private places. I'll show you later. Ouch . . .'

She grinned into the phone. 'That sounded painful.'

'Just a twinge.'

'A little unfit?'

She could almost hear him frowning. 'I wouldn't say that. How did last night go?'

'OK.' She said it casually, as though the event had been so-so, and no mention of John Rees . . . 'Saw a few famous faces.'

'Any professional rugby league players?'

'Possibly.'

'But you wouldn't know one if you fell over one. Right?'

'I know what they look like . . . generally.'

After admitting that he was soaking in a warm bath and inviting her to join him, they made arrangements to meet asap.

'I heard someone threatening to murder somebody else last night,' she told him.

She heard him make the painful sound again.

'Tell me later. I need to rub something in.'

'Wish I was there.'

'Wish you were too.'

After ten minutes beneath a warm shower, her head cleared. Various thoughts trooped through her head like a battalion of chocolate soldiers, mostly to do with the night before.

John Rees led the march followed by the famous and not so famous celebrities, the woman in pink and the threat to kill she'd overheard in the ladies' loo. Threatening to kill someone had to be taken with a pinch of salt. People made the threat all the time. Most of the time it didn't mean anything.

John Rees had been lovely, though a little distracted, a little out of character. She wondered if he had a new love in his life; not that she was necessarily his old love. Nothing like that. Well, not exactly. There was, or had been, a smouldering between them. Then Detective Inspector Steve Doherty had come along. She'd made her choice.

'Still,' she murmured, 'just because you're on a diet, doesn't mean to say you can't study the menu. Or have a little nibble now and again . . .'

She called a halt.

'No. That's naughty,' she said, shaking her head and going back for one more pass beneath the shower head.

Doherty's invitation to take a bath with him, plus John Rees, and sex in general, had made her hungry. Passing through the kitchen, she grabbed a sausage, a piece of bacon, and a fried egg, squashing the lot between two pieces of bread.

OK, it was unhealthy, but it was quick to prepare and devour between people checking out and staff checking in for the day shift.

All she had expected to see in reception were guests checking out after demolishing a hearty full English breakfast. Instead, she found toilet rolls.

'They have just been delivered,' said Anna, their hard-working Polish chambermaid. 'I think there are many more than usual. They would not all fit into the storeroom.'

Honey stood open-mouthed. The toilet rolls, packed in sets of twelve, were doing a fair interpretation of the Pyramid of Cheops.

'I don't believe it.'

'It's true!' Anna sounded almost hurt. 'See? Here is the delivery note Leski gave me.'

Honey frowned. 'Leski? Our usual disposable delivery guy is called George.'

'George has retired to go fishing in Scotland. We have Leski. He is Hungarian, I think. Or Romanian. I am not sure. Anyway. He is foreign and he speaks very poor English.' Anna tossed her head, her expression disdainful of somebody who hadn't yet mastered the language of his adopted country. 'And I think he is thick.'

Honey studied the delivery note. The total delivered was printed in ordinary everyday numbers that anyone could understand no matter their origin.

'You're right,' she said to Anna. 'He is thick. It says here one hundred and twenty packs of twelve toilet rolls. I think we have at least one thousand two hundred packs.'

The manager at Mister Mops Disposables was a man named Bernie Maddox. He used to be self-employed before working for them. Honey was privy to his history and ready for anything he might throw at her.

Number one excuse, he was telling Honey that their new driver had got himself lost.

'In Bath? Do you wish to elaborate on that?'

'Why the hell should I? He got lost. That's it. Right?' His tone was brusque. Telling him the customer was always right wouldn't cut the mustard — and mustard had a big part to play in Bernie's history.

'Bernie. Calm down. I'm not asking you for Dijon mustard on my burger. I'm asking you for the plain truth.'

'You know me?'

'You shot a guy between the eyes.'

'It was only ketchup,' he barked back, though sounded surprised that she knew about the scandal attached to his former profession of hot dog salesman.

His hot dog stand had been situated in a lay-by on the A46. He'd never done that well selling hot dogs, beefburgers and beverages on account of his attitude to the public. Bernie didn't like dealing with the public.

'I'm just reminding you. I'm Honey Driver, hotel owner. I know how the public can get to you.'

'The customer isn't always right, you know!'

'This one is. Do your current employers know that you shoot people?' Complaints hadn't been tolerated at Bernie's hot dog stand.

'I don't use a gun!'

It was true. He'd squirted the customers with mustard or ketchup from a squeezy bottle.

'I'm good at slanting things a certain way, and I'm a customer. They'd believe me.'

A promise was made to remove the surfeit of toilet rolls. Honey put down the phone.

'Oh. And we have no metal polish left,' Anna added.

'I don't care. We can nip out for some if we have to.'

'I need it for the knives and forks.'

'One can is enough and last time I looked, we had about a dozen. Is anything else missing?'

Anna shook her head, leaned forward and lowered her voice. 'It might be Sir Cedric. Sometimes he carries a sword. Ms Mary Jane told this to me.'

Being stunned by the comments of staff and customers was a common occurrence. Anna's fitted that category.

'A man phoned,' Anna said suddenly before Honey had any time to impart advice about believing all that Mary Jane said. 'I wrote down his number.'

Honey took the piece of paper Anna handed her, expecting Doherty to have phoned. She recognised John Rees's number and looked at her watch. It was a little early for him to be ringing her. She frowned. 'I'll take it in my office.'

Her office was situated immediately behind the reception desk and was a world apart from the rest of the hotel. It held a fancy desk she'd bought at auction, a mahogany swivel chair and oodles of filing cabinets. Not that she acquainted herself too closely with filing. Lindsey was best at that, though these days the records were mostly stored online.

Honey did have a computer, but it was linked into Lindsey's computer and Lindsey ruled the IT scene. Honey was content to leave things to her. Besides, this desk, this chair, were NOT ergonomic. The word hadn't been invented when they were made.

Anyway, the coffee pot was on the go, spitting on a triangular table that fitted neatly into an awkward corner.

While the coffee gurgled, she returned John's call. There was no response from John's phone, only a 'Hi. This guy isn't here at present. Be sure to leave a message and I'll get back to you.'

'I'm just returning your call,' she said after the beep. 'Ring me when you can.'

* * *

John Rees heard the phone but was otherwise engaged.

'Don't you want to answer that?'

John Rees shook his head. Adam Rolfe turning up on his doorstep hadn't been too much of a surprise. Even a worm can turn and poor old Adam had been crawling along on his belly for long enough, but he hadn't always been that way. John knew the man as he had been and he'd changed completely when he'd met Arabella Neville.

He guessed who'd phoned — he'd called Honey on a whim meaning to suggest they meet, have a bottle of wine together, or just a coffee. Then Adam had called and everything changed.

Adam Rolfe sat with head bowed, shoulders tense. He was clenching his fists so tight that his knuckles were as white as his face.

'I nearly killed her, John, I nearly did.'

'But you didn't kill her, did you. Here take a drink.'

Adam took the tumbler and sipped the Glenfiddich whisky. Glenfiddich was the only drink besides wine and coffee that John kept on the premises. He liked it so he figured everybody else could like it or lump it.

Thoughtful and calm, John poured himself a similar measure of the same drink. He was recalling the night before when he saw Arabella wearing a pink chiffon scarf around her neck.

'It was so easy,' said Adam. 'Easier than I ever envisaged. My hands were around her neck, and . . .'

His gaze was fixed on the bottom shelf of John's wall-to-wall shelves. Even here, in John's flat, books dominated the room. Most were here by choice, not purely overspill from the shop as some would presume. His favourite books were here, lovingly lined up and dusted frequently. They included early editions of Dickens, Homer's *Iliad, Ben-Hur* and the *Decameron*. There were others he hadn't read, but their spines were delectable. John Rees liked books for their looks and their touch as much as their contents.

Adam was stiff with tension. John refrained from patting him on the shoulder. He feared that if he touched him, he'd fall apart.

'You've had quarrels before.'

'Not like this,' said Adam shaking his head. 'I . . . enjoyed doing it. It made me feel so powerful, so very much in control, just as I used to be.'

Hearing this made John feel very much the opposite of being in control. He knew a great deal about Adam Rolfe's past. People who thought they knew Adam didn't really know him at all. They'd be surprised at the truth, amazed that the clever but bullied man had once been far from that.

John had met him at a veteran's club, a gathering place for people who'd served overseas with the UN. They'd hit it off immediately. However, there were differences between them. Whereas John had coped with his experiences, Adam Rolfe had not. He'd returned a different man, one that the likes of Arabella Neville had twisted around her little finger.

John hated what she'd done to his friend but couldn't, wouldn't interfere. *Not my business*, he'd said to himself. Deep down he'd known that in time Adam would revert to his old self and just . . . blow up.

'Leave her,' he said. 'You know you should.'

Adam knocked back what remained of the drink. 'I'm going to. I have to, for one reason if no other, for the look on my son's face.'

John smiled and judged now was the time to pat his old friend on the shoulder.

'Dominic looks like you.'

Adam gave a little smirk. 'He's more like me than you think. I really think that if I don't kill Arabella then he will.'

CHAPTER FIVE

Dealing with guests, Anna, and the toilet roll pyramid brought on a resurgent appetite and a buzzing in Honey's brain.

She told herself that her need for food was based on her energy levels. She burned off so many calories that they had to be replaced on a regular basis. It was a good enough excuse and she was swallowing it — along with the food.

Sometimes she was sure there was some kind of ley line her feet were automatically attracted to. Think food, feet travel. She headed for the dining room. Breakfast was served both to residents and passers-by until eleven o'clock. Only a few passers-by came in to take advantage of this new idea Smudger had come up with, so there was plenty left on the self-service counter.

Honey eyed the rashers of bacon, the sausages, mushrooms, baked beans, fried bread, and eggs. Her mouth watered.

Lindsey was already there, dipping into half a grapefruit and a bowl of muesli, hidden beneath the servery.

Honey glimpsed the contents of Lindsey's bowl and skirted the healthy stuff, going straight to the hot plates ranged along the server, piling rashers of bacon and an egg between two slices of white bread. She felt Lindsey's reproachful look even without raising her eyes from the sandwich.

'Mother, that sandwich is very unhealthy and will do nothing for your diet except wreck it.'

'I need the energy. My sugar levels are so low I think I may faint.'

She wasn't exactly lying. Unless you're a director of a large group hotel, owning one means mucking in when needed. Take yesterday morning, for instance. Honey hadn't expected to have needed to step in as a waitress, but Dumpy Doris, whose shift it was, had called in to say she'd got jammed in a taxi door and was still recovering. Because of the excess baggage she carried around her midriff, hips and thighs, Doris was always getting stuck in narrow and not so narrow places.

Honey took the cowardly dieter's way out and changed the subject.

'Has Anna been sick again? I didn't like to ask.'

Lindsey nodded. 'I haven't seen her throw up yet, but I figured it best that she did reception and I gave you a hand clearing down all this lot. Doris won't be back in until tomorrow. She's suffering trauma on account of getting stuck in the taxi. Anyway, I didn't think you'd want her vomiting in response to the smell of a full English breakfast.'

Anna, their Polish waitress-come-receptionist-come-chambermaid, was pregnant again and suffering from early-morning sickness. The father was Rodney 'Clint' Eastwood, their heavily tattooed casual washer-up. He'd told Honey that the most artistic and ribald of all his tattoos were hidden beneath his clothes. He'd also offered to let her take a look. She'd declined. Anna had not.

Talk of throwing up pre-empted the appearance of Mary Jane, their resident professor of the paranormal who shared a room with Sir Cedric, a long-dead ancestor reputed to live in the closet in the corner of her room.

She came bouncing in, a picture of garish nonchalance. Just for a change she had jettisoned the usual pistachio green and shocking pink for a floaty kaftan scattered with random patches of peach and orange. Bangles of the same alternating colours rippled up and down her skinny arms, and large similarly coloured hoops dangled from her ears. She resembled a garish tent, the sort they use on campsites to camouflage the Portaloo.

'I fancy a little snack,' said Mary Jane. 'I'm clear out of rice cakes and honey. Have you any granola?'

Honey fetched her a bowl of organic muesli. 'On the house.'

'Thanks. I could do with that. I think I expended too much energy yesterday. I was doing readings for a couple of people who have enrolled for your mother's dating site. It's a little extra service she provides for them online. A little psychic forecasting so they know whether they're compatible with each other.'

'Does it work?' asked Lindsey.

Mary Jane stopped dipping her spoon in the bowl and looked indignant. 'Of course it works. Good pairings are ordained, not manufactured. Opposites may attract, but it doesn't mean they stay the course.'

Honey gave that pronouncement serious thought. She and Carl, her first husband, had been complete opposites. She hadn't known it at the time, but with hindsight she could see it plain as day. He'd thought marriage was between two people who lived together in the same house. Once you were away from each other, then you were single again. Simple!

Lost in thought, she jumped when a set of spindly fingers landed on her arm.

'I have to tell you about the Australians,' Mary Jane whispered. 'Did you know that I heard them creeping around at three in the morning? What do you think they were up to?'

From past experience Honey would usually have said that they were preparing to check out without paying their bill. As it was, they had paid their bill and checked out at the appointed time.

'Ghost hunting?'

Mary Jane shook her head. 'They didn't believe in ghosts. Said it was all a load of baloney when I mentioned Sir Cedric to

35

them and the fact that I've joined the Bath and West Country Ghost Hunting Society. In fact they looked at me as though I was out of my mind. Would you credit that?'

The odd looks Honey had seen on the faces of the husband and wife were now made absolutely clear.

'They seemed nice enough,' said Honey. They were very understanding about the toilet roll pyramid, though she didn't mention that. If she did, Mary Jane was sure to set some meaning into why they'd been piled up in that manner. Instead, the Californian septuagenarian fixed her with one eye, eyelid fluttering halfway down over the other. It was very disconcerting. Honey was reminded of a chameleon called Clarence she'd once seen in a pet shop. Clarence had been unnerving too.

'They weren't just here on vacation, you know. They were looking for someone. They told me so.'

Honey shrugged. 'People do that all the time. A lot of people in Australia have relatives here or lose track of them and want to reconnect.'

'I overheard them saying they'd kill her if they ever tracked her down. Of course, they didn't know I was listening. They shut up real fast when they realised I was close by.'

Honey agreed that it was a harsh way to treat a long-lost relative. Whatever must the woman have done to them?

Up until now, Honey's comments had been wryly meant and wryly delivered. On seeing Mary Jane's hurt expression, she instantly apologised.

'Look, Mary Jane. They're gone now; flown to pastures new. People say things like that all the time. I mean, how often have you heard me threaten to murder the chef?'

'All the time.'

'But I've never carried out that threat.'

Mary Jane sniffed and helped herself to more muesli. 'And you're never likely to. He's the one with the knives.'

* * *

Doherty called first thing the following day to say that he was fine, that having to be helped off the bar stool at the Zodiac Club the night before was due to it being too high.

Honey had suggested that it could be that training for a rugby match wasn't a good idea for somebody of his age. The comment had gone down like a cast iron bathtub dropped from a tenth floor window. It hit heavy!

'It's the way I was sitting,' he insisted, 'leaning over the bar, reaching for the peanuts.'

'Nuts,' said Honey, and left it at that.

He was still rubbing his back when they got to her place but straightened up a little when she suggested getting Mary Jane to give him a lift home. Mary Jane's reputation behind the wheel was known — and feared — by all. Taking the coward's way out, he called a passing patrol car instead.

'How's the team shaping up?' asked Lester, one of the patrolmen. 'Can I put a tenner bet on our team winning?'

Doherty assured him that the game was in the bag. They were cheerful when they dropped him off, though less so when Honey had to help him out of the car.

'She hit me,' he said laughingly, gesturing at Honey. 'Packs one hell of a punch.'

They seemed to accept his excuse and he did put on a good show of walking the short distance to the door. Once there his back let him down.

'Ouch!'

Honey waved her hands in the air.

'Not me this time.'

Realising his work colleagues were watching him, he called over his shoulder.

'Count on me, lads.'

Their expressions had fallen. Honey suspected they'd be swapping their bet to the other side.

'So, who are you playing?' she asked.

'The fire brigade.'

'Are they good?'

He shrugged, wincing. 'So-so.'

His expression said it all. She knew instantly, beyond a shadow of a doubt, that they were good. Really good.

'Steve,' she said gently, not wishing for any further cast iron baths to fall, 'Don't you think it might be best if you pull out of this game and leave it to somebody a little . . . younger?'

A second bathtub crashed from a great height.

'Honey, I'm good. Real good . . .'

'For your age, you mean.'

'Hah!' he said dismissively. 'Just watch me move, baby! Just watch me move!'

* * *

She did. All the way to bed, though when he got there and she was there with him, he did give a pretty good performance. But she wasn't a rugby team and he didn't have to run fast or tackle a wall of masculine muscle. But it was up to him. His game. His body. His pain.

CHAPTER SIX

Mary Jane was more wrinkled than a year-old crab apple. When she adopted her psychic expression the crows' feet flowed into the rest of her face — like a crazy paving patio that had shattered into splinters. This was a psychic moment. Craning her scrawny neck, she narrowed her eyes and peered up into Honey's face.

'Your aura's a little wan this morning.'

'Is it?'

'You know it is.'

Their resident professor of the paranormal reckoned she could read people's auras just by looking into their eyes. This morning Honey was fully aware that her eyes were red-rimmed and tired. But anybody could read them. The chef could read them and know she'd been out on a jolly the night before. The man who watered the window boxes could read them and know it. Next door's cat could read them.

'Wanna tell me about it?'

'I'm just a little queasy . . .' Honey began and patted her stomach. 'It was probably something I ate . . .'

Mary Jane tutted. 'Feeling queasy is a sign of being off colour — or being pregnant. Let's take it that it's the former, shall we?'

'The former. Definitely the former.' Honey fanned herself with one hand, the other clinging to a pile of cereal bowls. 'I'm too old for the other.'

As Mary Jane made no comment on that particular statement, Honey assumed her psychic powers weren't picking anything up to the contrary. Thank God for small mercies — or rather the lack of small miracles.

Today was the day for viewing Cobden Manor, a clear candidate for conversion into a country hotel.

It looked good in the brochure, all mellow stone, mullioned windows and mauve spikes of wisteria drooping in tiers to first storey height.

Grand gates opened on to the yellow sweep of a gravel drive, swerving through trees and acres of verdant grass. The interior shots showed large rooms with elegant wainscoting, lofty ceilings and ornate fireplaces decorated with cherubs, grapes and hunting scenes. There were close-ups of Wedgwood tiles and the details on the frames of massive overmantles.

'Grand,' she murmured, imagining herself as Hannah Driver, Lady of the Manor.

As arranged, Glenwood Halley, the estate agent, phoned to say he would pick her up from outside the Zodiac at two thirty.

'I'm sure Cobden Manor will tick all the right boxes,' he added in a voice full of rounded consonants and an Oxbridge accent.

'I'm sure it will,' she responded.

He was the guy who'd invited her to the cocktail evening, had paused long enough to say hello before darting off to fawn over some TV soap star with a big hairdo and matching bank account.

She patted the glossy brochure before zipping it inside a lightweight briefcase, one that could be carried easily under her arm.

The briefcase would lend itself to the look; it didn't hurt to appear as though you could afford a sheikh's palace even if your cash only ran to a dilapidated farmhouse, though she knew Cobden Manor was a bit more than that. She reminded herself that the particulars stated the mansion had undergone 'recent refurbishment', though a little finishing-off was needed in some of the outbuildings. TLC, Glenwood had said.

She selected something suitable to wear for a girl about to consider parting with well over two million pounds — if she could get the mortgage, that is.

'Looking good,' she cooed at her reflection. She noticed the hint of a midriff spare tyre and breathed in.

The outfit was businesslike, smart and smoothed over the lumpy bits. If in doubt wear black. Her trousers were black, her jacket a checked design of black and shocking pink. A set of gilded buttons vied in brilliance with the gold studs glinting in her ears. A pretend Rolex, a Liz Claiborne handbag, and a dab of French perfume behind each ear and she was ready to roll. The big bag was hardly high fashion, but it certainly had purpose. Phone, purse, tissues and driving slippers all fitted in nicely. The driving slippers were especially important; four-inch heels could only be endured for so long. If she got really fed up with carrying the briefcase, she could shove that in there too.

Dark hair tousled around a studious face, her daughter Lindsey stood watching her, arms folded and looking thoughtful.

Somehow it always unnerved her when her daughter looked at her that way. It gave her the feeling that some criticism was in the offing.

She spread her hands, dividing her attention between the mirror and her daughter.

'Is my slip showing?'

Her daughter raised an eyebrow. 'You're not wearing a slip.'

'You're wearing that look.'

'What look?'

'The one that makes me feel as though I'm about to take up lap dancing.'

Lindsey shrugged. 'If that's your aim, feel free.'

Honey turned and faced her full on. 'Something's on your mind.'

There was a pause. Then she said it. 'Mum. Are you sure you should be doing this?'

Honey pulled a face, looked herself up and down, and tried to make out that she didn't know what Lindsey was referring to.

Pointedly she looked down at her feet.

'OK, I know these heels are a bit over the top, but I can wear my slippers until I get there.'

'That wasn't what I meant and you know I didn't. I meant selling this place and setting up a hotel in the countryside.'

Honey sighed. If anyone was going to detect her indecision, it was going to be Lindsey.

'It won't be easy. I know that, but I do like a challenge.' She hesitated. Was Lindsey likely to move with her, or would she stay in Bath? Was it possible that Emmett, the tin man in leather skirt and thong sandals, would whisk her away to his villa — or whatever a Roman impersonator lived in these days.

'Oh, Lindz. If you don't want to move out of Bath, you just say so now.'

'I'm not thinking about me. I'm thinking about you. Are you absolutely sure about this? Are you moving on for the right reasons? Will it be better than this?'

Stretching her arms, she indicated the old coach house they'd done up together, the collection of ancient underwear behind sheets of non-reflective Plexiglas, the carved oak coffer, the twin table lamps, made of brass and Baroque in design, that had started life as candlesticks; all had been gathered over a period of time, bought on a whim, each connected to a specific event in their lives, only small events, but precious to them.

'I just thought it would be fun to have a new challenge, and this city — I'd like to get away from it. That man that came in the other day unnerved me. You know they're out there, waiting to wander in and ask daft questions or run amok with an offensive weapon.'

'No one has yet.'

'There's always a first time.' On reflection the first time of being attacked with an offensive weapon, could also be the last, but Honey wasn't going there.

'The truth is that you're undecided,' said Lindsey nodding sagely. 'That's good. Keep an open mind. Don't let this estate agent bully you into buying status. That's what people hope they're getting when they buy a stately home.'

'Come on, Lindz. You don't really think Doherty would let him bully me, do you?'

'Weigh it all up. Watch what you say, and watch what you do.'

'I will. I'll keep an open mind, but, and I only say but, if it all works out you'll still be my right-hand man won't you? You'll have carte blanche with the new bookings system. New laptop. New printer. The lot.'

Lindsey sighed and threw her mother a look that made Honey feel about thirteen.

'I'm thinking of you, Mum. I'm thinking you might miss the buzz of the city.'

'But all that fresh air, all that peace and quiet . . .'

'That's what I meant,' said Lindsey. 'No Zodiac Club. No sausage shop around the corner. No popping into the Pump Room for a quick coffee and a Danish pastry.'

Honey groaned. 'Lindsey, mentioning the Danish pastry is so unfair!'

And before Lindsey could say anything else to deter her, she hurried out of the door.

Steve Doherty was waiting for her outside the Francis Hotel. He was wearing his usual three-day stubble, clothes casual, jacket scuffed leather. Doherty dressed up for no one.

'I see you've dressed for the occasion,' she said with just a hint of sarcasm.

Doherty didn't miss a beat. He wasn't one for conformity or gearing his appearance to the occasion.

'And I see you look very smart.' He glanced at his watch. 'You're not even late. You're always late for meeting me.'

'It's not for you. It's business. You know that.'

He raised his eyebrows quizzically. 'And that makes a difference?'

'Houses cost money. Especially manor houses suitable for turning into a country house hotel.'

'Point taken.'

'I take it this guy hung on to you like a leech the other night,' said Doherty.

'Of course he did,' she scoffed. 'He's an estate agent.'

'Good-looking?'

John Rees popped into her mind. She tried hard not to look guilty.

'It was an eventful night. Did I tell you that I overheard somebody threatening murder?'

'You did. While breathing in the atmosphere of the Roman Baths? How dare they?'

'You're making fun.'

'People threaten to murder other people all the time, but never mind. Tell me again.'

'There were two women. I was sitting in a cubicle—'

'Interesting picture . . .'

'After having had a phone call from my mother . . .'

'I'd hide too.'

'I know that. Anyway, they didn't know I was there. But get this . . . one of them was Arabella Neville, you know, that woman who used to be on TV a lot.'

'Well, there's a thing. And there was me thinking you were blushing because some sexy guy was after your body.'

'I was not blushing.' She shook her head emphatically while eyeing the surging traffic for a sight of Glenwood Halley, upmarket estate agent and as glossy as a conker. 'Someone was threatening to kill Arabella Neville. That's all I know.'

'She wouldn't be the first,' said Doherty.

Honey looked at him in surprise. 'She wouldn't?'

'Some time ago she was attacked in the street by a woman. Somebody's wife if I remember rightly. Arabella Neville was having an affair with her husband.'

'Was she badly injured?'

He shrugged. 'Shaken up rather than running with blood.'

A cyclist pulling a kiddie car behind him pedalled along the gutter. His presence preceded the arrival of Glenwood Halley in his dark blue BMW.

He got out and held out his hand.

'Mr and Mrs Driver. How lovely to see you.'

Neither of them corrected him.

A heavy gold bracelet slid onto Glenwood's wrist as he shook each of their hands. His hands were cold and silky, his handshake just a trifle limp as though touching them at all was doing them some kind of favour.

Glenwood had elegance and breeding written all over him. His father had dealt in top of the range antique furniture such as Sheraton and Chippendale. Like the furniture his father dealt in, Glenwood was top-notch and highly polished. He wore a navy-blue pinstriped suit and his sparkling white shirt collar emphasised his glossy complexion.

Glenwood held open the car door and, with a sweep of his elegant hand, invited them to enter.

'After you, Mrs Driver,' said Doherty.

'Well thank you very much, Mr Driver,' said Honey, emphasising the 'Mr' and smiling sweetly. He patted her bottom on the way in.

The car smelled as though it were this year's model, straight off the forecourt with tan upholstery, shiny chrome, the navigation screen set into the dashboard. It was fastidiously clean, polished and well presented — just like its owner.

The early-morning rush hour had long cleared. The engine purred into life and the car slid away from the kerb.

'Traffic's light. Shouldn't take us too long,' said Glenwood. 'If I recall, you're interested in turning it into a hotel; is that right?'

'That's my plan.'

'I suppose it's possible, subject to planning consent of course. I have to admit, most of my clients buy country estates such as Cobden Manor to serve purely as a private residence.'

'I don't have a bank account in the Cayman Islands,' snapped Honey. 'I pay UK tax.'

He gave no indication of hearing her tart response but went straight into the sales spiel which was vaguely disguised as casual conversation.

'Cobden House used to belong to a famous television star. Arabella Neville. She's married to Adam Rolfe, a property developer. It's a lovely place, but became too big for them so they decided to put it up for sale.'

No way was Honey going to let him get away with half-truths and downright lies. Fingers gripping the seat in front, she leaned forward, her lips adjacent to Glenwood's ear.

'Mr Halley. How about we cut the crap and tell it as it is? Following the demise of his business, the property was repossessed by the bank. Mr and Mrs Rolfe have purchased an apartment in the Royal Crescent. The bank is selling the house, Mr Halley, not Mr and Mrs Rolfe.'

'It's come on to the market with a very low reserve, might I add. There's quite a lot of interest; well, there would be, wouldn't there, Arabella Neville being such a big star.'

He'd totally ignored her!

Astounded, Honey exchanged a quick glance with Doherty, her mouth slightly agape and a killer look in her eyes. Doherty, not being so personally involved with this property purchase as she was, looked amused. The outer corners of his eyes turned upwards when he did that — the Cheshire Cat look.

If her tongue had been a pencil, it would have been sharp enough to stab someone, but she reined it in, ever so slightly.

'Mr Halley, there is no way I am purchasing this house at an over-inflated price just because some blonde . . .' the 'b' word bubbled over her tongue, '. . . bimbo used to own it.'

'Arabella Neville was at the soirée the other night you know. She complimented me on how well I'd organised things and how truly exceptional everything was. She suggested I could organise something for her perhaps — a party, reception . . . something where high-class catering was called for . . .'

Doherty hid the lower half of his face behind his hand and pretended that the concrete bastions holding back the land to either side of the lower A46 deserved his undivided attention.

Honey could see his shoulders heaving. She knew he was laughing.

For her part, Honey felt she was about to implode. She'd had enough of Glenwood's spiel; it was like an elongated ode to some celestial goddess, though goddess was hardly the right description for Arabella Neville.

'I adore celebrity,' he at last proclaimed with a heavy sigh.

'I don't,' snapped Honey. 'I have a headache.'

Doherty was now watching the trees go by and the wide expanse of countryside that was momentarily exposed between the Doddington House estate and Dyrham Park.

The sleek man in the sleek suit concentrated on driving his equally sleek car, though that was never quite enough. Every so often he forgot himself and mentioned something about another famous person he'd had dealings with, everyone a vignette of how much they'd admired something about him personally, or something he'd done. His conversation always went back to Arabella Neville.

High walls and mature trees screened Cobden Manor from the main road. Gold paint gleamed from the finials on top of the double ironwork gates. Beyond, the gravel drive curved and was lost amongst the trees.

Glenwood excused himself, got out of the car and proceeded to unlock the gates.

'Honey . . .'

Doherty was grinning.

Honey shot him a warning look. 'Don't say a word.'

'He's a groupie.' He laughed. 'A fame and fortune groupie. I bet he buys *Hello!* magazine. I bet he buys every single celebrity mag. He's celebrity-smitten.'

Honey sucked air through clenched teeth. 'Never mind. It'll all be worth it.'

Glenwood got back into the driving seat. The tyres crunched over the gravel, a sound not dissimilar to surf passing over pebbles.

Honey caught sight of the manor itself and heaved a big sigh.

'It's lovely,' she whispered loudly enough for Doherty to hear, but not their companion.

As elegantly pretty as a bespoke dolls' house, Cobden Manor glowed in the sunshine. Birds were singing in the trees and pale gold gravel scrunched reassuringly beneath the car tyres.

'I like the sound of crunching stones being ground beneath tyres,' Honey murmured as her eyes surveyed the surroundings.

'Years ago it was peasants being crunched beneath boots,' muttered Doherty. 'I hope you know what you're doing.'

She looked at him. It had already crossed her mind that things between them wouldn't be so convenient if she moved out here. But she'd taken the view that where there was a will there was a way. They'd still see each other. She was certain of it.

'Nothing's set in stone,' she finally said.

Four marble steps led up to a massive front door set within a stone-pillared portico. A four-sided lantern of ornate design, studded with leaves formed from copper or bronze hung overhead.

Glenwood Halley opened the door with a flourish. '*Voilà!*'

Mahogany doors, their colour warm, rich and complimented by brass fittings, made a hushing sound as they swung open.

If Glenwood Halley was aiming to impress — which surely he was — he was going about it the right way. Well,

Honey thought, he would do. He knew all the tricks of the trade.

Honey stepped inside followed by Doherty, Glenwood Halley hanging back, leaving them to be impressed without the impediment of him doing a twirl in front of them.

Honey looked around, the sound of her high heels echoing off the uncluttered walls. Overhead clouds raced above a curved glass cupola. Honey was impressed. OK, it wasn't the Sistine Chapel, but who needed a painted ceiling when a moving vista of sky and clouds was passing overhead?

Doherty was standing with his head back so he could see all the way up to the top of the staircase and a glittering chandelier.

'And just two people lived here?' He sounded incredulous.

'I do believe they used to entertain a lot,' remarked Glenwood, his chin held high, his agent's particulars rustling in his hands. 'There is a helicopter landing pad to the rear of the house and a panic room in the east wing. There's also a squash court, stables and ten acres of landscaped parkland and grazing, plus an indoor swimming pool.'

Doherty exhaled. 'Couldn't do without it, could you.'

Carried away by his own enthusiasm, Glenwood Halley appeared not to notice Doherty's sarcasm. He was into his stride and nothing could stop him now.

'The panic room has its own air and water supply. There's also a fridge and drinks cabinet, plus air conditioning and a remote-controlled bath filler. The master control is in the main bedroom. I'll show it you later.'

Plans on how to integrate panic rooms and remote-controlled air conditioning were far from the forefront of Honey's mind. Was there a big kitchen and were there enough bedrooms to make the venture worthwhile? she instead asked Glenwood.

'Twenty-five bedrooms including those in the attic. The kitchen is Smallbone, I believe. Very beautiful. American light oak, I think . . .' He checked the details. 'Yes. American light oak.'

'That's OK. I can sell it on eBay.'

Finally, she'd caught his attention. Glenwood's jaw dropped.

'Stainless steel,' she said to him. 'It's the rules. Environmental Health wouldn't have it any other way.'

Halley looked shocked. 'Oh!'

Doherty shook his head in disbelief as he gazed around. 'They must have rattled around in this place.'

Honey imagined this hallway with its grand cupola as a reception area. There were high windows to each side of her. She imagined a curved reception desk in front of them. Having something made to fit the curve of the wall would be exorbitant and she placed it firmly on the back burner. She was bewitched, bedazzled and bewildered as to why she hadn't thought of doing this before. Who needed to stay in the city when there was all this fresh air, all this beautiful architecture to enjoy?

'The possibilities are endless,' she said breathlessly. 'I can just imagine a tastefully proportioned reception desk fashioned from American light oak, a trendy table lamp nestling in one of the arched alcoves, and elegantly proportioned armchairs and sofas . . .' She turned to Doherty.

'You could cannibalise the American oak kitchen,' quipped Doherty.

Honey shot him a look. He was being facetious, though poor old Glenwood didn't cotton on to that fact.

'Subject to planning permission, it should be ideal for what you have in mind,' trilled Glenwood. 'I can just imagine your guests, sunning themselves in the conservatory or swimming in the pool. I'm sure they'd be very willing to pay top dollar for such luxury.'

The main lounge had floor-to-ceiling windows where sunlight fell like blankets on to a marble tiled floor.

'Sicilian marble, I believe,' cooed Glenwood, tapping the floor with one foot. Adopting a searching expression, he held his head to one side, his hands clasped behind his back. Bending purposefully from the waist he addressed Doherty. 'First impressions, Mr Driver?'

'I couldn't live here.'

Glenwood's jaw dropped in disbelief. 'Oh!'

Honey jumped right in. 'Don't mind him. He's my minder. He minds me and my money.'

'My apologies,' Glenwood gushed, rubbing his hands together like some latter-day Uriah Heep acting humble in a lowly dark corner.

For all his upmarket sheen he reminded her of a maître d' in a London restaurant, lingering with the intention of getting them seated with as little fuss as possible. Some seat, she thought. Some price tag!

'Right,' she said, swivelling on her heels and looking as though she meant business. 'Let's see what the rest of the house has to offer.'

'This way,' said Glenwood, indicating the direction he preferred they should go in.

Honey set a slightly different course.

'Mrs Driver?'

'Let her wander,' said Doherty cupping Glenwood's arm and guiding him in another direction. 'She likes to get a feel for the place and she's best left alone to do that. Fill me in on the details. I'm interested in old architecture and the technical aspects of this place. Tell me what you know, and I'll store the information for future reference. I can then advise Mrs Driver accordingly.'

The fact was that what Doherty knew about architecture, plumbing, plasterwork, and electricity could be written on the back of a postage stamp. He was a copper through and through, and when he wasn't being a copper, he liked to chill out. He did not venture into the world of 'do it yourself', gardening, or interior design. Doherty's interest could be captivated by a large gin and tonic, a comfortable armchair, and easy access to the TV remote, especially when there was a rugby match on.

Swallowing the suggestion hook, line, and sinker, Glenwood Halley allowed Doherty to guide him off towards the east wing and the oldest part of the house.

'Possibly dating back to an earlier house of Elizabethan vintage,' he was saying.

So far Honey hadn't found that part of the house where refurbishments had not been completed. If there were areas in need of attention, the bet was they were at the back of the house. That was where she headed.

Leaving the more splendid public rooms behind, she found herself skirting the dining room and entering the kitchen. The latter was just as Glenwood had described it, the light oak dazzling, the work surfaces unscarred by a busy cook or chef chopping, mixing, beating, or rolling. It looked like nobody had ever used the place; it was for show only, something to be photographed against for one of the celebrity magazines, or the showbiz section of a tabloid newspaper.

Sad as it was, the whole thing had to be ripped out and replaced by commercial fixtures, fittings and equipment. The cooker was too small, the extraction system was there but nowhere near the standard required in a commercial kitchen. Size, she realised, most definitely mattered, and this kitchen wasn't large enough to take two Falcon ranges and a host of stainless-steel kitchen fitments.

Exiting the kitchen, she doubled back and entered the dining room. Like something out of a vintage play, French doors dominated the room, though in this instance there were four pairs of them. Three sets looked out over a patio area where bursts of colour fell from ornate pots. The pots were fashioned to ape the look of broken Corinthian columns.

The fourth set of doors opened out into a huge conservatory, with a vaulted roof. Empty of greenery, the brightness was blinding.

Narrowing her eyes against the glare, she spotted a fountain. It was made of stone and had a fluted bowl, each flute resembling a single petal. She supposed it was a lotus, though botany was never her strong subject; she'd always preferred biology.

Disappointingly it held no water, but she had once seen it working, full to the brim with water.

She hadn't lied to Glenwood when she'd professed not to have an interest in celebrity. Sometimes she'd passed time in her aching-feet moments, sitting and thumbing through an old magazine. She ran her fingers over the rough stone-work wondering how many show business people had done the same while house guests of Arabella Neville and her husband Adam Rolfe.

The magazine she'd read which featured the fountain recalled one very specific event, the event that had destroyed Arabella's television career.

There they were, the two newlyweds, posing in front of this fountain for one of their wedding photos holding a tub of the sponsor's ice cream.

Adam and Arabella had once entertained on a large scale. Their world had indeed diminished, she thought, overwhelmed by the emptiness of it all.

The doorways in the house were wide and deep on account of the thickness of the walls. The windows brimmed with light. The library lent itself to converting to a bar — or remaining as a library. Some people would appreciate it. The dining room and drawing room would have to form two halves of the restaurant/dining room. The guests she envisaged staying here would demand plenty of space.

Plans on colours and furnishings came and went. The dining room was nice, the drawing room nicer. From there she retraced her steps, then back in there again. There was so much to take in, so many plans to make.

Wandering from one room to another brought her back to where she'd started. Glenwood Halley's voice weaved its ways through the empty rooms like a stone rattling inside a tin can.

It was the sort of voice best heard from a distance, she thought. She could do without him wittering on and on about the attributes of the house and Arabella Rolfe. No matter how often she hinted that the bank were the vendors, he continued to refer to Mr and Mrs Rolfe as the owners. It was as though he simply could not accept that the rich and famous sometimes made mistakes and had feet of clay, vulnerable to the same vagaries of business as anyone else.

Glenwood grated. Retreating from his voice, she came across the servants' staircase. The old staircase had been painted white. The walls were white, the treads covered in carpeting referred to in the trade as seagrass. It was tough, rough on bare feet but very fashionable.

Like the ground-floor rooms she had left behind, everything on the first floor was painted white, or pale mauve in the odd recess she came across.

It seemed that when it came to colour, Arabella was not at all adventurous. In fact, she thought to herself, she was downright conservative.

Never believe what you read, she thought to herself. The magazine had portrayed her as a capable interior designer.

Arabella Has a Cool Head for Colour. That's what it had said — well something like that. But where was the colour? Nowhere.

Proceeding back to the front of the house, she found herself on the wide gallery overlooking the spacious reception hall. Half closing her eyes, she imagined how the reception area could be, crisply white curtains draped at the windows, vast sofas of pale blue brocade, lamps with shades the size of buckets sitting on white marble tables, the unhurried ticking of an immense long case clock, and streams of blue light rising up from recesses hidden at ground level.

She sighed. *What a wonderful hotel*, people would say. The Cobden Manor Hotel is the best place to stay in the whole area. A brilliant hotel.

Suddenly Glenwood appeared at the bottom of the stairs, the light from the cupola shining on his upturned face.

'Do you require my input?' he asked almost plaintively. His white teeth flashed into a smile. His face was too shiny, too perfect, a bit like the head of a wooden puppet.

'I'm fine. I've seen everything up here.' She folded the brochure into a manageable portion and tucked her briefcase more securely beneath her arm. She had no intention of rejoining his little tour. She raised the folded-up brochure to eye level.

'It says in the particulars that there are various outbuildings including an untouched annexe suitable for a variety of purposes — subject to planning consent.' She looked up from the brochure she was reading and eyed him enquiringly. 'Where is this annexe?'

A pensive stillness froze his carved features and his skin didn't look as shiny as it had done. 'You wouldn't want to go in there,' he said shaking his head. 'It's not really up to standard.'

Honey surmised what he was thinking. The vendors had stressed that all prospective purchasers should be accompanied. On the one hand he wanted to adhere to their wishes. On the other he was naturally wary of alienating a buyer.

'I won't run off with the silver,' she said.

His face cracked into a flashy-toothed smile — designer teeth, she thought, too bright, white, and straight to be natural.

'Of course not. I can see just by looking at you that you are a very trustworthy person. It's just that there's really not that much to see out there . . .'

'Because Mr and Mrs Rolfe have stripped the place bare?'

'No. No. Of course not. It's just . . . it's empty and kept locked. You'll need the key, and I'm afraid I don't know where it is.'

'Why should I buy something I haven't seen?'

'Well, of course, if you insist, I can search for the key, and dependent on me finding it we can all go together.'

'No need. I'll find it.'

He didn't look too pleased at her peeling away from his guided tour, but she went anyway.

Being a hotelier, she had a penchant for finding lost things. Guests lost things all the time, anything from expensive jewellery, to false teeth, family photos, and misplaced underwear.

The underwear was usually the easiest to find. Some was merely tucked down at the foot of the bed, flung off during a burst of passion. False teeth were misplaced as a result of memory loss, though a pair had once been found at the foot of someone else's bed in an adjoining bedroom. Sleepwalking was a common excuse.

At the back of the kitchen was a utility room. To the right of the utility room door was a cupboard and inside that cupboard a bunch of old keys hung from a wooden rack.

The largest key was about five inches long, made of iron, and big enough to use as a lethal weapon if need be. The size of it, and the fact that it was forged from solid iron, was slightly alarming, though not surprising. Only places that hadn't been used for years retained keys like this. The other two keys on the ring were similar in style though not nearly as big. There was more than one outhouse, she knew.

The group of outbuildings was located across the yard at the back between the main house and the stables. Like her private quarters back at the Green River Hotel, the annexe had once housed coaches plus room for the horses. What was now pleasant living accommodation had once smelled like a cesspit. The builder had told her it was a tip and that she'd never get it in order. Would this be a tip too? She stopped to toss a coin.

'Heads it will be an irreversible wreck, tails it will lend itself to be the best conversion ever.'

Tails won, but she went on anyway. Only a shrinking violet would turn back. She was more of a Valkyrie.

CHAPTER SEVEN

The biggest of the buildings was the most intact, though moss almost obliterated the clay-coloured roof tiles and a forest of cobwebs clouded the dirty windows.

Neither the door nor the window frames had been painted in years. Patches of dull blue flaked off like dried skin. Mostly there was only bare wood weathered to silver and rough to the touch.

She sniffed when she reached the door and wrinkled her nose. Something smelled bad, possibly drains. On the whole this place had nothing going for it. The rest of the house was top-notch crash pad. This old place had woodworm and giant spiders' webs written all over it. Still, since when had she been scared of spiders?

Taking a deep breath she tapped the big key against the palm of her hand. Did she want to go in?

Her feelings were mixed and confused. All that work of renovating somewhere to live. What was she doing here? Did she really intend buying it and creating a country hotel? Would she miss city life? Would the spiders really be that big, and would there be mice? She eyed the key pensively. It was big enough to bash spiders aside, no problem!

The key clunked into place. The door creaked open. The smell of dirt, dust, and general neglectful mustiness wafted over her; it was like being smothered with a dirty old blanket, one a dog used to sleep on — and had died on.

Swallowing a mouthful of dusty air, she stepped inside.

Just as she'd suspected this was mission control for spiders. Their cobwebs were everywhere; some hanging like small hammocks across the windows, clustered in corners, and all twitching with nearly dead flies writhing in shrouds of semi-white gauze. It occurred to her that the flies should have seen the traps. Surely the nearly dead flies should have signalled warning; keep away. Were flies that stupid? Obviously, they were.

The smell of something nasty was stronger inside than out. This place was grim. For all its luxury attributes, Cobden Manor itself would need some serious capital expenditure if she were to turn it into a hotel. And this place, this so-called annexe, was in serious need of being knocked down.

Think positive, she told herself. This place can be sorted and Cobden Manor does have some definite attributes. For goodness sake, there was a panic room complete with air conditioning and a fully stocked fridge.

But instinct was kicking in. Take the blurb in glossy brochures with a large pinch of salt.

She kicked at a clump of nettles, stunted and whitish in colour, that had made the bad decision to grow indoors, the seed probably dropped there by some burrowing vermin.

The main house was liveable. This place, glibly described as an annexe, was like something out of a Hammer horror film.

She found an old broom and attacked the cobwebs across the windows while muttering, 'Let there be light.'

Once that was done, she brushed something creepy off her shoulder, and took a look around.

At one time the building might have been used as a big old prep room complete with Victorian pine dresser, huge cook's table and pot/meat hooks hanging from the ceiling. This was where the butchering and butter making would have been done before being transferred in smaller containers into the kitchen proper. The far wall was taken up by a huge inglenook fireplace complete with oak Bessemer and a few dusty logs looking lonely in one corner.

She checked the agents' particulars. *'The adjoining annexe is untouched and retains a great deal of character.'*

'Along with the dust and cobwebs,' she added, flicking at a spider that appeared to be doing a trapeze act from an overhead beam.

The floor of red clay tiles was uneven and not high-heel friendly. Should have worn your driving slippers, she thought. You shouldn't have been so vain.

The fact was she'd wanted to look as though she could really afford this place. And she could! Couldn't she? The final decision lay with her bank manager, once she'd brought Lindsey along for a look before taking the leap. Lindsey had already voiced doubts. They gnawed at the back of her mind.

'What about the shops? What about your social life?' And what about Doherty, her own voice added.

She sighed and told herself again that no decision had yet been made. So let your imagination run riot. Take a good look round and do your research.

The inglenook fireplace was a big draw. She'd always wanted a place with an inglenook fireplace, a place of blazing logs in winter and a voluptuous flower display in summer. Its dark void cried out for closer inspection.

Her footsteps left smudged imprints in the dirty floor and sent beetles scurrying for cover as she made her way across the room. Something bigger than a spider scuttled beneath the dresser.

Mouse? *Rat?*

She didn't like vermin, full stop. Not even hamsters.

For a moment she held her breath and waited for the scuttling creature to show itself. Nothing. Hopefully the little critters would keep out of sight while she was around.

Another rustling sound came from behind her. She saw a pile of old rotting feed sacks.

Mouse! Rat!

As hyped-up as a sprinter ready for the off, she pivoted like a ballerina, though in her case she wasn't wearing ballet pumps. Moss and general dampness had made the floor slippery and uneven. The heel of her high-fashion heels snapped off between two uneven floor tiles.

She looked down at the floor. 'I do not believe it!'

Her foot was still in the main part of her shoe. The heel was stubbornly stuck between the tiles, sticking up like a lopsided mushroom.

There was no way she could balance on one leg indefinitely. Balancing on one leg was for ballerinas and skateboarders. There was also the price of the shoes to be taken into consideration. Heels could be glued back on, and at the price she'd paid for these babies, she sure as hell was up for that.

There was nothing for it but to get down and get that heel out. The floor was filthy but the price of the shoes kept her focused. Dirt washed off, she told herself. She got down and tugged too hard and tumbled backwards, hands, heels, and bottom connecting with moss and dirt.

'Sod it!'

Her shout and sudden movement sent whatever had been hiding beneath the rotting feed sacks heading for the fireplace.

Normally she would have rubbed the dirt off her hands and heaved herself to her feet, but something had caught her eye. Then her heart began to race. Her stomach cleaved to her spine.

She sucked in her breath and remained on all fours. If she'd been standing she wouldn't have seen anything but sprawled across the floor she could see a little way above the heavy beam that held up the stonework.

An expensive shoe hung level with the Bessemer of the old fireplace. To see a shoe hanging there would have been odd, but this was worse than odd. There was a foot in the shoe, and where there was a leg there was bound to be a body.

CHAPTER EIGHT

Honey was shivering. Like the estate agent standing next to her, she watched as the body of Arabella Neville was ferried from the dusty building and into the meat wagon.

Strange the other things she noticed; like the medical examiner taking a tissue from a box beneath his arm and giving his nose a good blow. Police incident tape was fluttering everywhere, like bunting at a village fete.

The ebullient Glenwood Halley was silent. His carven features reminded Honey of the stone statues of Easter Island. Since the moment the body had been found, he'd either simply stared ahead or asked questions of anyone who would listen.

'Who is it?' He'd asked the same question of Honey three times. She'd answered three times that it was Arabella Neville.

'No,' he'd said, shaking his head. 'It can't be.'

Just like her comments coming up here in the car, the responses were not sinking in.

Friendly fingers gripped her shoulder and gave her a gentle shake.

'You OK?'

Doherty was grim-faced.

Honey shivered and took a very deep breath. 'I've never found a dead body before — not a murdered one anyway.'

He smiled, only a half-smile but she appreciated its warmth.

'Take it easy. Think calming thoughts. Think about anything except her. Think of me if you like. I don't mind.'

His sentiment hit the right spot though her smile was weak. 'That might help.'

'Only might?'

His grin was swift though reassuring.

'You'll need to come into the station to give a statement. Are you up to that right now? If you're not, we can leave it till the morning.'

Shaking her head, she ran her fingers through her hair and gripped the blanket that some thoughtful soul had put round her. She'd never known that shock could be so chilling.

'I'll be OK. I suppose you'll be making a statement too.'

He nodded. 'Under the circumstances, yes. Him too.' He jerked his chin in the direction of Glenwood Halley who was now looking more lost than lofty. He had left Honey's side and was now loitering around the area between his car and the place where the incident tape was fluttering and blue lights flashing. He couldn't take his eyes off the vehicle taking Arabella away from the scene.

It had been some hours since the body was discovered. Honey had phoned Lindsey to tell her what had happened. Most noticeably, Glenwood had phoned nobody. He seemed in a state of shock of the kind usually suffered by the nearest and dearest of the deceased.

Suddenly he spotted Doherty and rushed over. 'You're a policeman. I've been told you're a policeman. I'm sick at heart, Mr Doherty. Sick at heart. She was a lovely person. That's all I'm saying.'

Doherty shifted position. Unless you knew him you wouldn't really notice that his stance had changed, that he was studying you carefully. But Honey noticed. Honey knew him well.

'How close were you to her?' His tone was enquiring though not piercingly so.

Halley never wavered. 'Very close. But she was married.'

Doherty looked at him then looked away. 'She had a husband. It's usually the husband that's to blame.'

'Is that true?'

It was difficult to tell whether Glenwood Halley looked surprised or intrigued. Either would have sufficed.

'It is. We weren't expecting quite such a surprise,' said Doherty. 'I hope it wasn't down to you. I hope you didn't lay it on especially on my account.'

It was a joke and although the incident was a serious one, in his experience Doherty believed a little humour helped lighten the load. Glenwood Halley took it the wrong way.

'I didn't know she was there!' he said angrily.

'Never mind. We'll be speaking to everyone we need to speak to. In the meantime, I would appreciate you calling into Manvers Street to give a statement.'

Glenwood's chin firmed up. 'Yes. Of course.'

Doherty stood squarely between the estate agent and his car.

'Just one thing, Mr Halley. This house is on the market for two and half million. That's a lot of bread. How much commission do you charge?'

Glenwood looked very much affronted. 'I'm sorry, but I really don't think . . .'

'How much?'

'Three per cent. It's a little above the norm, but we do give a top-drawer service. We have our clients' privacy to consider and we do place advertisements in very upmarket glossies . . .'

'I bet you do. It seems common knowledge that Mrs Rolfe — Arabella Neville — was not keen to leave this place. If she had somehow got the means together to pay her husband's creditors and stop the sale, you stood to lose a great deal of money. How do I know you didn't bump her off to hold on to your commission?'

There was no mistaking the sudden flush spreading up from Glenwood's ultra-white shirt and on to his cheeks.

'How dare you!' he spluttered. 'I didn't kill her. I had nothing to do with this. Nothing at all!'

Honey listened with interest. She hadn't considered the motive that Doherty was now expressing, but it seemed perfectly logical. After all, money was always a good motive.

Doherty was into his stride. 'How many buyers do you have for the house, besides Mrs Driver that is?'

Glenwood hesitated. 'One or two . . .'

'Specifically?'

Again that nervous licking of lips. 'There's been a great deal of interest. Cobden Manor is suitable for a variety of uses . . .'

Doherty persisted, edging that little bit closer so that their chests almost touched and Glenwood could see the glittering determination in his eyes. Doherty was good at passive intimidation. Halley had to cave in.

'Ten,' he said eventually. 'Six very interested.'

'I doubt I will need to question them but I definitely want a list of the guests who attended the do at the Roman Baths. Names and addresses. As quickly as possible.'

'Why? I mean, what do you want them for?' Glenwood's eyes were round with horror.

'Mrs Driver attended the Roman Baths event. She overheard a woman threaten the deceased. I may need to contact them. Plus the names of those people who have already viewed the property. I take it there have been some?'

Glenwood sucked in his breath. 'Well, yes . . .'

'I want them.'

'But our clients don't always handle a purchase personally,' Glenwood protested. 'Sometimes they use a buying agent in order to keep their identity a secret. Indeed, buyers of such a mammoth property without an agent are the exception, and they are usually trade and on a tight budget.'

'Ouch,' whimpered Honey.

'Their names too. The agents, I mean. Anyone who viewed the property fairly recently. Say two months. You do keep records of viewings, don't you?'

'Of course.'

'Then get them to me.'

CHAPTER NINE

News spreads fast in Bath. By the time Honey got back to the Green River Hotel, her employees and Mary Jane were hovering around, desperate to know the gory details, faces bright with interest.

She couldn't oblige them. She felt distinctly sick and was still shivering.

'She looks very pale,' she heard Mary Jane say as she let herself into her office.

She double checked the door was tightly shut before she sat down in her big old comfortable leather chair, lay her head on her folded arms and closed her eyes.

At the sound of the knob turning, she opened her eyes. It was Lindsey.

'Mother, you've had a shock, so I've brought you a drink.'

'If it's sweet tea, you can take it out again.'

After all, wasn't sweet tea the antidote to all shocks and traumas?

'I wouldn't dream of it. It's vodka and tonic. A large one.'

Leaving one arm curled under her head, she reached out, grasped the glass and knocked the lot back in one.

Lindsey perched herself on the corner of the desk. Honey felt her eyes on her.

She repeated what she'd said to Doherty. 'I've never found a dead body before. Not someone who's been murdered.'

'A once in a lifetime moment, never to be repeated.'

Hopefully Lindsey was right.

'I didn't like the woman when she was on telly, but I didn't wish her any harm. All I wanted was for her to get out of my TV set.'

'Well, she certainly did that — if you don't count the repeats.'

Lindsey poured her another vodka and tonic.

Honey eyed the glass stealthily. 'If I go on like this I'll be in bed before midnight. That'll certainly make a change.'

'It wouldn't hurt. You've had a rotten experience.'

Honey took a sip from the glass. The chilly feeling was leaving her bones, but something else was taking over. Unlike all the other investigations she'd been involved in, this one was personal. She was the one who'd found the body.

She pushed the glass away. 'Do you know what the worse thing is about this case?'

'Tell me.'

'I feel as though the murderer did this on purpose to upset me.'

Lindsey frowned and folded her arms. 'I see.'

'Do you though?'

'You're taking it personally. I know you are which means you're going to be like a hound after the fox until the killer is found.'

Honey nodded. 'Hmm.'

Smudger was next to appear, his golden-red hair flattened onto his head by sweat and the chef's toque he'd just removed from it.

'Hey boss. Is that right you found somebody famous stuffed up a chimney?'

'Arabella Neville's dead body, no less,' said Lindsey.

Smudger looked unimpressed. 'Arabella Neville?' He shook his head. 'Never heard of her.'

Footballer or pop star. That was the limit of Smudger's interest. He left and the door slammed behind him.

The phone rang. Even before Lindsey had picked it up, her mother instinctively knew that it was either Casper St John Gervais, chairman of Bath Hotels Association, or her mother.

The chairman of Bath Hotels Association made it his business to keep on top of criminal matters that dared to occur in a city as elegantly civilised as the one he lived in.

However, when it came to gossip, Honey's mother, Gloria Cross, was second to none. If anyone was ever to give her an apt title, it was chairperson and general news and gossip gatherer of Bath Senior Citizens Conservative Association.

'Hannah. I'm ringing you from Top to Toe TLC. You'll have to speak up because I'm having my nails painted in rainbow hues with gemstone inserts and Courtney has to hold the phone against my ear. The polish isn't dry yet. She dialled the number too.' There was a pause. 'That is you, Hannah, isn't it?'

Mouthing, *it's Grandma*, Lindsey handed the phone to her mother.

Honey rolled then closed her eyes. This she could do without.

'I'm here.'

'Oh, good. Now you haven't forgotten to buy the present for Wilbur and Alice, have you?'

Wilbur and Alice? Who the devil were Wilbur and Alice? Was he or she a relative? Were either or both of them old friends of her mother? And why was she buying them a present? A golden wedding perhaps? She didn't have a clue but hated to admit it.

'I'm sorry, Mother. It's been an extraordinary day. I'm really having trouble getting myself together . . .'

'You've forgotten,' Gloria replied flatly.

'Mother, how can you say that?'

'A *wedding*. The first wedding between two of my clients and you've forgotten! I'm hurt, Hannah. Extremely hurt.'

Honey slapped her forehead. 'Of course. The wedding. Wilbur and Alice. I bought them Champagne.'

'They don't drink.'

Her mother's tone was icy cold.

'Of course not! Silly me. I bought them . . .' She paused while making frantic sign language to her daughter. Lindsey waved a copy of the hotel brochure opened to a very lovely photo of the honeymoon suite.

'The honeymoon suite. Free overnight accommodation in the honeymoon suite.'

Her mother's response was damning. 'Oh, that's no good at all. They can't possibly sleep together! He's got arthritis and she's prone to night sweats. People have delicate bodies once they reach their eighties.'

Although tempted to ask her mother why these two were bothering to get married, she didn't go there. The details might be too lurid.

Lindsey was banging her head against the wall in mock exasperation. But she was laughing as she did it. Honey contemplated doing it for real. No hotel guest could be as exasperating as her mother. She made a career out of being exasperating.

There was nothing for it but to admit defeat and hope for forgiveness.

'So what do you suggest, mother?'

'A footbath. One of those that vibrates and aids circulation.'

'A footbath,' Hannah repeated. 'What a good idea.'

Honey nodded at her daughter. Lindsey stopped banging her head and sniggering. She made the OK sign and slid down in front of the computer.

'The wedding's at eleven. You do remember that, do you?'

'Of course I do.' She didn't have any recollection of the details, but followed the old adage, if in doubt, lie! Or make a shrewd guess.

'This Saturday, eleven o'clock, Bradford-on-Avon.' It was a good guess, but not the right one.

'No. This Thursday at eleven o'clock. Wear something suitable.'

'What's not suitable?'

'White. The bride's wearing white so nobody else may.'

'Just like Miss Havisham,' Honey murmured.

'I don't know any Miss Havisham,' her mother said suspiciously. 'Is she a member of the Conservative Club? Did I go to her wedding?'

Honey answered no to each question. Her mother had obviously never heard of *Great Expectations*.

Once the connection was cut, she leaned against the wall with her eyes closed. 'Wrinkles in white. It'll look like a shroud.'

'Handy if the bride drops dead at the altar,' Lindsey observed. On seeing her mother's expression, she apologised. 'I'm sorry. It was the wrong thing to say.'

Honey said nothing. A vision of a dead woman had flashed into her head. Her thoughts went back to the very dead Arabella Neville and the glossy photos in *Hello!* She too had been wearing a white dress, though her face was unwrinkled. Was her death a revenge killing for splitting up a family? Or was there something else going on here?

'Penny for your thoughts,' Lindsey said. 'You're looking dour.'

'I could really do without attending a wedding, especially a wedding where the bride and groom are total strangers and likely to keel over before they've even had a honeymoon.'

'Well, you certainly can't wish them a long and happy marriage — well you can, but it doesn't really suit.'

Honey sighed, her shoulders aching with the weight of it all. 'I was thinking about Arabella Rolfe née Neville. I bet she had a load of luxury wedding presents.'

'But not the ultimate wedding present. I bet they didn't have a footbath. Pink for her, blue for him.'

* * *

Later that evening, once the diners had finished dining and Mary Jane had read the last palm and made her way to bed, Honey phoned Doherty. She asked him about the preliminary results of the autopsy.

'Arabella Rolfe was strangled with a strip of pink material before being stuffed up the chimney,' said Doherty. 'Most of the scratches and bruising came from being wedged against the old stonework. The ligature marks were totally consistent with death by strangulation. She was also dressed to the nines and wearing sexy underwear. I thought I'd just mention that in passing.'

'Not quite the occasion she was dressed for.'

Doherty was in agreement. 'Women like to dress to suit the occasion. Dress to impress. We checked her movements prior to the murder. She was at a programme rehearsal but took off in an apparent tantrum. No one's quite sure why except that she did accuse somebody of stealing her handbag.'

'Wish I could afford her style. Did you find a bag with her?'

'A small one containing money and credit cards.'

'Not a receptacle, then.'

'There's a difference?'

'A woman of means needs a travelling office.'

She asked how the husband had taken it.

'I can't say. We can't find him. Looks like he's done a runner, which of course makes him the prime suspect. I'm interviewing some of his business colleagues tomorrow once I've checked out the possibility that Arabella had life insurance and he would benefit from her death. As far as I can make out, they kept their finances separate. He went bust; she held on to her cash. Not so much cash as him, but enough to keep them in smoked salmon and silk bed sheets.'

'Did they really have silk bed sheets? I've always wondered what they felt like to sleep in.'

'Something to be explored,' said Doherty.

'How about the woman I overheard? Any fix on her yet?'

'Not yet. I'm waiting for the guest list. In the meantime, I'll ask the work colleagues and the relatives, the ex-wife for a start. I've pinned her down to tomorrow morning. Care to accompany me?'

* * *

Arthur King told lies as easily as he told the truth. What's more, he told them with a smile on his face which was also reflected in his eyes. This in itself was very unusual. It made him that much more convincing, so people believed everything he said. That was why he was such a successful psychic, beloved of cable TV, talk shows and whistle-stop psychic fairs.

At present he was doing his best to charm the producer of *Fate and Fortune*, a new series being made for one of the satellite channels.

'I did a spot on *Most Haunted* and my books have done very well, also, my speaking tours have been sell-outs. Standing room only. Even if I say so myself, I'm one of the top, possibly THE top psychic in this country. You couldn't do better than to have me present the whole shebang. What do you say to that, Paulette?'

He heard an intake of breath, a sure sign of impatience. Paulette Goodman was the television producer he most wanted to impress. The fact that she was a total stranger to him was neither here nor there.

'So what do you say?' he added after pressing as much information in her direction as he could. This was the first time he'd ever spoken to her, but Arthur King didn't believe in letting the grass grow under his feet. He was first in, had got her mobile phone number purely by chance from the little pink diary he held in his hand. No way was he letting a good chance pass him by.

'I'll think about it,' said the young hussy on the other end of the phone. Anyone under thirty was a young hussy and in need of a good rogering, as far as Arthur was concerned.

'Let me give you my direct line and my mobile number,' he said. 'Is there anyone else in line for presenting the programme?'

He heard her hesitate. Arthur sensed she was holding her breath while deciding whether she told him or not.

'Well, I suppose I can tell you. It's likely to be Arabella Rolfe. She's well known and is looking for something like this to relaunch her career.'

The young hussy on the phone would not be aware that he was grinding his teeth at the mention of Arabella. Neither would she know that he hated her, though she wouldn't be that surprised. Arabella had never been the most popular of people with past production teams. She was one of those people who loved herself above all others.

'Ah, yes. I did hear she was looking to relaunch her career. There's no doubt that she's been on the slide for some time. But I don't think you'll get her to do it. I think in fact, you'll find she's unavailable.'

'Oh. What makes you think that?' Paulette sounded surprised.

Arthur King threw a small pink diary into the ladies' handbag he gripped between his knees. 'Just call it a professional premonition. It's what I'm known for.'

* * *

Doherty arrived early the next morning looking tired and scruffy.

'Too many hours,' he said gruffly.

'Here.' She handed him the key to a room plus a bottle of pine-scented shower gel. 'Take a shower. You'll feel better.'

He sloped off, bereft of his usual energy, just glad to be able to take his clothes off and stand being buffeted by a torrent of warm water.

'Won't be able to do that when we move to this country house hotel,' said Lindsey.

'I'm not sure . . .' Honey began.

73

'Good,' said Lindsey, butting swiftly in. 'I wasn't sure from the start.'

'How did you know what I was going to say?'

'You're my mother,' said Lindsey, slapping a pile of brochures down on the desk. 'You get an idea in your head that won't really suit, but you have to work it through for yourself. It's the only way.'

If Honey had had any doubts about her future, they were all done with now. Who knows what might have been? The fault lay with the murderer of Arabella Neville.

'It could have been good,' she muttered. 'Just wait till I get my hands on whoever did it.'

'Cream them,' said Lindsey, and went off looking a lot happier than she had for a long time. The funny thing was that Honey hadn't noticed she'd not been looking happy. Her daughter was right; she'd persuaded herself that developing a country house hotel was a great idea without really planning things.

Would have been an experience too, she thought to herself. Would she have gone for it? It was hard to say, though she thought it was very likely. It had taken a murder to stop her in her tracks.

Doherty reappeared smelling good though still looking dishevelled; shirt crumpled, jeans creased, hair clean but uncombed and leather jacket slung over his shoulder. The casual street cred look came naturally to him. It was his personal look, it suited him, and it suited Honey too.

He settled himself on the big brown sofa in the dining room. The sofa was usually used by guests enjoying an aperitif before going to their table but Doherty was lying full stretch, his elbow resting on the arm of the sofa, his hand supporting his head.

'You look as though you've just got out of bed,' she said to him.

'Care to go back upstairs and tidy me up?' This was delivered with a suggestive arching of eyebrows.

Before she had a chance to respond, he was on his feet, his lips on hers while reaching behind her for a piece of buttered toast.

'I'm starving,' he said once he'd set her to one side and reached for more food. The paying guests had already dined, but there was plenty left. Serve plenty of food, get no complaints. That was Honey's number one mantra for running a successful hotel.

'When did you last eat?'

'Last night.'

She frowned. 'Not healthy.'

Doherty sighed. 'Too much work, not enough time. I've been trying to squeeze in more training.'

'How's the back?'

A grin slowly creased his face. 'Fine, though a little massage wouldn't go amiss.'

She snorted. 'Eat your porridge.'

Only the two of them in the dining room, they pulled chairs up to the breakfast bar, helping themselves to what was left. The smell of grilled bacon overwhelmed everything else. The sausages were delicious, the tomatoes were squashed and the fried bread had dried out, but still tasted good.

'So this piece of pink material Arabella was wearing; was it an Alice band or a chiffon scarf?'

'Not sure. I need to check. Is it significant?' asked Doherty.

Honey nodded. 'She was wearing a pink Alice band and a chiffon scarf when I saw her the other night at the baths. I'm not sure whether she was wearing them when she left, but she was certainly wearing them while she was there.'

'That argument you overheard. Are you sure you didn't recognise the voice of the woman who threatened to kill her?'

Honey shook her head. 'She talked about taking over Arabella's career. That's got to be a lead, don't you think?'

'Very likely.' He looked thoughtful. 'We've made enquiries of her agent and the people who produced the last programme she presented. The former shouted abuse. The second didn't really throw any light on her prospects except to say they'd been considering her.' He frowned thoughtfully, swallowed and said, 'Were there many other people she spent some time with the other night?'

'Every man who was there.'

He did that nodding, screwed-up eyes thing that most men do when they suspect something or someone they'd failed to meet might have proved intriguing in a fairly sexual way. 'OK. Was there anybody there who obviously disliked her?'

Honey was emphatic, choosing to ignore his previous look. 'Every woman in the room. Arabella Neville didn't care much for other women, and other women clearly didn't care much for her. Anyway, you don't think a woman might have strangled her, do you?'

He shook his head. 'Strangling isn't usually a female thing. Poisoning has historically been the preferred method of the murdering woman-about-town. And then there's stuffing a whole body up the chimney. That takes strength. No, I think we're looking for a male perp, though it might have been useful to talk to the woman you heard. She did mention getting the job done by a professional . . . It could have been hot air, but on the other hand, she may have meant it.'

'Have you received the guest list yet?'

He nodded. 'I have, but apparently not everyone who was there is on the list. There were gate-crashers; friends of friends and hangers on. Pity you didn't recognise that voice. What her tone like, did it sound like she meant what she said? For real?'

'It sounded as though she did, but you can never tell, can you?' She stopped eating as a thought occurred. 'Just think. It might have happened there and then if I hadn't flushed.'

'A flush in time so to speak,' said Doherty. He shook his head. 'Women! Fancy having a set-to in the toilets.'

'Men don't do that sort of thing? Not even your streetwise alpha males?'

He shook his head. 'Too busy trying not to mess up their shoes.'

Honey took a bite of sausage sandwich. 'I wonder how many men she'd pissed off, besides her husband, that is?'

'What makes you think she'd pissed him off?'

'Are you kidding? Last night, every red-blooded male was over her like a rash. Or, to put it another way, she was the meat in the sandwich surrounded by a whole loaf of bread. Men fall to pieces over women like that.'

'Specify "women like that"?' said Doherty, as he buttered another slice of toast then reached for the marmalade.

'Well,' said Honey. 'Very girlish. Very pink, and very capable of massaging a man's ego until one part of him is stiff and the rest turned to mush. And she enjoys doing it. And her husband wasn't with her, so no doubt she'd done it before and he'd got sick of watching her do it. That's my opinion — for what it's worth.'

Doherty thought about it. 'Point taken. She was at the party, he wasn't, and she gets a lot of male attention. I'm guessing he's more of a stay-at-home type, not in TV like she was.'

'You sound curious about her.'

'Not me. Not my type,' said Doherty shaking his head. The lid of one eye drooped as he slid a sidelong look in her direction. 'But, hey, I like that bit about massaging a guy's ego and stuff; if you want to try it out some time . . .'

'I'm not that type,' she retorted with a toss of her head and a swipe at the bread crumbs clinging onto her chin.

'You sound as though you think she deserved to get murdered.'

Honey grimaced. 'Anyone over forty caught wearing a pink Alice band is definitely in the fashion police danger zone.' She tsked. 'Good taste gone bad.'

'You're just jealous,' he said ruefully. 'I'm listening to your opinion that there's an element of passion to this crime, but I'm not discounting the greed element. Adam Rolfe had financial problems and marriage problems, and now he's gone missing. On the other hand, Arabella didn't endear herself to the people she worked with, of that we're pretty sure. And socially . . . well . . . I sense an element of feminine dislike for our TV celeb.'

Honey elaborated on his analysis, confirming that on the whole, it was pretty accurate. Even without knowing the woman, Honey could feel her hackles rise and her talons come out for sharpening. Arabella Rolfe was the sort who got up the noses of women and down the pants of men — figuratively regarding the former, and physically as regards the latter. How many pants she'd got down was open to conjecture; rumours abounded. How many female noses she'd got up was a natural phenomenon.

'Did you hear about the personal trainer?' she said, relishing the prospect of stirring up just a little dirt.

Doherty had finished the toast and had poured himself a large black coffee. 'Fill me in.'

'Rumour has it that he was giving her more than a thorough fitness regime. She wanted a good body, and she got his as well as some improvement to her own.'

Doherty reached across to flick at some crumbs that still adhered to her chin. 'Is that jealousy I hear, or puritanical disapproval?'

She immediately stopped eating. Food always took second place when Doherty touched her, and his voice was like velvet. It was her body's natural response.

'Neither,' she replied, accepting the fact that she was a pushover as far as Doherty was concerned. 'It's just gossip.'

'And gossip by definition has to be juicy.' His eyes glinted with merriment. He was enjoying this.

'And where there's some gossip, there has to be more,' Honey pointed out.

Despite the fact that Doherty was wearing his usual three-day stubble, not one single crumb had adhered to his bristles. She made a mental note to check her own chin hairs; p'raps they'd grown longer than his.

'Hmm.' Doherty stroked his jaw. There was a sound like heavy grade sandpaper rasping over wood. Doherty's stubble had a sound all of its own. It sounded harsh, but she knew differently, the bristles seeming to lay back and surrender when pressed against soft places, which, as far her own soft places were concerned, they did pretty frequently.

'So the husband didn't accompany his wife to the estate agents' jamboree? You never saw him there.'

Honey shook her head. 'She didn't seem to be with anybody and I think someone told me that he wasn't there and that the reason was because they were moving house; which of course we know about. We're talking here about Cobden Manor, the place I envisaged turning into a country house hotel.'

'I take it you've changed your mind.'

'Too right I have. Who's going to want to stay in a place where murder happened?'

Doherty shook his head. 'Honey Driver. You're a one-off and that's for sure. For anyone else viewing an old house with a view to buying, the worst thing they might find is woodworm or rising damp. You found a dead body.'

Honey grimaced and reassessed the situation from the business angle. 'I suppose it could still work. How about murder weekends? They're pretty popular.'

On the whole Honey considered herself a pretty tough cookie, but then she'd never found a dead body before, not a murdered one anyway, and not someone she'd seen alive and quaffing cocktails just a few nights before. Her expression must have reflected what she was thinking.

'Don't dwell on it,' said Doherty and hugged her. It was such a good hug that she swore she'd remember it until right up to bedtime — possibly beyond. Definitely beyond. 'It isn't healthy,' he added. 'Think of something else. Do something else today to take your mind off it.'

She took his advice and began making a list. She was good at making lists; prided herself on them in fact. They helped her concentrate; helped her plan what needed to be done.

Usually her lists were about staff rotas, food and beverage ordering, rooms, and snagging (such things as fluff balls under the bed and spiders in the corners). But this list was different. This list was about murder suspects.

'OK. Husband, personal trainer, agent, and television rivals. That's a pretty fair selection I think.'

'Plus the husband's business rivals. Was she having an affair with any of them? And what about the first wife? I suggest we pay her a visit tomorrow. She's already been questioned, but it wouldn't hurt to give it another pop.'

* * *

Talking to Adam Rolfe's first wife turned out to be a nonevent. A neighbour came out to say that she was visiting somebody in Leicester.

'I think it's something to do with the son,' said the neighbour. 'He's got a place at Leicester University.'

It occurred to both of them that it might be a lie; that the husband and the first wife might be together.

'The second marriage did turn bad,' Honey pointed out.

'But she was a woman scorned,' said Doherty. 'I hear tell that she packed all his clothes in the same suitcase as three pounds of tripe and half a dozen kippers.'

Honey laughed but said, 'Not nice.'

'Especially when she refused to let him collect it from the house. Instead she put it in a safety deposit facility and posted him the key. It was a week before he tracked its location. Pretty high by then.'

She had expected Doherty to wind his way back to Bath, but instead he swept past Bath across the Severn Bridge.

'Where are you going?' she asked in surprise.

'To see a man about a crime.'

'Right,' said Honey, burrowing herself down into her turned up coat collar. Yet again, Doherty was driving with the top of the car down. 'Did he commit the crime?'

'That's what we're going to find out.'

CHAPTER TEN

She guessed whoever they were about to meet had some bearing on the case. Judging by Doherty's terse manner, she wasn't going to be told who it was and what they knew until they were face to face.

The little car flew up the A40, then on to side roads thick with trees and the smell of damp earth. Doherty turned into a minor road and then into a dirt track. A large sign read: 'Forestry Commission — Forest of Dean.'

At the end of the track the trees diminished and they were in a grassy clearing with parking spaces; a building used as a yacht club. A navigation light blinked above a concrete pier jutting out into the River Severn. The tide was out, but the sea-gulls didn't seem to mind, bobbing about on what remained.

Small boats were moored in a silky green slip of water protected from seepage by a pair of lock gates. A cool breeze blew across the water. Honey tucked her chin deeper into her coat collar and her hands into her pockets.

'It's pretty exposed here. Is this person we're meeting already here, or do we have to hang around, in which case I wish I'd brought hot coffee — and maybe a hot water bottle.'

'Over there,' said Doherty, pointing at a promontory in the river where a man sat fishing.

The man was wearing a quilted jacket the colour of which could best be described as mud, though it might once have been moss green. Like the man wearing it, the jacket was faded.

The man turned when Doherty's shadow fell over him. His face was crumpled, a bit like an old leather football with all the air squashed out.

'You're the police officer that phoned me earlier.' He sounded defensive and his expression was surly.

Doherty was cool. 'That's right. I wanted to talk to you. Your daughter gave me your mobile number. I tried phoning you but couldn't get through.'

'Too bloody right you couldn't. It's in there,' he said, nodding towards the river. 'With the bloody fishes. And they don't take phone calls. Bloody phone. I told her I didn't want one. Told her I didn't want to be contacted. You know that, don't you?'

Doherty settled himself down on a large rectangular rock that looked as though at some time it might have stood upright. 'I hear tale that following the folding of the development company you threatened both of them – her especially.'

The man turned and glared at them. He was in his fifties, his squashed face flush from being outdoors. She guessed his hair was probably thinning beneath the sludge green hat he was wearing.

'Mr Albright, would I be right in saying that you lost money when Adam Rolfe and Associates folded?'

The man emitted a low growl before beginning to speak.

'The business was well funded. No doubt about it. It shouldn't have gone under. But it did. The money that had been there wasn't there anymore, though God knows where it went. I didn't get mine back, that's for bloody sure. Left me barely enough to afford a decent rod. Put me off investing ever again. I want the simple life in future, Mr Policeman. Enough to live on and no worries. That suits me fine.'

'Aren't you curious as to where the money went?'

Evan Albright blew nigh on a raspberry through his pursed lips.

'No need to ask. There was plenty of cash in the bank until she came along, that TV star. He fell for her hook, line and sinker. And then she sunk him, the silly sod. She went through his private cache and then went through the company money. Well, that's my theory and no one will convince me otherwise. No one!'

His eyes were hard with hatred, as though daring Doherty to try and convince him otherwise. Doherty had no intention of doing so.

'I understand there were a number of other investors? I imagine they were pretty sore too, though they didn't threaten bodily harm as you did,' said Doherty. Although he appeared to be studying the still surface of the water, Honey knew he wasn't looking for fish. He was listening intently.

'I can't speak for them. I'm only an ordinary Joe who had a bit saved but no big corporation or old boy network behind me. Some did. I just lost my rag.' He shrugged. 'So what?'

'Arabella Rolfe has been found dead, murdered and her husband is missing. When was the last time you saw either of them, Mr Albright?'

'Ages ago,' he snapped, his attention now fixed on his float which had just disappeared beneath the water. 'And good riddance,' he muttered.

'When exactly did you see them?'

'I can't remember . . .'

He flipped the rod, played with the fish, dragging the float carefully towards the bank.

Doherty grabbed the rod. Holding it firmly, he prevented Albright from reeling in his catch.

'When?' He repeated, his voice grim and if Albright had had any intention of putting up a fight, one look at Doherty's face was enough to make him change his mind.

'You'll make me lose my fish!' He sounded alarmed, though Honey deduced that was more to do with Doherty's swift action than the thought of not frying fish for supper.

'*When*?'

'Fourteen months ago at the Theatre Royal. I was invited to a gala evening courtesy of Rolfe Investments. I saw both of them there.'

'It sounds quite grand.'

Grim-faced, yearning for his rod and the fish he'd hooked, Evan Albright grunted a response, his annoyance all too obvious.

'It was a gala night. Everyone was there.'

'Everyone who'd invested money with Rolfe Investments?'

'Everybody!'

Doherty let go the rod and stepped away.

Albright stayed with his back to them as he reeled in his fish.

Doherty thanked him. Albright made no response.

'I can't see that he would have killed her,' Honey whispered as they walked away. 'I mean, he's old, and although fishing doesn't float my boat, it seems to float his.'

'Floating a boat. Very apt of you, Honey Driver. Evan Albright used to have a big house once. Not as big as Cobden Manor, but big enough. His daughter told me so.'

'And?'

He paused at a spot where a weeping willow flowed like water over the prow of a small wooden sailing boat, mast laid down for canal use. 'Now he lives on that.'

CHAPTER ELEVEN

Honey lugged the footbath to the Zodiac Club where the eccentric old couple were to have their reception and where Doherty was there waiting for her. Once the footbath was safely stowed with the other wedding presents, she hopped up onto a bar stool.

'Here,' said Doherty. 'Let's drink to success.'

'The case is solved?'

'Hardly. We've spoken to other investors. It's not easy,' he said. 'Some of them are very private people with a lot of money. They don't like being taken for fools.'

His blue eyes were dark and distracted. Honey knew that look and took a stab at what he was thinking.

'So they could afford to have their revenge — kill them — both Arabella and Adam.'

Doherty nodded, cradling his drink. 'We still haven't tracked down Adam and we're thinking he could be a victim too. Murdered elsewhere. Hidden elsewhere. Perhaps he was killed first, his wife interrupted the killer, and he didn't hide her as well as he's hidden the husband.'

'Is that possible?'

'Anything's possible.'

Honey rested her chin on her hand. 'I'd like to be that rich. Not that I'd pay to have somebody bumped off — well not just at this moment in time. Just to be able to buy anything I wanted.'

'Not all of the investors were ultra-rich. A few, like Evan Albright, were just comfortably off. And John Rees. That guy you used to know. The bookshop owner.'

She felt herself go hot and hoped it didn't show. Luckily the Zodiac was a very dark place.

News that John Rees had been an investor in Rolfe Investments was a total surprise, though it did explain his acting out of character. Losing a lot of money was enough to make anyone behave differently.

'He was at the Roman Baths,' she said flippantly as though she'd only said 'hi' in passing.

'I know. He was on the list.'

Phew! For once she'd chosen the right time to tell the truth.

'I could go along and talk to him, seeing as I know him.' It seemed the least she could do. Besides, she had a yearning to get to the bottom of John's involvement. Not that he's guilty of killing anyone, she told herself. OK, he had been in the army or something, but he just wasn't the type to kill. He'd probably just been an army cook or a stretcher bearer. Not a killer. Not John.

'Give me time,' she said to Doherty, coming back to the present. 'I'll go and talk to John Rees and Arabella's personal trainer — though not tomorrow.' She rolled her eyes. 'Tomorrow I have to attend the wedding of my mother's first well-satisfied customers.'

* * *

Honey kept muttering to anyone that would listen that she really didn't have time to leave the hotel and a murder case to attend a wedding of people she didn't know. The only person she didn't convey this to was her mother. Gloria Cross had already announced that she would be very upset if her daughter did not attend. After all, this was the first pairing of lovebirds who'd met via her online dating site.

'At least it's not far,' Honey said as she pulled a broad-brimmed black hat onto her head. The hat had been purchased on a trip to Covent Garden. It was plain black and therefore useful. Add a red rose or a pink scarf, anything that matched the outfit, and the hat matched too.

The plan was to get there, hand over the card, explain the present was being forwarded to the Zodiac Club where the reception was to be held, then leg it as fast as she could back to the hotel. A coach full of tourists was due to arrive at noon for tea, scones, jam and clotted cream. The fact that midday was not usually the time to partake of a cream tea was beside the point.

'They watched some costume drama on TV where all these women in big frocks were tucking into a cream tea,' the coach operator had explained. 'They thought Bath would be the place to do the same, so if you could oblige . . .' Naturally, she would oblige.

'I'll be back asap,' she said to Lindsey. 'Cover for me.'

'Never fear. I'm on the case,' said Lindsey.

So here she was, suitably dressed and ready for a wedding.

'What do you think, Lindz?'

Her daughter looked her up and down. 'It's very you.'

'That could mean anything.'

'It suits you.'

She'd gone for something jazzy and bright. The red suit she chose had a panelled skirt with a small black motif and a panelled top with a keyhole neckline. She added a red rose to her black hat. Handbag and shoes were also black.

One look in the mirror and she could see she looked decidedly cheerful. Not a hint of Miss Havisham — more Moll Flanders perhaps?

'Don't ask. Just go,' said Lindsey when it looked as though she were having doubts.

'Oooow. You look nice,' said Mary Jane as she tottered through reception on four-inch heels. 'Very bright!'

The comment about her outfit being bright was decidedly unnerving. Mary Jane had a penchant for *very* vivid colours, so if she thought this was bright . . .

Honey glanced at her watch and sucked in her breath. There was no time to change.

The moment she left the hotel, she did the decent thing and switched off her mobile phone. How many events had she attended where people had forgotten to do that? Including herself, hence being one jump ahead and switching it off now. The day was fine, cooled with a breeze, though not enough to swipe off hats and make a mess of a hair do.

She decided to walk there. Luckily the wedding of Wilbur Williams and Alice Prendergast was to be held at the Duchess of Huntingdon's Chapel, a lovely old place perched up on a parapet of a pavement at the side of the A4 road.

The air outside was bright, the pavements shiny and slippery with recent rain. Speed was not really an option, though might have been if she'd taken the sensible approach and worn low-heeled shoes.

Tourists thronged the pavements. *They* were all wearing sensible shoes and casual clothes, glancing at this woman so formally attired in red and black. One or two smiled at her and she smiled back.

Two cups of coffee plus fruit juice had been consumed before leaving and nature accordingly took its course. She popped into the ladies' cloakroom at the Roman Baths, did a quick check in the mirror and nipped out again. One toilet being out of action and a long queue made it a long wait. But she had to go. She just had to.

Outside the air seemed cooler and even more people were smiling at her.

It's the colour, she thought to herself. It's making them happy.

Back at the hotel, Lindsey was going spare. Her grandmother had phoned on her mobile to check whether Honey had left.

'I left a message on her phone last night. She did get it, didn't she?'

'What message?'

The moment she was told what had happened, Lindsey phoned her mother's mobile. There was no reply.

Smudger was in reception having written down the changes to today's *table d'hote* menu.

'Problem?'

'Big problem. My mother has not got her phone turned on and my grandmother has just phoned to say that the venue is the same, but the form of service is changed. Wilbur and Alice will not be getting married.'

'Ah! Cold feet or cold as in . . .'

The look on Lindsey's face said it all.

Smudger offered to run after her. 'I'm a good runner, though not as good as Clint.'

Lindsey grimaced. The less said about Clint the better. Anna was pregnant again and Clint had run — fast.

'Try,' she said to Smudger.

'Is the world going to stop if I don't?'

'No. Just my mother's heart!'

CHAPTER TWELVE

Late arriving at the Duchess of Huntingdon's chapel, Honey realised she'd probably missed the wedding march. She couldn't hear any music, the vicar had probably now moved on to the tried and tested words of the wedding service.

There were no big silk bows and bouquets of flowers decorating the wrought iron arch that girdled the gateway as she'd been expecting. Her mother had assured her there would be. An oversight, perhaps? Or maybe funds hadn't stretched that far.

The moment she pushed open the door, she fancied something was wrong.

Everyone was dressed in dark colours. She put that down to the warning about not wearing white. Most of the people there were elderly. She guessed they'd gone for the opposite of white. Black was always a good standby.

Searching for her mother, she saw her three pews back from the front.

She slid into a pew at the back, and found she had it to herself.

The vicar spoke quietly and she had to strain to hear the words. Though tempted to urge him to speak up, she refrained. The poor man was getting on in years himself. The atmosphere was odd for a wedding: you could have dropped a pin and heard it roll over the floor; that was how hollow and silent it was. Nobody was making a sound. There were no funny comments about the bride and groom as is usually done at weddings. Nothing. Nothing but the incessant drone of the vicar.

And then it struck her. She couldn't see Alice at the front in her frothy white gown. The only splash of colour was her own outfit . . .

Just as the penny dropped the door behind her opened. A figure in white stepped through, his face pink with effort. Gazing around he spotted Honey in her solitary pew and slid in next to her.

Once he'd caught his breath, Smudger whispered into her ear. 'The bride died after dancing on the table at the Zodiac Club.'

'Oh, my God!' she whispered, and quickly stood and rushed out, followed by Smudger.

Once outside, her chef told her of the change of plan.

'The old geezer about to get wed couldn't bear to cancel the service entirely, so he got it changed at the last minute. It's a kind of tribute to the bride — a bit like footballers when they finally hang up their boots. So. You're not quite dressed for a wake, boss,' he said, running his eyes over the scarlet suit.

'It can't be called a wake if she's only just died! Anyway, it just wouldn't be right. It should have been a wedding. Besides, it's a wedding I'm dressed for, not a wake.' Honey swept her hat from her head. 'How embarrassing. Everyone was looking at me when I was walking here. Was my outfit a bit too colourful?'

Smudger grinned. 'It's not about the colour. The back of your skirt's tucked in your knickers.'

She could have gone back to the hotel there and then, after her embarrassing morning she really did want to, but for the second time in two weeks, she was dressed to impress.

'I'll be back later,' she said, once she'd rearranged her skirt. 'I've got to see a man about a dead woman.'

* * *

91

The frontage of the upmarket agency Glenwood Halley worked for was glossy with glass and shiny with chrome. Honey looked for a door handle but couldn't find one. The door was just one sheet of glass; very trendy but, she reasoned, a magnet for mucky finger marks.

The interior was breathtakingly pristine, all clean, clear surfaces and lots and lots of glass. Two inches of her high-heeled shoes sank into a creamy carpet. Soft music was playing and the air smelled of lemons.

A young woman displaying the orange skin tone of a sun-bed-addict wafted across to greet her.

'Mrs Driver, isn't it? So nice to see you again. Would you like tea, coffee, Champagne? We always have some on ice for valued clients.'

A little surprised that the receptionist had recognised her, Honey shook her head thinking that Champagne at this time of day was too decadent.

'I want to speak to Mr Halley. Is he here?'

'I'll just see,' she said, her voice prim and her expression slightly condescending.

A few moments later, Glenwood Halley swept towards her with outstretched hand, his shirt crisply white, business suit smartly navy. The gold chain slid around his wrist.

'Mrs Driver. How lovely to see you. Would you like coffee? Tea?'

'No. I wouldn't want to trouble you.'

'Oh, you wouldn't be troubling me, Mrs Driver. Ruth will make a cup if you wish for one.'

'No thank you. I'm sure Ruth has other things to do.'

She smiled sweetly. Ruth showed no sign of being either surprised or hurt by Honey's rejection of beverage. She just smiled in a professionally bland manner and betrayed no emotion whatsoever.

It struck Honey that Glenwood Halley hadn't asked if she would like Champagne, not that she wanted any. She preferred red wines, full bodied clarets just like the men in her life. Not fizzy and crisp – like Glenwood.

'Do come into my office.' With a flourish suited to a Buckingham Palace flunkey, he opened a glass door. Like the main door, it was fashioned from plate glass, the handle a bronze pad inset. The door closed with a hush behind them.

His office was cool, the walls lined with beige fabric, the carpet almost as white as his shirt. The chairs and sofa were of navy-blue leather and plush enough to drown in. The rest of the furniture was chrome and glass. Framed photographs of 'hot' properties lined the right-hand wall. Photographs of famous people were bunched into groups on the opposite wall. The two were obviously tied together; vendors and buyers ranged opposite the properties they'd purchased or sold.

'I see you've noticed my display,' he said with an air of superiority. He sprawled himself at one corner of a settee, his long legs unfurled.

Looking at his legs brought to mind the spiders in the old outhouse. When he invited her to join him, she settled herself in the opposite corner. A two-foot gap opened up like a moat between her knee and his. Her hat — now crumpled — sat between them.

'You've met all these people?' She nodded at the photographs.

'Indeed I have! Lovely, lovely people, all of them.'

Like the people he hero-worshipped, Glenwood Halley was overwhelmingly theatrical.

'Arabella was an angel. I absolutely adored her. How sad. How very, very sad.' He sighed like a love-sick teenager.

'You sound as though you held her in high regard — not just on a business footing, I mean.'

'Why wouldn't I? She was beautiful. Such people have electrifying auras, don't you think?'

'Not really.'

Most of the people in the photos were instantly recognisable. One of them was the recently deceased Mrs Arabella Rolfe, and this struck Honey as strange.

'Excuse me for asking, Glenwood, but I notice Arabella Neville is up on your wall, though you haven't yet sold Cobden Manor. Did they purchase it through you?'

His eyes narrowed defensively. 'Yes. She also recently purchased an apartment in the Royal Crescent through us.'

'You say "she". Does that mean it was her money that bought it, not her husband's money?'

A closed look came over his face. 'I couldn't possibly comment on our client's financial arrangements. It would be a breach of privacy.'

Honey cleared her throat. 'Glenwood, it's a question the police are very likely to ask you. It might be beneficial both to you and your client list that the facts were relayed by me to Steve Doherty. I mean, how would your clients react if the police brought you in to answer more questions?'

His response was sharp and immediate. 'Private money. From a private source. There wasn't a mortgage or anything like that.'

'What do you mean by private?'

He paused as he tried to make up his mind whether to bluster around the truth or declare it openly. There were options to weigh up. Then he obviously decided to tell what he knew.

'Her solicitor would know, though of course they're less likely to tell you than I am. Client confidentiality and all that.'

Honey toyed with the big fat rose still clinging to the side of her hat. The fact that the purchase money had come from a private source was interesting. Glenwood Halley was probably telling the truth. As an estate agent he wasn't likely to be privy to that information. The solicitor, on the other hand, would know.

'So who was Arabella's solicitor?'

Glenwood ignored the question. Eyes shining, he was staring adoringly at Arabella's photo-friendly smile.

'She was so wonderful. Did you know that she was being considered for the *Celebrity Big Brother* House?'

'No. I didn't.' She didn't tell him that reality shows were her reality. She ran a hotel. All the world and his wife came through those doors, their behaviour good, bad and somewhere in between.

Glenwood sighed deeply. 'After that first meeting when her eyes met mine and she shook my hand, I watched every programme she ever appeared on.'

Honey eyed the side of the sofa arm just in case it had magically turned into an aircraft seat complete with sick bag. Then she had a thought.

'When did you first meet Arabella? Was it *before* she bought the apartment and the bank ordered you to sell Cobden Manor?'

'Yes. We first met when she and her husband bought Cobden Manor.'

'This was — how many years ago?'

'Five, I think, though I could check the records for the exact date.'

'And do you know anybody who would want her dead?'

'Of course not. She was lovely. So lovely.'

He suddenly seemed close to tears but Honey ploughed on:

'And her husband; what did you think of him?'

It was barely perceptible, but she was sure she detected a sudden look of dislike in his velvety brown eyes. But he rallied, unwilling no doubt to sully the memory of Arabella Neville in any way.

'Mr Rolfe was quite the gentleman. His wife loved the house and although he was a little reluctant at first, she easily won him round.'

I bet she did, thought Honey.

Glenwood carried on. 'She was so excited about the house and had great plans for it. They were newlyweds back then and her husband indulged her every whim. They were so in love, and she was so gorgeous! So very, very gorgeous!'

'Still, she was only human,' Honey said.

'But very attractive!' The comment was delivered vehemently. Poor Glenwood was totally star-struck. If Arabella had been a rock band, he would have been a groupie. But what had been Arabella's feelings for Glenwood? She could guess, but for now the fact that Adam Rolfe had not been keen to buy the manor was interesting. Had it contributed to the downfall of his business? Had he hated her for buying it?

'Do you think Mr Rolfe would have bought the manor if his wife hadn't persuaded him to do so?'

Glenwood eyed her balefully. At the same time, he fingered his chin as though tracing an imaginary line. Unlike Doherty there was no whiskery sound. Glenwood was shiny. Glenwood obviously went in for a regular and very close shave.

'I really couldn't say.'

'What was her reaction when the bank took possession?'

'Upset,' he snapped. 'Wouldn't you be?'

She had to admit she would. Glenwood was tapping his knee with his fingers, looking impatient. If she was going to end this interview having learned something, it made sense to return to what seemed to actually interest him.

'So, Glenwood. You like rubbing shoulders with the rich, the famous and the glamorous.'

Conviviality was instantly restored. Glenwood's dark eyes shone as he surveyed the bevy of beauties hanging on the wall. There were more women than men.

'Excuse me for asking, but did you actually have any . . .' Honey paused as she searched for the right word. 'Liaisons with any of these beauties?'

He froze and for a moment he was like an engine that had stalled on start-up. Then he was all subdued laughter and shaking of head.

'That would be telling. I couldn't possibly comment.'

'I'm not a tabloid journalist, Glenwood,' she said, smiling fit to seduce an archbishop. 'Just out of interest — and envy of course. I would love to know . . .'

He shook his head and came over all coy. 'Well,' he said. 'Between you and me, let's just say that I became intimate friends with a few of them.'

'How intimate?' she cooed, narrowing the gap between them and lowering her voice.

'Let's just say, some became quite close.'

'Was Arabella one of those you became close to?'

Whether she'd sounded too eager or he'd suddenly remembered her policeman boyfriend, a light clicked on in his brain. He sat back, looking suddenly aloof again. 'I really don't think I should say any more. Shall we stick to the subject of Cobden Manor?' he said coldly.

'I thought that's what we doing. That's where I found Arabella, remember? She was dead. Strangled with her own Alice band. Her murderer had to be a pretty strong guy to stuff her up that chimney. How big are you, Glenwood. Six two? Six three?'

'I didn't do it.' He glanced towards the office door, aware that he'd raised his voice. 'Not her. Not Arabella! How could I?'

'How close were you two?' said Honey, rising to the occasion and to her feet. 'Did you arrange to meet there? Did you try to force yourself on her? Did she reject you?'

The torrent of questions caught the estate agent unawares.

'No!' he burst out.

He shot to his feet, towering over her. A nerve ticked below one eye, spoiling his smooth complexion.

'I don't have to answer any more your questions. You're not a police officer.'

'No. But my boyfriend is. Any suspicions I have will be relayed straight to him. Plus, of course, I am Crime Liaison Officer on behalf of Bath Hotels Association. I'll be reporting on the progress of this investigation to Casper St John Gervais. He's chairman of the Hotels Association. If you happened to mention to Casper that you've met the Archbishop of Canterbury, Casper will inform you that he's met the Pope. Casper knows everybody. He has lines of communication all over the place. So it's not a bad idea to tell me *precisely* what you know. I'll keep it under my hat, so to speak. Unless it has direct effects on the murder case.' She gave him a pointed look. 'Got it?'

She wondered what Casper would think if he'd heard what she'd just said. Puff up with pride or explode with indignation? Her money was on the former.

Frustratingly, the tactic backfired big time.

'Get out! Get off these premises right now. Even if you had ten million to spend, I wouldn't deal with you!'

The game was up, the party was over. Honey sauntered slowly for the door twirling her black-brimmed hat around one finger. Before opening the door, she turned round, held her head to one side and said, 'Just one last question. Why didn't you offer me Champagne? Ruth did.'

'I only offer Champagne to . . .'

'Famous and fabulously wealthy people?'

Glenwood Halley really was a victim of celebrity culture. He couldn't help himself. She had gone to view a property with regard to a commercial venture, but not because she was rich, famous, or both. People who bought mansions to turn into country house hotels were obviously pretty low in the pecking order as far as Glenwood was concerned. He would tolerate them for the money it would bring in, but that was as far as it went. It was the celebrities he loved to deal with, the beautiful people with their fantastic lifestyles and instantly recognisable faces. Basically, he was obsessed, and that in itself was worrying. She recalled Doherty referring to a stalker and Arabella being attacked.

'I'll find my own way out.'

He didn't come after her. She hadn't expected him to. It was clear by now that she wouldn't be buying Cobden Manor. Would I ever have gone through with it? she asked herself. She didn't know the answer to that. All she did know was that Glenwood Halley had been rattled by her questions, and yes, she truly believed that he had got close — too close — to some of his clients. She had no proof of it, but perhaps a few questions of some of those women — stars she'd recognised — wouldn't hurt. Glenwood Halley was in the frame, and she didn't mean a picture frame!

CHAPTER THIRTEEN

Doherty came round to park himself in her office, talk about the murder case and indulge in a cup of black coffee.

She told him how obsessed Glenwood was with celebrity and asked whether there had ever been complaints about stalking reported against him.

'Not as far as I know, and remember, Glenwood was as shocked as we were when her body turned up. In fact, I'd say he was even more shocked.'

Honey knew he was right. Glenwood had been totally thrown off balance.

Doherty declined a Danish pastry on account of his training schedule.

'I'm fitter and leaner than I've been for a long time,' he said. 'I might start playing rugby regularly.'

Honey was doubtful. OK, he was sticking to the training schedule. There were only three days to go before the match and although he complained about his back, he refused to drop out of it.

'It's for the honour of the boys in blue,' he said to her.

'Steve, it's a game of rugby, not the defence of Rorke's Drift.'

After he'd made himself comfortable in her leather-up-holstered, swivelling bosun's chair, Honey told him about the wedding that turned into a tribute and the reception that turned into a wake. She omitted the details about her skirt being tucked into her knickers. Such information was on a need-to-know basis only. Smudger had been sworn to secrecy on pain of her cutting off his bonus entitlement — 'or something more painful' – if he dared tell.

He'd soberly responded that his lips were sealed. When he wasn't sober could pose more of a problem.

'My mother said that they're hoping to bury Alice in her wedding dress,' Honey told Doherty, 'though it does mean taking the hoops out of her skirt. She made the mistake of choosing a Little Bo Peep-style dress and it won't fit in the coffin if they keep them in.'

Doherty shook his head. 'You've certainly been up against it just lately.'

'I wish,' she said with a sad grin.

He looked at her. 'That's a double entendre, I take it.'

'You bet it is. I can do with some light relief.'

'Things can only get better.'

He was right about that. Just the act of him leaning over and kissing her forehead felt pretty good. Tingly feelings spread all over.

'So how's the coach house looking?'

'Same as usual? I haven't redecorated it or anything.' Suddenly she got the gist of the true subject here. 'You mean you want us to go over there and study the bedroom ceiling?'

'It probably needs studying. That mattress too.'

The occasion called for a clinch so they had one.

It had barely ended when Lindsey barged in.

'Hey, I hate to interrupt a truly beautiful moment, but we have a problem.'

Honey smoothed her hair and pulled her shirt back down over her waist.

'Something wrong?'

'Grandmother phoned and asked if you would like to attend the funeral, the proper one. The one the other day was just to make use of booking for what should have been a wedding. It turned out to be something else, but now it's the proper one with a coffin and everything. She also asked what should she do with the footbath?'

Honey's mother took advantage of any occasion to dress up, even if it was in black. Out of everyone attending she would look the most glamorous. Gloria Cross was not the sort of grandmother who sat knitting and looking after grandchildren. At the time of Lindsey's birth, she'd just married her fourth husband. She'd buried him four years later. Fortunately he'd left her a considerable sum of money, enough to keep her in designer clothes, cruises to foreign countries, and a very nice apartment where nothing was out of place.

Honey knew she wasn't being invited to the funeral, she was being ordered to attend. Her mother actively encouraged people at such events to guess her age and invariably to make the comment that mother and daughter could easily be sisters.

'No, I am not attending the funeral. I suppose I could donate the footbath to charity. People quite often donate things to charity instead of sending flowers, so that's what I'll do.'

'That's usually money, Mother, not footbaths.'

She shrugged. 'It's the thought that counts.'

Doherty tugged his leather jacket back on. 'I'll leave you to it. Shame about the wedding. I would have liked to been there. It sounded like fun.'

He was grinning broadly. The vision of her wearing scarlet in a church full of people wearing black had tickled his funny bone. Or was it more than that? Had Smudger gone back on his word.

'It wasn't *that* funny,' said Honey. 'My mother didn't think it very funny at all. That wedding was a milestone for

101

her online dating business. She'll have been so disappointed. Wilbur and Alice met, fell in love and were getting married.'

'And then one fell dead. It could happen to anyone,' said Doherty, his expression fighting between amusement and solemnity. 'My uncle Sam remarried at ninety-two.'

'My God. How old was his bride?'

'Seventy-two. He outlived her by three years. Their children outlived both of them.'

He regarded their puzzled expressions with amusement. 'They both had children from past marriages. Get it?'

'So this murder. Arabelle Rolfe,' said Lindsey, absolutely refusing to acknowledge Doherty's sense of humour and instantly changing the subject. 'The husband did it. It's always the husband. Or the butler.'

Doherty had been heading for the door, but stopped abruptly. 'Funny you should say that. The Rolfes used to have a butler, but they let him go a few weeks before they moved.'

'But the husband's the prime suspect. Always is, isn't he?' said Lindsey.

'I think the butler might be worth a question or two,' said Honey. 'But first there's that personal trainer. I'd like to get my teeth into him. I really would.'

Lindsey raised her eyebrows. 'By biting his buttocks?'

Honey didn't answer. She'd never enjoyed exercise and couldn't understand those who did. On top of that it was a personal trainer who had once told her that without his help she would remain pleasantly plump for the rest of her life. It was like a red rag to the bull; she had wanted to put her horns down and charge!

CHAPTER FOURTEEN

Visiting a gym was not something Honey did very often, but she certainly knew how to dress the part. Delving deep into her daughter's wardrobe, she had purloined the use of a pair of navy-blue jogging pants, matching sweatshirt and white trainers with 'go faster' navy-blue stripes along the side. Her hair was swept back into a ponytail and held in place with elasticated white sweat band specially made for the purpose.

She looked fresh-faced, sporty and ready to go — except that she had no intention of doing anything remotely energetic. She just figured that if she was going to ask this guy some questions, wearing the right outfit would put him at ease, even catch him off guard.

The woman behind the reception desk queried her asking for him and him alone.

'Are you sure Amelia or Cosmo wouldn't suit you? Only Victor is terribly sought after. I take it you're looking for in-depth attention?'

'It must be Victor. He comes very highly recommended. I need him. Badly.'

The woman sighed as though she were asking for something really difficult, like George Clooney's email address.

'I'll see what I can do. Can I have your name, please?'

'Mrs Driver.'

'First name?'

'Hannah. Hannah Driver.'

The blonde young thing with her even tan and her flawless complexion looked her up and down before picking up the phone. Honey paid her the same compliment as she informed Victor Bromwell that a lady insisted on seeing him and him alone.

The woman's breasts thrust like ice cream cones beneath her white polo sweater. Honey concluded that her sports bra must be paper-thin. Unlike her own which had thick straps and ample cups; there was no danger of overflow.

'If you'd care to wait over there,' she said once she'd hung up.

Honey sat down on a black leather settee tucked to one side of a clutch of tropical palms but jumped back up again when a man entered the reception area.

Victor Bromwell was the colour of a Sheraton sideboard, though with better legs. His teeth flashed pearly white when he smiled.

'Hi there. Pleased to meet you.'

He was all testosterone, his body was encased in skin-tight Spandex. Over six feet tall, with defined muscles and the dentistry of a superstar, his thigh and arm muscles bulged from the leg and armholes of his shorts and cutaway vest.

Honey shook the outstretched hand. His eyes gave her the quick once-over. She returned the compliment, her gaze falling ever downwards, then returning, pausing on the upward sweep. Spandex held everything in place, but some things just couldn't be hidden.

'I need your help, Mr Bromwell. I need your help very badly.'

He spread his arms. 'Hey, lady. There's no problem that I, Victor Bromwell, can't help you with. Reshape. Define. Deflate.' He stepped closer to her and lowered his voice. 'There ain't no part of your body that I can't do things

104

to make you feel real good. Forget about becoming a new woman; babe, I can do wonders with the old one.'

Honey felt her jaw tensing and her teeth set on edge. Was it her imagination, or was she really feeling his body heat?!

'That sounds very interesting, Mr Bromwell,' she said, carefully averting her eyes from below his equator. 'Do you think we could talk in private?'

His face lit up like a Christmas tree. 'Hey. If you want to talk it through in private, that's OK by me.'

Boy, this guy was full of himself. At least, his Spandex certainly was!

He took her through a door in the corner of reception. The room they entered was little more than a cubicle. A height chart was painted on the wall. To the right of that was a small table and chair, to the left a pair of scales.

When he closed the door, the room grew smaller. There was no window, no light except for that for that provided by overhead halogen.

'Right,' said Victor, standing real close. 'Now where would you like to start? Is there any particular part of your body that's giving you real concern, if so, show it to me now. Right now.'

'Right, Mr Bromwell . . .'

'Please. Call me Victor, or even Vic.'

'Right. Victor.'

She gave him another once-over. At least, she thought, there was no gold medallion warming against his chest, though a thick gold sleeper gleamed in his ear lobe. His big feet were enlarged by top of the range Nike trainers and he stood with legs braced, crossed arms enhancing his bulging muscles. His biceps were as thick as her thighs, but definitely firmer.

She knew this stance was for her benefit. He had poser written all over him.

'So, babe. Can I ask you your name?'

'Honey Driver. Can I ask you a question?'

'Shoot!'

'Do you shoot that line to all the women that come here for your body workouts?'

He grinned. 'Only the really sweet-looking ones like you, babe. I've got respect for older women. They know what they want. Know what I mean?'

She knew what he meant alright.

'Did Arabella Rolfe know what she wanted?'

His face clouded over. 'Arabella? What you asking me about her for?'

'I'm making enquiries regarding her murder.'

The veins in his naked arms swelled like tree roots. He gazed at her steadily.

'Did you hear what I said, Victor?'

'I heard. Are you a cop?'

'I'm a Crime Liaison Officer.' She mulled over whether she should state anything else and decided she would. 'I found Arabella's body. It wasn't a pleasant experience. I really want to find out who did it and why.'

Any doubts he had about co-operating were cancelled out by her telling him that she was the one who'd found the body.

'Look, lady,' he said, his eyes deep and dark. 'I know nothing about it and I definitely didn't do it.'

'I didn't say you did.'

'So what are you here for?'

'There are rumours that you were giving Arabella more than physical fitness advice.'

His arms fell to his sides. The biceps lost their bulge and the thick veins shrank to half their previous size. The confidence fell too.

'Look, there was nothing in it. She came on to me, asked for a little extracurricular activity, and I gave it to her. Hell, she wasn't the first to offer it up on a plate. That's the way it is with older women. Everyone knows that. They've done relationships. They know what they want.'

'Is that so?' Her skin was crawling. Was that really the way older women were apprised when they worked to keep their bodies trim? 'Older women just want sex? I never knew that.'

'That's the way it is,' he said, failing to notice that she was far from impressed with his assessment. 'Pure physical, sister. That's all they want. Pure physical.'

'So you're admitting to a sexual relationship with Arabella?'

'That isn't what I said. I said she didn't want a relationship. Neither did I. That's not what I'm willing to do.'

'Was she OK with that? Physical intercourse only?'

He shrugged. 'She had to be. Take it or leave it. I play a team game. No favouritism.'

Honey folded her arms, her dislike for Victor Bromwell growing by the minute.

'Did she demand your singular attention?'

He hesitated, swallowed and then answered. 'She liked to be the centre of attention.'

'So she wanted you to herself.'

'I told her no can do. She fretted a little.'

'Is that so?' she said, nodding thoughtfully. 'So, tell me, can anyone verify where you were on the eleventh of last month at around eleven at night?'

He paused for a second. Beads of sweat gleamed on his close-shaven skull. He looked like a TV competitor in gladiator games. Though more nervous.

'Look. I was with someone, but hey. It was a special someone. Can we keep this between us? My reputation is at stake here.'

Honey raised her eyebrows insidiously. 'The bad reputation, or are you insinuating you've got a good one.'

He gave her a dark look. 'Look. OK, I keep most of the women I date on a physical level, but not all of them. I do have a special someone, and she's cultured. You dig?'

It crossed Honey's mind that if this special person was 'cultured', what the hell was she doing with Mr Muscle. On second thoughts though, a hot dog was sometimes a welcome change from chicken chasseur.

'OK. I'll accept that. You're Mr Rough Diamond to her Lady Penelope. You can't tell me who you were with, but can you tell me where you were?'

'Hey, babe,' he said, glancing nervously around him. 'I just told you . . .'

'Come on. Were you in a pub, for example, and would the barman remember you?'

He chewed his lips a bit and looked down at the floor. He mumbled something. At first she didn't quite catch what he said, he was saying it that quietly. She asked him to repeat it.

'I was at the opera. *Madame Butterfly* by the Welsh National Opera. The guy behind the bar would remember me. I was that dehydrated, he poured me two glasses of tap water.'

'And your girlfriend. What did she drink?'

He swallowed and his eyelids flickered. 'She didn't drink. She was on the stage. She's an opera singer.'

OK. Now it was Honey's turn to blink. This dude with the rippling biceps was dating an opera singer. Not only that, but he then assured her that he'd sat through the whole thing from start to finish and had actually had tears in his eyes.

'Pinkerton was a bastard. He should have come back for Butterfly. I felt real sorry for that chick.'

Honey made a note to check where the opera had been performed and talk to the barman on duty, but could guess the answer. A dude like Victor had to have sat all the way through it to even hint at the plot. It disappointed her to have to do it, but for now she was crossing Victor Bromwell off her list.

On the way out she followed her reflection in the plate glass windows. Not too bad at all, she thought to herself. Navy blue suits you. Lindsey had bought the outfit on sale or return. The size was wrong and she'd been about to return it. Honey was in two minds whether to buy it off her. The truth was self-evident. She nodded at her reflection. It makes you look slimmer, and let's face it, girl, a few pounds from the purse buying this little number sure beats pounding the treadmill!

CHAPTER FIFTEEN

'Why have you brought me here?'

There was no answer. Sean Fox was scared. It was dark, pitch dark; not a light in sight. He began to run. He didn't know where to but it didn't matter, just so long as he made distance between himself and the man who had brought him here.

The track beneath his bare feet was soft; the scents and sounds of the forest were all around him. Wild garlic, pine trees, and the heavy smell of damp peat filled his head. An animal, probably a rabbit in the jaws of a fox, screamed before dying.

As he ran he cursed his shameful behaviour. He'd got into a car, something he'd done many times before, with mostly strangers; straight men by day, something different when they were away from home, family, and everything 'normal' by night. This time the driver had looked familiar. He'd said, 'Hello. Long time, no see.'

They'd talked like old friends, neither actually pressing to enquire where they'd seen each other before. The journey here, to the forest, had passed in friendly anonymity. Once they'd turned off the narrow road and on to a forest track, everything had changed. The friendly face had turned threatening. The words that had been so warm had turned cold and hateful.

At knife point, Sean had been ordered out of the car, told to leave his shoes, jacket, and warm sweater behind. And now he was running for his life.

The ground that had been soft turned stony and scattered with the debris from windblown trees. Though his feet were cut, he continued to run. He was frightened, he was breathless and he couldn't see where he was going. Like a drunken man, his legs were shaking and he veered from side to side in darkness.

Suddenly he fell. There was water beneath him and his hands clutched at muddy earth and clumps of fern. His forehead connected with a stone and the darkness deepened.

* * *

After a little old-fashioned research which consisted of picking up the telephone, Honey had acquired the address of Arabella's agent, Faith Page. She normally frequented Covent Garden in the heart of London's theatre district, also happened to have a cottage in the Wye Valley, and that was where she was at present.

She had never meant to get Mary Jane involved in going to Wales, but somebody had vandalised Honey's car. The old Citroen usually lived in a corner of the car park next to the bus station at the bottom of town. Unfortunately, building works were ongoing on the new shopping centre down there, so space was at a premium. Honey had parked the car in Forester Avenue instead. And that was the last she'd seen of it.

'Stolen!' said Smudger. 'Who would want to steal an ancient Citroen? I'd go for a Beemer myself.'

It occurred to Honey that if Smudger hadn't chosen a career in catering, he would have made a pretty good car thief.

'I'll pass on the BMW. My old Citroen had a wheel at each corner. That suits me,' Honey retorted hotly, miffed that the car was gone and even more miffed that Smudger was slating her car's desirability, albeit to a car thief.

Unfortunately her first choice of driver, Doherty, wasn't free so Mary Jane had enthusiastically stepped up.

Mary Jane stipulated that if she was to drive to the Wye Valley, then she couldn't possibly go unless she got to take a peek at Tintern Abbey. 'I hear it's haunted,' she added.

Honey rolled her eyes upwards as she tossed a mental coin on whether to go with Mary Jane or stay and travel another day — when she had a car or when somebody — anybody — else had a day off and could take her.

But there was no time. That was all there was to it. Arabella's agent had the reputation of being scary, volatile and hard to get hold of. With the help of someone who worked for the agency and was a friend of a friend of a friend of her mother's, she'd had managed to pin her down. There was nothing for it but to go.

Once she'd sorted out the transport situation, she phoned Doherty to let him know her plans.

'I'm going to tell her that I've written a book that's been optioned by Miramax and she's been recommended to me as the right person to sell it for me.'

'Let me know what you find out. Drive safely.' He paused. 'By the way, do you really want your car back?'

This was so exasperating. Was she the only person to place more value on getting from A to B than sitting in a spanking new car?

'We all get stuck in the same traffic jams, no matter how great our wheels,' she said to him.

'Your funeral. Ooops! Sorry. Figure of speech. Have a great time. It's great scenery over there. You could take a lunchbox with you.'

At mention of a lunchbox, she thought of the personal trainer's bulging bits. 'Oh, by the way, Victor Bromwell has an alibi. He was at the opera.'

'Is that so?'

'Yes. The lead soprano was having him for supper.'

If she discounted the fact that Mary Jane's driving made her sick, she had to admit that luck was definitely riding with her. She'd phoned Faith Page via her secretary and was told she was at the cottage and would see her.

'So this woman has something to do with programmes about haunted houses and all things paranormal?' said Mary Jane with great enthusiasm. 'Do you think she could get me on the show? I mean, I am a natural psychic. The spirits speak to me regularly and I'm mightily tuned into the earth vibes. Do you know that Wales and England are criss-crossed with ley lines? Especially Wales. It's a very haunted, spiritual land.'

'I thought it was the Land of Song,' said Honey absent-mindedly. 'Oh, and coal mines. It used to have a lot of coal mines.'

'Those too, but first and foremost it's full of spirits.'

Honey had armed herself with a notebook, a pen and a folder of blank paper so that she really looked the part of an about-to-be-famous scriptwriter.

The day had started fine, but the sky clouded and the rain began to fall the moment she hit the A466. There was a saying that it was always raining in Wales, but she reckoned that the luck would stay with her and it would brighten up.

Just as they swooped down into the valley the rain stopped and a patch of blue followed her along the road.

'That was lucky,' said Mary Jane, and Honey wondered whether she'd been reading her thoughts.

The abbey, a long-standing ruin thanks to Henry VIII, loomed large and imposing on their right-hand side.

The directions to the cottage took her to the far end of the village, a left-hand turning and a road that eventually led into the forest.

Narrow and lacking any sign of pavement or parking, there was just enough room for parking Mary Jane's car. Mary Jane had shipped the pale pink Cadillac from California. Like her, it was getting on in years, but still capable, though a trifle thirsty on the fuel front. With a bit of shunting backwards and forwards, enough room was left for other road users to pass by.

She told Mary Jane to stay put.

'Sure,' Mary Jane replied, closing her eyes and settling back on her seat. 'I'll commune with the spirits of the woods. It should be interesting.'

The cottage looked pleasant enough, thought Honey, though smallish and built of dull grey stones. Summer flowers exploded with colour from a series of window boxes and the leaves of a horse chestnut rustled from across the road.

She was half in, half out of the car when her phone rang.

'Where are you?'

No introduction. No 'how are you today'. Casper prided himself on having a uniquely recognisable voice — a touch of the Noel Coward who he tried hard to emulate even down to an ebony cigarette holder. The cigarette was unlit. Casper didn't smoke.

'I'm in Wales.'

'Wales? My dear girl, why? Do you have relatives there?'

'I'm on the case of Arabella Rolfe — stage name Neville, the woman I found very dead and very stuffed up a chimney. She used to be a TV presenter.'

'I know that. And a would-be singer, her main failing being that she acted like a diva even before she'd actually become one. And she couldn't sing. But why Wales?'

Honey explained about Arabella's agent having a country cottage in Tintern.

'It saves me going to London to question her. I'm incognito of course. Arabella's husband is prime suspect. He hasn't helped his situation by doing a runner. We still can't find him. I thought she might know where he is.'

She didn't mention that John Rees was a friend of Adam's or of her sneaking suspicion that John might be involved.

'I say again, my dear, what are you doing in Wales banging at this other person's door?'

Honey cleared her throat. 'Hmmm. I thought her agent might be able to shed some light on her character. She was a very pink person and rather aloof. I wanted to know whether her actual character matched her true persona.'

'You met her? This Arabella?'

'Yes. At the Roman Baths, courtesy of the Federation of Local Estate Agents. You must have seen her too — dressed in pink and white and wearing an Alice band.'

'Ah yes! I do recall such a creature. Granny trying to be girly.'

Honey thought Casper's take on Arabella was a bit harsh, and she said so. 'She's a stepmother, not a granny.'

'Do carry on with your little shindig in Wales, but do hurry back before you develop a chip on your shoulder. They have a lot of them in Wales.'

'You hate Wales that much?'

'Only since the mines closed and those grubby, gruff men singing in gorgeous choirs were no more. There's still the rugby players of course; very butch though not very dirty.'

She hung up, shaking her head.

Faith Page filled the doorway, her body like a cloth-wrapped pudding of billowing black. A Hampstead Bazaar label protruded from the neckline.

After initial introductions, she invited her in.

The interior of the cottage was unexpected. Like the TARDIS in *Doctor Who*, it really was far larger inside than out, though it wasn't filled with gimmicky electronics. Far from it. A large tapestry showing a hunting scene dominated one wall. Two brass table lamps, lit even at this time of day, sat on an oak coffer in front of the tapestry.

Faith led her through to a bright conservatory at the rear of the house.

'Do you take tea?' asked Faith after inviting her to sit down on an antique chair.

Honey said that she'd love a cup.

'Great.'

Faith Page pushed a tea tray in her direction with a pudgy hand and rings on all fingers.

'I've just made it. Help yourself.'

A quick survey of the tea tray revealed only one cup and saucer.

'Aren't you having one?' Honey asked.

Faith reached for a tall tumbler, a green glass bottle and a plastic bottle of tonic water.

'Gin,' said Faith. 'I don't like tea. I only drink gin.'

'Ah,' said Honey. Interesting.

After a few years in the hotel business, assessing what and why people did things became second nature. She had Faith Page sussed; Faith's escape to the country was to unwind away from London, clients, and anyone wanting a slice of her time. The gin was her solace and the reason an appointment had been so easy to get. Faith and her bottle of gin were bosom buddies.

'So!' said Faith, her snub nose lifted high, and her small, deep-set eyes as piercing as a surgeons' scalpel. 'You were recommended to me. Anyone I know?'

'Casper St John Gervais!'

It was the first name to fall into her brain and from there fell easily onto her tongue. Casper had such an impressive name.

Faith paused as though searching her memory banks. Honey hoped and prayed the gin had befuddled her recollections of names and events.

'I believe you met at a Noel Coward event,' Honey said breezily. 'Casper is such a sucker for Noel Coward. His greatest fan I should say.'

Faith's soft jowls relaxed as the suggested recollection was considered and accepted.

'Ah yes. Noel Coward.'

Of course, Noel Coward. Honey congratulated herself on using Casper's name then linking it to the noble Noel. Faith was taking her at face value.

'He said you impressed him greatly when you met and suggested you were the best agent I could possibly approach with my project. In fact, he added that nobody else would do,' said Honey, the fanciful explanation pouring like treacle from her tongue.

Already of generous proportions, Faith digested the flattery and swelled as though she'd eaten it whole.

'Ah!' she exclaimed, throwing back her head, her chest heaving with the enormity of it all. 'A man who knows what he's talking about. How refreshing. Most men talk out of their rear end. Well, they certainly think below the waistline.' She pulled a face and took a swig of gin.

'Do you know that I'm one of the top five agents in this country,' she continued, waving her glass around. 'If you write me a bestseller, an excellent script, or can act your ass off in front of the right producer, then I can make you rich. Give me the right material, leave me to promote you or your work, and you'll go straight to the top. Just don't bother me while I'm doing it. I don't like being bothered. I've got better things to do.'

The fact that Faith was supposed to be representing the artiste's work in all this was totally smothered by her highly inflated ego.

'Well, you do seem to have quite a reputation,' said Honey going out of her way to massage it a bit further.

The fact of the matter was that she'd made enquiries of a few people who knew of Faith Page, and none of them had had a good word to say about her. 'Faith Page is a right cow,' was the average comment.

'So was there anyone else who recommended me to you?' asked Faith.

'Another friend of mine, Arabella Rolfe informed me that you were the person to speak to if I wanted to get on in the world of TV, film and theatricals. She used to be Arabella Neville. I believe you were her agent.'

The gin paused on its way to Faith's mouth before resuming, the contents swigged back in one gulp.

'That fucking cow. She's dead, you know.'

Honey feigned horror. 'How dreadful!'

'I heard somebody did for her. Fucking cow. Had no talent anyway. Wouldn't listen to what I said. Thought she was better than what she was. Told me I wasn't doing my best for her. Ungrateful bitch! I should have dumped her years ago.'

'So she left the agency before she died?'

'Bitch! Thought she could do better elsewhere. Phoned me last week and told me so. The *cow*. Couldn't tell me to my face. Couldn't march in and tell me to get stuffed!'

Ignoring yet another stream of expletives being used to describe the very dead Arabella, Honey sipped her tea. Over the rim of her cup she scrutinised Faith's bitter expression, the pink cheeks, the red-rimmed eyes, and down-turned mouth. Faith was brutally honest, erring distinctly on the side of brutal. She also had meaty shoulders that looked capable of tossing a caber at the Highland Games or putting the shot in the Olympics. So was she capable of shoving a body up the chimney? Did she hate her ex-client that much?

'It sounds as though you didn't like Arabella very much — even before she left you. Do you think there was any justifiable reason for her leaving?'

Faith fixed her with slitty, mean eyes.

'It was all too late. She'd already done the damage. She wouldn't listen. OK, she wasn't the first to open her legs for a married man, but hey, that's fine for a pop star or someone with a femme fatale reputation. But the public believed she was all sugar and spice, the cute, innocent girl next door. They couldn't contemplate her being capable of breaking up a family, stealing the father of three kids.'

'But she wouldn't listen to reason?'

'Would she hell! I kept telling her that the public have to be kept sweet even though their lives are far from perfect. They want somebody to look up to and be the person they deep down want to be. Look at it this way, they felt betrayed and sorry for the kids and the abandoned wife. They've got enough of that sort in their own lives. They wanted Wonderland. The silly cow wouldn't listen. Jumped off the gravy train and hit the buffers.'

'I sympathise. It couldn't have been easy for you — I mean professionally as well as financially.'

Up until now, Faith Page's eyes had been narrowed and fixed on some point on the other side of the room where a flowering impatiens glowed from a willow-patterned soup tureen that had long ago lost its lid.

Now, Faith regarded her sidelong.

'What are you trying to say?'

'Well . . .' Honey couldn't help the length of her hesitation. 'Do you think she regretted marrying him? Adam Rolfe?'

'You bet she did. She was thinking of leaving him. It wasn't as though she'd be alone for too long. Not Arabella. Not the way she operated.'

'Do you think he killed her?'

She shrugged. 'If he didn't, he should have. The silly cow deserved it.'

'So I suppose you didn't speak much or meet up like you used to even before she left the agency.'

Faith Page leaned across the side table and poured herself another drink even though the ice cubes were steadily turning to water. After taking a sip, she lowered her head and looked up from beneath orange hair and jet-black eyebrows.

'If I'd met up with her and the circumstances were right, I would have murdered her myself.'

Honey made the 'oh' shape with her mouth, though no sound came out.

'Me and a whole army of other people,' Faith added, a creepy smile spreading over her face like a malignant rash.

'TV people?' asked Honey.

'Especially TV people. Amiable Arabella was a smile a minute on TV. Once the camera stopped rolling she was arrogance on legs. Ask anybody. Ask any of the poor sods who worked with her.'

'Interesting. Still, you're out of it now you no longer represent her.'

The malignant smile returned. 'Sweetie, I still do represent her. She owed me ninety days' notice, even if she is dead.'

'But you've just told me, and her husband would be aware . . .'

'You don't count. I can call you a liar. As for Adam, well that weak-kneed excuse for a man wouldn't dare stand up to me. If ever a man left himself open for intimidation, it's Adam Rolfe. Wimp! That's what he is. A wimp!'

Faith leaned forward, eyes hard with hatred. 'I'm telling you now, there's a fair chance she'll make me more money dead than alive. She was murdered. If she'd died from an illness — pah! No chance. But,' she said, her eyes gleaming as she reached for another shot of gin and tonic, 'she was murdered. All publicity is good publicity but getting herself knocked off is more than likely to repair all the harm that she did. I can just see all the TV streaming sites rushing to sign a contract for the repeats . . .' She raised her glass in a toast. 'Happy days are here again . . .'

She sang in a high rasping voice, a voice matured in a mix of alcohol, rich food, and French cigarettes.

'I know a psychic you might be interested in having on one of your shows,' she offered, suddenly remembering her promise to Mary Jane.

Faith waved a careless hand. 'Speak to my secretary. She deals with all that crap.'

'Thanks.'

'See yourself out.'

'One more thing,' said Honey, remembering what Casper had said. 'Did she ever have any children of her own?'

Faith laughed into her drink. 'Ask Sean. Ask Denise.'

'And they are?'

Faith's open expression closed shut like a door slammed against an intruder.

'People she worked with. People who snuggled up to her.'

This case, thought Honey, is getting more and more confusing. Now should I ask her what she means by these comments? Or should I let it be. Sozzled people can get pretty cranky at the slightest comment. Oh, what the hell . . .

'Literally?' she asked, caution flown out of the window.

Faith fixed her with a glassy-eyed stare. 'Her personal doormats — for whatever reason.'

It wasn't long later that a very confused Honey slid into the passenger seat of the pink Caddy.

Mary Jane was all eager eyed enthusiasm. 'Did you get me a slot on a TV programme?'

'She said she'll bear you in mind.'

It was far from the truth, and even if Faith Page had said that, Honey doubted it would happen. Faith, she reckoned, looked after Faith. Honey's take on the woman was that if a client achieved success through their own effort, Faith took the credit — and her percentage.

CHAPTER SIXTEEN

Lindsey was yawning at her computer screen when Anna came down from upstairs frowning hard at a piece of paper and chewing a pen.

'This list,' she said to Lindsey. 'It isn't right.'

'Really?' Lindsey stifled the urge to yawn again. She'd been away for two days and all the excitement and outdoor activities — which included getting to know new boyfriend Emmett in a very physical sense — had taken their toll. 'What list is that?'

'Polishers. Not wood polisher. Metal polisher.'

At the mention of metal polish — for that was what Anna was referring to, Lindsey woke up.

'Let me see.' She snatched the list.

Anna looked peeved. 'There is no need to snatch. You can see there should be six cans of metal polish, but there is only one. I have not used five. I could not possibly use five. I only do silver and brass with that polish. Anything shiny. That does not include toilet handles or towel rails, things like that. Damp cloth for them.'

'Ah,' said Lindsey. 'It's just a blip.'

Anna held her head to one side and frowned. 'What is this blip?'

'A blip is usually down to a one-off occurrence — such as if my mother suddenly bought a large brass monkey from the auction rooms. If it was dirty we would use a lot of metal polish to clean it.'

'Mrs Driver has not bought a brass monkey from auction. I have heard of these brass monkeys. She would not buy one, especially one made of brass, because bits drop off brass monkeys in cold weather. I have heard this.'

Lindsey's smile was pained but patient. 'That isn't what I mean. What I mean is . . .'

'That Mrs Driver used metal polish for brass monkey. But she did not buy brass monkey. I would know this if she did. She would tell me, Anna, I have bought brass monkey for you to clean, but be very careful not to put it out in the cold.'

'Never mind, Anna. If you run out of metal polish, let me know I'll nip out and buy some from Waitrose. Like I said, it was just a blip.'

Anna didn't look too sure about this whole business of blips, but Lindsey was the owner's daughter and Anna liked her job, liked the family, and had a growing family of her own to think of. Whatever her employers wanted to do with their metal polish was up to them. And if they wanted to buy a brass monkey whose balls fell off in frosty weather, well that was up to them. Clint had said, 'It's cold enough to freeze the balls off a brass monkey.' She'd taken it on board with as much gullibility as she had taken up his offer to view his new tattoos. Hence another baby in the offing.

Mumbling in Polish, Anna went back upstairs to attack the bedrooms with her brand-new Dyson cleaner and a whole plethora of cleaning fluids.

Lindsey, feeling a bit annoyed and also a bit guilty, reached for her phone and dialled a number. Emmett and the Twelfth Roman Legion were on a budget, but she really had to draw the line somewhere.

'Emmett. It's about the metal polish.'

Emmett said something about his performance during their weekend break. For a moment Lindsey was thrown totally off track. However, once she'd pushed the vision of his bare thighs out of her head, she got back on course.

'I said you could have *one* can of metal polish, not enough to shine up an entire Roman legion.'

'Hey! You've got a great polishing action.'

'Flattery will get you no more metal polish,' she said sternly. 'Buy your own.'

'I meant it. You can't deny we had a great weekend. And it took in a lot of polishing.'

'That's no reason for you to take advantage of an amenable situation.'

He pointed out that the legion he belonged to lacked the sponsorship and resources of the Ermine Street Guard, who had been going for some time and were quite well known.

'We have to make do with second-grade metal. Only metal polish and Vaseline keeps us from going seriously rusty — just like the Tin Man in the *Wizard of Oz*.'

'Oh yeah, and I flew in from Kansas. Only I didn't. So quit the sob stories. Anyway, I thought the Tin Man was a bit of a wimp.'

'True, but then I'm a lion inside,' he said.

Lindsey silently counted to ten. 'X,' she said at last.

'I'm forgiven,' he said exuberantly. 'I can tell. You counted to ten in Roman numerals.'

'Yeah, and X marks the spot.'

'Hey, babe. I'm only a humble waiter.'

* * *

'Have a good time over the weekend?' asked Honey, a few minutes.

'Great,' said Lindsey automatically.

Unfortunately, the check list for polishes, toilet cleaners, and sundries was still on the desk between them. Her mother scrutinised it.

Honey frowned. 'We seem to be going through a lot of metal polish.'

Lindsey pretended that there was something needing her serious attention on the computer screen.

'Dirty finger marks. There were a lot of dirty finger marks on the brass stair rails. We ended up using a lot more than usual.'

'Hmm. Has everyone been down for breakfast?'

Lindsey did a serious scrutiny of the list produced by the dining room.

'Everyone has had breakfast with the exception of Mr and Mrs Milligan.'

'Ah!'

Honey recalled the overweight gentleman and his very much younger bride. The bride had dancing eyes and a penchant for wearing clingy leather outfits.

The obvious thought had occurred that as a spring/autumn relationship, they weren't married at all, but just out for a fun weekend. Mrs Milligan had put her right, flashing her platinum wedding ring and the knuckle duster of a diamond that was her engagement ring.

'It cost Reginald *thousands*,' she'd breathed while fluttering her eyelashes at her less than nubile husband. It occurred to Honey that the poor man couldn't possibly have sighted his wedding tackle for many a long year — except with a mirror.

'Nothing is too expensive for my sweet little Bagpuss,' he'd gushed, his face pink and his pudgy hand holding hers.

Bagpuss! Yuk! How and why did people come up with names like that?

First things first. 'I think I'll check with Emmett to see how they were last night, or do you want to?'

Emmett had been on duty the night before. Honey wanted to get his feel on the couple before disturbing them, barging in when no barging in was called for.

Lindsey pretended that she didn't really care to phone Emmett, which of course she didn't. She'd only just put down the phone on him.

'No thanks. I'll leave it to you.'

'Do you find his outfit attractive?' Honey asked her suddenly.

Lindsey looked at her wide-eyed. 'I take it you mean the short skirt, metal breastplate, and plumed helmet. Not his starched shirt, bow tie, and neatly pressed trousers.'

'You know what I mean.'

'Yes. I've always had a thing for Roman soldiers. And knights in shining armour. Especially knights in shining armour,' said Lindsey, nodding affirmatively.

Accordingly, Honey phoned Emmett, who yawned into the phone before saying, 'Am I forgiven?'

'Why? What have you done?'

He laughed. 'Oh, Mrs Driver. It's you.'

'Do I need to forgive you for anything?'

'Um. No. I thought you were somebody else.'

'Obviously.'

She waited until she was certain that he was tuned in. 'Milligan. Mr and Mrs. Did you see them go up to bed last night?'

'Oh, him. Yeah . . .' Another yawn. 'Champagne. Two bottles.' Another yawn. 'To wash down the Viagra.'

Honey took this as a young guy's attitude to the older, overweight bridegroom. 'You're surmising. Just because he's a little older than you is no proof that he's not physically capable,' said Honey.

'I'm not surmising,' he protested. 'He told me that thanks to Viagra his soldier still stands to attention.'

'Okay. Too much information.' Honey rolled her eyes then looked directly at Lindsey. 'While we're on the subject of soldiers, is it possible that I can sponsor your soldiering weekends rather than merely provide the metal polish?'

Lindsey sunk lower in front of the computer.

'That would be great,' Emmett gushed. 'If you sponsor us, we can buy our own. You won't regret it, Mrs Driver.'

'I know I won't. It's tax deductible.'

'I'll pay for the polish. Sorry.'

Honey shook her head. 'Let's put it down to sticky fingers and leave it at that. Goodbye, Emmett. Get some rest. See you at six.'

She turned to Lindsey who was gradually unfurling herself from behind the computer screen. The metal polish fiasco was over. Honey judged she now had her daughter's full attention.

'Now, about Mr and Mrs Milligan. I think their non-appearance needs further investigation and I don't want to tackle it alone. Come with me.'

They headed to the drawer behind the reception desk where the master key was kept and bolted for the stairs.

'Thanks for sponsoring Emmett,' said Lindsey whose spirits seemed to have risen. 'He'll be dead pleased. He looks great in his uniform. You'll have to have a closer look at it some time. Maybe come along to one of the enactments. They really go all out for authenticity. And all well-built men that really look like soldiers. You'll love them.'

Honey stopped dead, obviously not listening. 'I think we need a man with us.'

Lindsey cottoned on to what was going through her mother's mind. She made a hissing sound through her teeth. 'I'll get Smudger.'

Wearing chefs' whites and a red bandana around his head, the chef accompanied them to the Milligans' room.

Honey knocked at the door. 'Mr Milligan. Mrs Milligan. Is everything all right in there?'

Someone responded, though weakly.

Honey looked at Lindsey and Smudger. 'Did you get that?'

Both looked blank and shook their heads.

She pressed her ear against the door.

'Someone is saying something,' she said, brow wrinkled in concentration.

Smudger nudged her aside.

'Let me.'

He did the same as Honey had done.

'I think I heard something,' he said.

'Yes, but was it "*come in*"?'

He shook his head. 'No. I don't think so. Hang on. I can hear something. I think it's . . . yes . . . that's it . . . "*Help me*"! Someone is saying, "*help me*".'

Honey made a quick decision and opened the door of the Green River's honeymoon suite which boasted a six-foot-wide oak four-poster bed. Drapes of light blue and gold brocade adorned each turned post, tied back with thick ropes, each ending in a heavy gold tassel.

'Help me.'

On the bed, lay Mr Milligan. Honey could tell instantly that he was dead, his weight pinning his new bride to the sheets. A cry of distress emanated from beneath Mr Milligan and a pair of feet wiggled out from beneath the naked body.

Smudger smirked. 'Like a giant duvet. Puts a whole new meaning on the phrase dying for . . . love,' he put in quickly after seeing Honey's warning look.

Mrs Milligan's head was turned sideways, possibly the only reason why she hadn't suffocated. Mr Milligan's weight alone was a potential killer; his kiss would have finished the poor woman off.

Honey pushed at Mr Milligan's shoulder so she could get face to face with his wife — his widow as she now was.

'We'll lift him off you. OK?'

'Is he dead?' she gasped.

'Most definitely.'

'I thought so. One minute he was steaming like a train, next he was . . . well . . . out of puff.'

'Yes. Well, he'll never be coming in on platform nine again, that's for sure. Just wait a minute while we try and lift him. My daughter's gone to get more help.'

'Just make it quick as you can. I'm busting to use the bathroom.'

'I bet you are.'

Mrs Milligan's casual treatment of her husband's demise came as no great surprise. Hotel residents were a micro-world of human behaviour.

'Luckily I packed a black dress.'

Mrs Milligan would make a very merry widow.

'Right,' said Honey smacking her palms together as though she really meant business. The three of them would lift and roll Mr Milligan off Mrs Milligan. Then she stopped. Smudger was pulling on a pair of the fine latex gloves he used in the kitchen. He saw her looking at him.

'What? I'm not touching a dead body without these on. It's not hygienic. Do you want some?'

He pulled two more pairs from his pocket.

Honey rolled her eyes. 'Give me strength. The man's dead,' she added in a whisper. 'Think of the widow's feelings.'

'No worries,' said Smudger. 'She gets to keep the diamonds.'

CHAPTER SEVENTEEN

Mr Milligan was duly collected by The Co-operative Funeral Service; apparently he'd been paying in for years.

Mrs Bunty Milligan had showered, changed and looked peachy in a plain black Viyella dress with a triple rope of pearls around her neck. She sipped Champagne and asked Honey to join her.

'He was a good sort, old Reg, and it weren't a bad marriage, though a bit too short. We were going on a cruise next month. Now I'll have to go on me tod, though I could take me old mum. She'd come as long as they play bingo and got a roulette wheel. She does like a bit of a flutter, does my mum. How about yours?'

Honey wracked her brains. Quite frankly she could never recall seeing her mother place a bet. It took a lot of persuasion to get her to buy a raffle ticket. She told Bunty that.

'Well, how about you? Do you fancy coming with me on a cruise? I think we'd get on OK, you and me. Bit of a laugh, like. What d'you reckon?'

Although the thought of going on holiday with Bunty Milligan was actually attractive, Honey declined. 'I've got this place to run.'

'You've got staff.'

'Difficult at present. I'm working on a murder case with the police. I'm Crime Liaison Officer for Bath Hotels Association.'

Bunty Milligan looked terribly impressed, her eyes round with interest.

'Never! Is that the Arabella Neville case?'

Honey nodded and sighed.

'That's it. Arabella Neville.'

Bunty Milligan slapped her thigh with a set of well-manicured fingers flashing red, apricot, blue, and purple nail varnish.

'Well I'll be blowed! I did hear old Arabella was dead — well — her that was Arabella Neville on television. Then she married that bloke,' said the widow Milligan. 'I knew her when she wasn't the big star. Fur coat and no knickers, as my old mum would say.'

Bunty Milligan — stage name Priscilla Pussy, exotic dancer — made no bones about her own background, nor her reasons for marrying Reginald Milligan.

'I wanted to be a ballet dancer when I was a kid, but what with my accent and my big boobs, it was never to be. With my figure and my need to dance, it was obvious I'd end up as an exotic dancer. Danced all over the place I did. Disrobed in front of Saudi princes, Italian counts, German barons, and God knows what other royalty. Texan millionaires as well. But there comes a time when you get tired of all that dancing and my knees were beginning to go. Not that you'd have noticed, mind you. They still look good, don't you think?'

Honey agreed that Bunty's knees were indeed still pleasant to behold.

'It must have upset you to give it all up,' she said, not sure whether it had, but thinking it the right thing to say.

'Not really,' said Bunty, Champagne in one hand, compact mirror in the other. 'I wanted a big 'ouse and loads of money. Reg Milligan wanted a warm belly and a pair of big tits to snuggle up to. Fair exchange is no robbery, as my old dad used to say. Nothing wrong in that, is there?'

Honey had to agree that Bunty's 'old dad' was probably right. From time immemorial, women had married men for security, and men had married women for regular sex. Bunty had also stated that she was no hypocrite about his death and that she would gain from it.

'He wouldn't mind,' she'd told Honey. 'As long as I was 'appy.'

'He's left you quite a lot?'

She nodded. 'Over ten million. That should keep me in silk sheets.'

It certainly would, thought Honey.

Bunty expressed her intention to stay a few extra days for the autopsy and the funeral, though the outcome was predictable. Too much fat coupled with too much exertion brought on by too much Viagra. After that she was off on this world cruise they'd already booked as their honeymoon treat, though only after a glut of shopping in Harrods.

'Did you know Arabella's husband?' Honey asked.

Bunty threw up her hands and almost mooed her contempt. 'Dodgy bleeder, 'e was. Wore a big ring through 'is nose. If he'd been a bull, they'd've put a rope through it — and cut off his balls. 'E certainly needed them cutting off!'

Not sure she was hearing right, Honey blinked and asked her to repeat what she'd said. Bunty obliged.

Honey slumped back in her chair. 'I never knew that. I understood Adam Rolfe to be a property developer.'

Bunty roared with laughter. 'Her last old man might 'ave been that, but the husband she 'ad when I knew her wasn't named Adam and he weren't no property developer. The bloke I knew as her husband was a gangster, a right bully boy. God knows why she fell for the likes of him, though she did hint it was a family thing; their dads being mates and Matt being the son. It was expected that they'd get together. I s'pose that's what it was. Oh, and her name back then weren't Neville. It was Casey. Tracey Casey.'

'Poor girl. Whatever were her parents thinking of, to lumber her with a name like that?'

Bunty grimaced and nodded. 'Yeah. Tracey Casey. What a handle!'

Honey grimaced. 'Poor kid. So this husband; I take it he lit out before she became a big name on TV.'

Bunty retouched her lipstick and nodded.

'You got it.' There was a rattling sound as Bunty threw make-up and mirror back into her bag. It sounded as though she were carrying a whole beauty parlour around with her. She held up the bottle of Champagne against the light from the window. 'Mustn't waste it,' she said, and she didn't. The Champagne went into the glass and what remained at the bottom of the bottle was chugged down in one gulp.

'Lovely,' she sighed, dabbing at her lips with a napkin.

'Did she hit the big time before the divorce from the first husband or after?' Honey asked, silently trusting the laundry firm to expunge bright red lipstick from the square of white linen.

Bunty looked at her as though she were stupid. 'Divorce! Are you kidding? He wouldn't have none of that. Beat her up when she asked for it. Oh no. He got knifed on 'is way 'ome from a club one night. Police reckoned it was a gang-land killing.'

Honey instinctively knew there just had to be a 'but'.

Bunty took a big bite of a jam and cream doughnut that she'd ordered as a chaser to the Champagne.

'But . . .?' she asked, feeling and probably looking too curious for her own good.

'Her dad was a gangster. Maybe he decided his daughter would be better off without her old man, but kept the problem in the family, so to speak.'

Bunty smiled. She had an expressive smile that flowed like warm chocolate. Honey understood why Reginald Milligan had married her; Bunty was a born entertainer, and Reginald had liked being entertained.

As for Arabella/Tracey Rolfe, she had more sympathy with the woman now she knew the details of her first marriage. She hadn't been *all* bad and hadn't deserved to die like that.

CHAPTER EIGHTEEN

Steve Doherty gritted his teeth and swore. The doctor was telling him he'd be on his back for at least two weeks.

'You've pulled a muscle. Badly, I'm afraid. Par for the course on the rugby field. Most definitely a game for young men.'

Doherty's back hurt; that was the bit of the diagnosis he had no argument with. But he totally disagreed with the being too old bit.

'I'm not old.' The muscle in his lower back jerked into a spasm when he protested.

'Old enough to know better,' said the doctor. Aged around fifty, the doctor was chewing gum and wore a black T-shirt with a slogan written in white. The slogan said 'Eat Me. It's Christmas'.

The police fifteen had been playing against the fire brigade fifteen. Pure machismo, the prospect of singing victory songs over a few beers in the Pulteney Arms, took over from common sense. They were going to whip the fire brigade; they were sure of it.

Doherty's enthusiasm had overruled his good judgement. Some of his colleagues were of the same age and similar mind set. Pride, as they say, comes before a fall — or a pulled muscle.

133

Full of confidence that experience could win, the police team had stepped onto the field only to find themselves confronted by fifteen stalwarts of less than twenty-nine years of age.

It was up to Doherty as team captain to give the pep talk.

'Don't worry lads. Young blood is green blood. Mark my words, they can't have the experience.'

A groundsman overheard, chuckled and spat out of the side of his mouth.

'You're wrong there, mate. They've won their last eight games. They're a champion side.'

'Only on a local level,' said one of Doherty's colleagues tersely.

'You wish,' said the smirking groundsman. 'One more win and they're South-west champions and off to the finals.'

The men of the fire brigade absolutely slaughtered the Bath police team.

Irked by the thought that the victory celebration would now be a case of drowning his team's sorrows, Doherty put in that bit more effort, tackling a man with the physique of a silverback gorilla. Clinging on for grim death, Doherty hooked his leg around the tree-trunk thigh of his opponent, meaning to send him crashing to the ground. His tactic proved successful. Unfortunately, he got it slightly wrong in that he landed underneath his opponent. The moment the big guy was hauled off him, Doherty knew he'd done himself a mischief. His ribs shouldn't be feeling that flat. He shouldn't be having such pain breathing and a muscle in his back felt spread over a wider area — as if squashed.

Two paramedics got him home, reiterating the warning already given.

'Stay in bed. Give it time to heal.'

He was none too polite on that front. 'F.O.'

The paramedic was used to offensive patients. He was brown, lean, and had elegantly long fingers which he posed on his hip. His face was expressive.

'I'm guessing your meaning but won't take offence. You're confined to bed. For two weeks.'

'One week and I'll be fine,' he protested as the paramedics prepared to leave.

They were having none of it. 'F.O. to you too. TWO weeks.'

The medic with the elegant fingers gave him a two-finger salute before leaving. Grimacing — with annoyance as much as pain — Doherty reached for the phone.

'Honey. I've injured my back. Properly this time. I'm in bed.'

He held the phone at a safe distance from his ear to avoid injury from the verbal tongue lashing. She'd warned him not to play. It had served only to make him more determined. Now she was saying, 'I told you so,' though in less than ladylike terminology.

'Hey! How about some sympathy here?'

She came back with, 'How about some common sense. How about growing up.'

'How about joining me? We can chill out while swapping information about the life and loves of Arabella whatsername and why she was stuffed up a chimney. There could be something symbolic about it. What do you say? I bet I've got some information that you haven't got.'

At the other end of the phone, Honey stabbed the point of a pen at the latest business rate demand from the city's treasury department. It might just as well have been Doherty. To get busted up was downright careless and inconsiderate and she told him so.

'Rugby is a young man's game.'

'OK, OK. I hear you. So what do you say? Care to join me?'

She imagined him lying there, helpless and hungry. Unless the pain was totally intolerable, the hunger would be for something more physical than information about Arabella's death.

'You can be my eyes and ears,' he said unnerved that she was taking her time answering.

So far she hadn't mentioned John Rees and his friendship with Adam Rolfe. It could be something, it could be nothing. In her heart of hearts she hoped that Doherty would throw her some piece of information that would totally exonerate any involvement on John's part.

'How about you tempt me with some little morsel to get me salivating? Tell me something that I don't already know.'

'Come on over and I will. Use your key. I can't get up. Then once I've told you what I know, and you've told me your conclusions, then I can show you mine and you can show me yours.'

She glowed pink at the thought of what he was suggesting.

'I take it we're talking physically.'

'Honey. What else?'

'You're injured. I don't think I should encourage you.'

'Hey. Encourage me. Please.'

* * *

Mary Jane was off to see a psychic friend who lived in a semi-derelict cottage in Lansdown. 'I'm going your way. I'll drop you off.'

'Murgatroyd doesn't believe in refurbishment and repair. It upsets the elementals,' she'd stated when Honey had asked her why her friend didn't give the place a facelift.

'So if the roof leaks?'

'The elementals have crossed over. They don't notice.'

So Murgatroyd was impervious to rain or at least put up with it because the spirits didn't mind.

The city passed in a blur of scattered pedestrians and angry car drivers. Even white van men, the centrifugal force of bullying motorists everywhere, looked through their windscreens with open mouths as Mary Jane wove in and out of the traffic.

Honey waved at them with both hands — a terror-inducing action until they realised that the steering wheel was on the left-hand side.

'Take this. Give it to your cop friend,' said Mary Jane as she got out of the car. Honey took the small leather pouch. It had Native American embroidery all over and the draw string was attached to a 'dreamcatcher', one of those string nets stretched over a small hoop.

'What does it do?'

'Well, you've heard of the tooth fairy?'

Honey nodded. 'The one that leaves money under your pillow after losing a tooth.'

'That's the one. Well, this one isn't a fairy. It's a kind of unseen spirit that massages painful bits when you're asleep.'

'But doesn't leave anything under the pillow?'

Mary Jane looked blankly upwards and shook her head. 'Not that I know of, though there's always a first time. Hang the totem above the bed. The spirit will get caught in the dreamcatcher and get to work on your cop friend's broken bits in no time. I guarantee it.'

Tucking the pouch beneath her arm, she let herself in with the key Doherty had given her. The surroundings were as familiar to her as the place she shared with her daughter. The décor was plain, black and white tiles, walls sage green, and a half-moon hall table on which was a dish where keys were dumped. She dumped hers, thought about dumping the totem there too, but changed her mind. Totem went with her to Doherty's bedroom.

He was lying flat on the bed, as wooden as it was possible to be.

'Hey, Honey.' He smiled and managed to wave his fingers — just two as it worked out, though not with the same meaning as the paramedics had done.

Honey smiled and waved back. 'Hey, you.'

He patted the space beside him. 'Care to join me?'

'Sorry, I'm working.'

His face fell. Then lines of amusement creased the corners of his eyes.

'You're giving me that hard stare.'

'It's my working face. You've got a working face. I've got a working face too.'

'Have I? I never knew that.'

'You got my message about my visit to Faith Page?'

'I did. So what's with these two characters she mentioned? Sean and Denise?'

Honey sat herself down on the bed, but at the foot, too far for him to reach her.

'They were colleagues of our murder victim, though I can't work out exactly how and why they were close to her. I'm not sure Faith Page knows herself.'

He frowned and looked thoughtful. 'I don't know, but I know something about Arabella's dad from when I worked in London. No one's seen him for years, though there are rumours he shot off for one of the Spanish Costas. Could be he's running rackets in Malaga. On the other hand he could be there for his health. Not the sort you upset if you want to keep breathing.'

'Interesting.'

It wasn't just the information that was interesting. The bedclothes only reached his chest. His shoulders were bare. She guessed the rest of his body was equally bare. It was hard, but she resisted temptation.

'Me or the information?' Doherty asked.

'That was some.' She ignored his remark. 'But there's got to be more. I won't come any closer until you give me anything that might be useful.'

'And then? When I've been a good boy and handed it over . . .'

Already warming to a few ideas, she folded her arms and smiled. 'Let's see where it leads.'

He grinned. 'I'm at your mercy. Do with me as you will.'

'Hmmm.'

'OK. Arabella Rolfe was done up to the nines when she was stuffed up the chimney at Cobden Manor. Right. I've told you mine, now you tell me yours.'

'I already knew that. I told you that myself.'

'His children were not allowed to visit. The eldest is eighteen. It's not beyond the bounds of possibility that he shoved his step-mum up the chimney.'

'I know she hated the kids.'

'You know?' He looked surprised, raising his eyebrows so much that it caused a twinge in his back. 'Ouch!'

'Serves you right,' she chastised. 'You shouldn't try and play with the boys. You're not a boy. You're a middle-aged man.'

'Hey,' he said, pointing sharply. 'I resent that.'

'So who is prime suspect?'

'My bet is still on the husband. Has to be.'

'But you don't know where he is, so can't ask him outright.' She began pacing the room, eyes down, fingers thoughtfully tapping her lips.

'No. But we do know there was a big insurance policy on her life.'

Honey looked at him, thought about it then shook her head. 'I don't buy it.'

Doherty winced as he folded his arms behind his head and frowned. 'Why not? You know damned well that the husband is always the prime suspect, especially when there's a prospect of financial gain.'

Honey shook her head again and continued to pace, tossing the embroidered pouch between her hands as she did so. Where did John Rees figure in all this? OK, if he didn't come clean when she asked him direct, she'd investigate indirectly.

Honey took a deep breath. 'So Arabella Rolfe used to be known as Arabella Neville, but was born plain old Tracey Casey and was married before. Back then her name was Mrs Tracey Dwyer.

'And the ex-husband is dead. If I recall, the word along the Old Kent Road was that Tracey's father didn't take kindly to Mr Dwyer beating up on his daughter and meted out his own brand of justice.'

Doherty fell silent. Honey looked at him and saw that the serious face was in situ; he was staring at the ceiling, chewing things over.

'How about the showbiz side?' he asked.

Honey filled him in on the details.

'Ms Neville — or Mrs Rolfe if you like — made a lot of enemies. She had a chat show at one point. A very cultured chat show. She was rude to the crew, rude to the sponsors, and rude to the people she interviewed. Seems she thought herself better than all of them.'

Their eyes met. 'It's perfectly believable that someone might hate her enough to kill her,' said Honey. 'What's the feedback?'

A number of Doherty's colleagues had been out and about asking questions of people who had worked with Arabella. They'd all been pretty much agreed that she was far from being the nice girl next door.

'I still think she was meeting a lover. It's a no-brainer. Lacy thong, stockings, perfume, and ridiculously high heels. She must have been meeting someone pretty special. Not her husband. Stockings are only worn for lovers.'

'Is that so?' Doherty looked hurt. 'So when do I get that sort of treatment?'

Honey stopped pacing. 'I will if you want me to. But not when I'm working. Anyway, you've got a bad back. I wouldn't want to cause permanent injury?'

Doherty's grin said it all. He was perfectly happy to accept permanent injury if the moment was worth it.

Honey gave him the evil eye. 'Stick to the subject.'

He sighed. 'OK. We've asked the first Mrs Rolfe, who has now returned home, where her husband might be hiding. She says she doesn't know, doesn't care, and is having a party to celebrate the fact that the second Mrs Rolfe is dead. She reckons they'll probably have a bonfire and burn an effigy of her.'

'No love lost between those two then. Do you think she did it?'

'Who knows? And there is the son to consider. At this stage everybody that knew her is a suspect. What's that?' Doherty nodded at the pouch Mary Jane had given her, distracted.

'A talisman, a totem if you like. According to Mary Jane I have to hang it above your bed and then this fairy . . . well not exactly a fairy — a spirit — will come along and massage your muscles while you're asleep.'

'I can't wait,' he said, warily eyeing the bag as she attached it to the headboard.

'What's in it?'

She sniffed it, sneezed and the contents went everywhere. Peering inside confirmed that there was nothing left in it.

She heaved a big sigh. 'I'll hang it up anyway. I wouldn't want to go back to the Green River with just an empty bag. Questions would be asked.'

They agreed he would keep his phone by his side and she would contact him.

Kissing him was kind of dangerous on account there was nothing wrong with his hands, but she kept it cool, ducking back at the right moment.

She told him to rest.

'But I could do with a massage?' he said and grinned.

'Just lie there and let nature — and Mary Jane's dream-catcher — do its work. Your back will be fine in no time.'

His grin widened. 'I wasn't talking about my back.'

* * *

Honey was still grinning on her walk down Lansdown Hill when the phone rang. It was John Rees. 'Honey. I need to speak to you in confidence. Can we meet?'

He sounded anxious. She guessed the subject matter wasn't going to be books.

Intrigued, she agreed to meet him.

'Though not until this afternoon. I'm having lunch with my family. It's my mother's birthday.'

CHAPTER NINETEEN

It was indeed her mother's birthday. And Mrs Gloria Sabine Cross, Honey's mother, had expensive tastes. Not for her the close proximity to other diners, wipe-down tables, or three-ply paper napkins offered by a high street restaurant such as Café Rouge. There was only one place that suited her tastes; the Dower House of the Royal Crescent Hotel.

The Dower House restaurant was approached via the main entrance to the Hotel. The hotel takes up a large portion of the middle section of the crescent with its sweeping views of the city. A more direct entrance existed at the rear off Julian Road. Honey knew her mother well. There was no way she would enter at the tradesmen's entrance. She entered via the front door or not at all.

Dressed to impress in an outfit usually reserved for evenings; the dress was of olive-green silk, its plainness offset by a gold brooch pinned to one shoulder. Her shoes and handbag were navy blue and matched the stones in her gold earrings.

Gloria cooed over the presents Honey and Lindsey had bought her. Nothing cheap would do. Honey's mother didn't do cheap, and there was no getting away with pooling funds and purchasing just one expensive present. Gloria Cross expected separate gifts from her daughter and granddaughter.

Just because they might be strapped for cash was neither here nor there.

The late eighteenth-century miniature of a sweet young woman in a blue dress had gone down well. Alistair at the auction rooms had tipped her the wink that it was for sale and at a very fair reserve. Unable to attend the auction herself, Alistair had bid on it for her.

'You'll not be disappointed, hen,' he'd said to her in his broad Highland accent. Honey knew the accent was mostly put on and that he actually came from Glasgow, but what was a bit of fantasy between friends?

'Never mind me. As long as my mother isn't disappointed.'

He captured the gravity in her voice and assured her that she'd made a canny purchase.

'How're you going on with the murder case by the way?' Alistair had asked her.

'My workload has doubled. Doherty's laid-up after playing rugby. I'm on this alone as far as the Hotels Association is concerned.'

'Rugby's a tough game suited to younger laddies,' said Alistair, his Scottish accent accompanied by a sage shaking of his head.

'I told him that.'

'So how goes the purchase of a country hotel?'

'Oh, not very well. I think I would have gone for Cobden Manor, but finding a dead woman in the chimney flue put me off.'

'Ah,' said Alistair with a backward flick of his head. 'Cobden Manor. Of course. They were moving to smaller premises and had to get rid of a lot of furniture. Nice items for the most part, but a few rum ones too. We're putting them up for auction.'

'You would be.'

There didn't seem much point in knowing anything more about the furniture. It couldn't have any relevance to the case. Anyway, she had a present and that was all that mattered.

Lindsey had dared to be more practical in her purchase of a birthday present. She'd purchased an option for chauffeur driven car to be used on twelve separate occasions.

Honey admired her pluck and guessed it came from being one generation removed from her mother — granddaughter rather than daughter.

'What is this,' her mother said when she first perused the stiff piece of card with embossed lettering. Her frown was deep enough to plant potatoes in.

All was sweetness and light once Lindsey had explained what it was.

'And you can take your friends,' said Lindsey.

Gloria looked absolutely appalled at the idea. 'Certainly not. I shall indulge alone.'

The meal was pleasant, the surroundings elegant and everything went swimmingly. The conversation was mostly about her mother's online dating business and obviously got round to the wedding that had turned into a funeral.

'Poor Wilbur. He was so disappointed that I just had to do something to ease his pain. Losing Alice on the day before the wedding.'

'Rotten luck,' said Lindsey. 'So what did you do to ease his pain?'

'Free introductions for twelve months. I assured him that women looking for men far outweighed men looking for women. He bucked up at that. It was the least I could do.'

It was on the tip of Honey's tongue to point out that good old Wilbur Williams was knocking on a bit and not likely to last twelve months. On reflection she decided that her mother was shrewder at business than she was. If Wilbur didn't last twelve months — highly probable at his age — then her mother had lost nothing; plus she'd placated a client.

'We're actually in the process of joining a group relationship site. It's when all different groups of like-minded people intermingle online and attend each other's social events.'

Honey was poking at an escargot that was proving reluctant to emerge from its shell. A quick slurp of the Krug she'd

144

ordered to celebrate her mother's seventy-fifth year — exactly the same figure as last year — was a welcome alternative.

'That sounds fun,' she said casually, with another poke at the snail.

She meant what she said. Her mother's latest business venture was going pretty well. OK, so it hadn't quite worked out for Wilbur and Alice. But you win some, lose some. Literally.

The plus side as far as Honey was concerned, was that she didn't get as many visits from her mother, and she didn't have to go round there so often. It was good that her mother was busy.

'I could do some good for you, Hannah,' her mother was saying.

Honey cringed. 'No you could not. We've talked about this. I'm already spoken for.'

Her mother turned to Lindsey. 'How about . . .'

'Me too, Gran.'

'Don't call me Gran!'

'Sorry, Gloria.'

Gloria Cross could not envisage herself as either old or a grandmother, hence she insisted her Lindsey called her by her first name.

Lost in myriad thoughts, Honey looked out of the window. A man and woman were making their way along the path leading away from the Dower House to the rear of the main building. Along a corridor, through reception would take them out onto the cobbled crescent itself.

They were holding hands. The man was dressed in light blue trousers. The woman was wearing stockings — seamed stockings, just like the ones Arabella Rolfe had been wearing.

It was no big surprise that Arabella Rolfe had had a lover, Honey thought. Everyone she'd spoken to acknowledged that she'd played the field. The trick was to track him down. The personal trainer had been something of a surprise. She'd fully expected him to be all meat and no brains. He'd certainly looked the part in his tight black vest, Spandex shorts, brown

145

hairless legs, and top of the range training shoes — that was when he was wearing clothes. Without them, he probably had a hairless chest, the result of regular exfoliation, plus honey-brown skin made glossy by the application of olive oil . . . but to find out that he was squiring — if that was the right word — an Italian opera singer of generous proportions and with the lungs to match was a shocker. She checked the woman's name from the website poster for the event. Sofia Camilleri. That was her name.

'Hannah!'

Gloria Cross fixed her daughter with glassy-eyed suspicion.

'Are we acceptable company, or were you expecting somebody else? George Clooney perhaps?'

'My mother is having a frozen moment,' Lindsey declared to her grandmother.

The word frozen seeped through into Honey's brain, fitting in nicely with what was already on mind.

'She was pretty cold though she hadn't been up there that long according to the Medical Examin . . .'

That was when she noticed the catlike expressions — like a pair of Siamese cats, one determinedly inquisitive than the other. Her mother and granddaughter were not amused.

'What?' she asked.

Gloria Cross, never one to refuse a glass of Champagne, waved at the second bottle which as yet was unopened.

'Is that there for decoration or is it about to make a speech?'

'Sorry,' said Honey placing the bottle on the table. 'My mind was elsewhere, but yes, we'll drink this one too.'

The waiter did the honours once Gloria had waved at him. Nobody could wave like Honey's mother, except the Queen. That wave that wasn't quite a wave but a regal acknowledgement — or command.

'So?' said her mother once her glass was brimming with bubbles.

'Yeah, Mother. So?' echoed Lindsey, for once seemingly swimming in the same stream as her grandmother.

146

Heaving a sigh, Honey raised her glass. 'Why not indulge in a second bottle? It's not every year we celebrate your seventy-fifth birthday, Mother.'

She caught a slight uplifting at the corners of Lindsey's lips. They'd celebrated a seventy-fifth last year and the year before that. Oh, what the hell . . .! Another one or two seventy-fifth birthdays wouldn't matter as long as it kept her mother happy. Neither would another glass or two of Champagne. And it was good. Extremely good.

CHAPTER TWENTY

The Champagne had, in fact, been uncommonly good. It was so good that she tingled from the tips of her toes to the top of her head.

Even though it was late afternoon, the air was warm or at least it felt warm. Though it could be my cheeks, thought Honey, testing their warmth with the back of her hand.

No matter. She felt good. Lunch had been good. Now she was back in the swing of things. Crime that is. Not hotel. Not until she'd seen John Rees just as she'd promised she would do.

'That's funny,' she muttered. Had John told her that he'd moved his bookshop? She didn't recall that he had, but it did seem that way. She was having a devil of a job finding it, so decided he must have done.

Thanks to the fresh air inhaled on a few circuits of Queen Square, her head gradually cleared. The route to the bookshop was finally remembered with greater clarity, though accompanied with a slight wobbliness of the chassis. She put this down to the heels of her shoes, not the Champagne. They were high heels, after all. Classy and sassy.

The door to J R Books had withstood three centuries of wet British weather, and no matter how many times John Rees took a plane to its hardwood frame, it was always reluctant to open. Two hands plus a nudge from a shoulder was the norm.

The old-fashioned brass bell jangled loudly heralding her arrival. The bell had always been there, though John insisted it had been used to summon the butler at a country house. She'd never believed that particular tale. The bell was as much part of the old building as the books were — or John Rees himself come to that.

Inside the air was thick with the smell of aged parchment and leather bindings.

John had his back to her, in deep and animated conversation with someone she could not see. He turned at the sound of the bell.

Honey smiled broadly. 'You said you wanted a word? It sounded very secret,' she added.

The man John was with stared at her unsmiling, his face hard and as serious as his clothes — expensive clothes with razor-sharp trouser seams and gold cufflinks.

She smiled at him too. 'Sorry to interrupt.'

'No matter,' he said curtly and glanced at his watch. 'I was just going. I'll be in touch, John.'

His smile was tight and he didn't linger, brushing past her, focused firmly on leaving.

Honey's antenna was working overtime. She'd definitely interrupted something.

She stood there grinning stupidly, waiting for John to ask if she wanted a coffee, a chair or even a cuddle in some dark corner. 'Was it something I said?'

His smile was forced. 'Of course not. Whatever made you think that?

'Did he buy anything?'

'From me? No,' said John, his smile more relaxed now as he shook his head. 'He's not interested in books.'

'Or maps?'

'Sometimes.

'Are you going to tell me about this man, or is it some big secret?'

Once she'd said it, she remained silent, arms folded, eyes fixed on his face, noticing the wrinkles at the corners of his eyes, the wisps of grey hair on his upper lip quivering as though he were about to say something but hadn't yet decided what.

He finally gave in. 'Gabriel Forbes. He owns an art gallery.'

'Oh. Well, what was it you wanted to see me about?'

It was only a split second, but she knew he'd been taken off guard.

'Oh, it was nothing. Just wondered whether you were still going to do the move out of town.'

'Are you kidding? Haven't you heard about Arabella Rolfe? Her of the pink Alice band and West End fashion? Strangled and stuffed up the chimney of her own house. Well, what used to be her house. Apparently the bank foreclosed.'

'Yes. I did. So that's that then. You're not buying the house. That's all I wanted to know.'

She didn't believe him. Perhaps it was the way he half turned away from her as he spoke.

He made a show at being busy, pretending to put some books in order. He'd never ever done that before when she was in the shop.

'Are you sure there was nothing you wanted to see me about?'

'No, I phoned you on a whim. I thought I'd have time for a coffee with you, but it so happens I'm now rather busy.'

The fiddling with books continued. It was getting downright irritating. Should she hang around or be direct? Or should she just throw in the towel, at least for now. She decided on the latter option.

'You knew Adam Rolfe quite well, didn't you?'

He paused, two books in his right hand, his left hand covering them as though wanting to hide the titles.

'How did you know that?'

'You told me so at the Roman Baths event. Arabella was there, but her husband wasn't. You hinted they'd probably had a row, so on that score I guess you knew both of them pretty well. You said Adam used to collect maps.'

His face fell and he looked embarrassed about being found out.

'So I did.'

Arabella had been there. John had been there. Arabella had been looking at John. This was one of those occasions when she couldn't help putting one and one together and . . . well . . . making two.

The question had to be asked. But she couldn't do it.

'She was dressed to the nines when they found her. Right down to her underwear. They were the sort of clothes a woman wears when she's meeting a lover.'

'Not me,' said John. 'She wasn't meeting me. So don't ask me that. Certainly not me. Adam is my friend. I wouldn't do that.'

She immediately regretted what she'd said. John wasn't the sort to have illicit affairs.

'Sorry,' she said. 'I should know better.'

John put down the books and heaved a huge sigh. 'I suppose you had to ask.'

'But she did have a lover?'

He nodded. 'Arabella *always* had a lover, though who the latest one was I don't have a clue.'

'The police are desperate to ask Mr Rolfe about his wife's death, but he's disappeared.'

Suddenly John started stacking books again.

'Look, Honey. You'll have to excuse me. I really am behind schedule. We'll catch up next week sometime. OK?'

She gave him a hard look. 'OK.'

It was hard to leave. John Rees was agitated about something, but wasn't letting on what it was.

Adam Rolfe is a friend of his. He's worried about him. She'd waved at him. 'OK. If you change your mind about whatever it was, feel free to get in touch.' She glanced at her watch. 'Oh well, I'll be off then.'

He waved a hand, one side of his mouth curving upwards into a half-smile. 'See you.'

Once outside she took a deep breath. John was being evasive and she'd promised herself that if he continued to be that way, she'd switch to plan B. If he wasn't going to be direct with her, then she wouldn't be direct with him. She'd go undercover. She'd discover what he was up to.

The thought of going undercover was pretty exciting. In a sudden need of external advice, she thought about phoning Doherty but stopped herself. There he was, lying supine and all alone in bed, and in receipt of a phone call regarding John Rees. She'd have to explain too much and had no wish to. Being close to John in any respect might make Doherty jealous.

Visiting John's book shop had only ever been for pleasure and he'd been pleased to see her. Just now he'd been edgy as though waiting for an axe to fall — or more likely a question to be asked. He'd admitted to her that Adam Rolfe was a friend of his. That night at the Roman Baths, Arabella had waved and smiled at him.

A horrifying thought struck her: did John have anything to do with her death?

On reaching the end of the alley she glanced back at the shop. One part of her wanted to tell the police (aka Steve Doherty) that she suspected John knew more than he was letting on. The other half of her refused to believe he could possibly have a criminal bone in his well-toned, highly desirable body . . .

Stop that! She wasn't sure whether it was the voice of her conscience or Doherty sending her telepathic messages. Whatever, she couldn't bring herself to shop such a dear friend to the police. Not until she was sure. So she had to make sure.

CHAPTER TWENTY-ONE

The arched framework and brass sill of the window had been the height of shopfront fashion during the reign of Queen Victoria. Before that the windows had been bow-fronted and made up of small panes of perfect and not so perfect glass. The latter were known as Bullseye glass, mutated at the firing stage by a ripple effect.

John eyed the people jostling in the alley, squashed together where the alley was narrowest, some stumbling over the crumpled flagstones that were almost as old as the buildings. Overhead a mere sliver of summer sky showed between the buildings.

When viewed through the dimpled glass the faces of those in the crowd were distorted into odd shapes, their features elongated or hopelessly spherical.

John came away from the window, the familiar contents of the shop soothing his jangled nerves.

Two gentlemen from Rotterdam had come in immediately following Honey's exit. They had spent over an hour perusing the collection of atlases for sale and, uncharacteristically, he'd left them to it.

The way they had pored over his stock, heads together, shoulders hunched, had reminded him of a painting by an

Old Dutch master, of gentlemen wearing black hose and doublets.

Leather-bound books, their titles etched in gold on padded spines, gleamed from the shelves to the right of the door. To the left hefty atlases lay on a lectern arrangement running the full length of the wall. Jostling for space above the atlases hung a series of maps in ebony frames.

John Rees exuded a passion for the items he sold and had an aversion to selling his stock to someone who didn't share this passion. On the other hand he was honest about his stock, open should the authenticity of an item be somewhat questionable.

The bookshop was his life. He never tired of the smell of dusty books and old ink. Seeing as he had no other love in his life — not one who was currently available anyway — his affection stayed focused on his books.

Narrowing his eyes, he turned his gaze away from the world outside and on to a particularly lovely eighteenth-century atlas. Not that he was really taking in the fine detail or the overly flowery language. No. Instead he was thinking of Honey Driver.

He'd felt bad being so offhand with her, his own fault for considering betraying his secret. He'd almost done it too but stopped before things had gone too far. He'd never been so cold with her before and all because he'd stepped out of line to help an old friend.

Eventually the two gentlemen from Rotterdam bought a number of ancient maps plus an excellent atlas from the early nineteenth century.

On the dot of six o'clock he shut and locked the door, slid between the shelves to the back of the shop, picked up the phone and dialled a number. The call was answered almost immediately.

'Look. I want nothing to do with this. If I had known what you were up to . . .'

The voice on the other end offered him the world — if only he would do what was asked of him.

'No,' he said. 'No!'

He put the phone down and closed his eyes. He could feel sweat congealing on his forehead, soaking into his hair. Honey must have guessed that something was up. He'd seen the look on her face, and no wonder. He'd not greeted her like he usually did. He hadn't offered her coffee. He hadn't communicated with the usual spark that seemed to flash between them. In short, he hadn't been himself and she'd cottoned on. He was sure of that.

CHAPTER TWENTY-TWO

Being sneaky wasn't nice. Neither was it part of her nature, but Honey Driver had made her mind up. She was going to be sneaky. In fact she was going to be super-sneaky, like a Cold War spy, or one of her mother's old friends who sneaked into neighbouring gardens and allotments to dig up spuds or slice off the head of a cauliflower. She'd never been caught. That's the kind of sneaky Honey wanted to be.

There was one major reason for doing this; John Rees was acting suspiciously and out of character. He was admitting nothing. Neither was she come to that, at least, not to herself. She liked him. That was the plain fact. He wasn't telling her what the problem was, so she felt obliged to find out for herself. To do that, she had to be sneaky. Kind of like an undercover cop. If he wasn't going to help himself out of the hole, then she had to do it for him.

At twenty-five past five, she slipped into the charity shop on the corner of George Street and Gay Street. Scurrying swiftly between rails of limp cotton dresses, knitwear, and outsize trousers, she found a box of scarves nestling beneath a shelf of affordable accessories. Following a quick rummage she sourced a silk headscarf from the box and a pair of cheap sunglasses from the shelf of accessories.

After paying for her purchases, she put both on straight away explaining to the elderly assistant that the silk cooled her head and the sunglasses eased her aching eyes.

'It's been a warm day.'

The assistant craned her neck like an egret wondering about the best time to leave the nest. The weather outside didn't look that good.

Honey rushed out looking like a refugee from Badminton Horse Trials. A quick glance at her reflection in the gleaming window confirmed that she'd made a good choice. Headscarves sporting hunting scenes were famously worn by the royal family and owlish sunglasses by the late Jacqueline Kennedy Onassis. She didn't look like either. Best of all, she didn't look like herself.

Disguise complete, she hurried along George Street, down into Milsom Street and beyond, finally taking a left turn into the narrow alley where John Rees's bookshop was located.

The two last customers of the day emerged first, one clasping a large book beneath his arm, the other something equally large wrapped up in brown paper. Purchased books came out in a dark green carrier bag displaying the shop's emblem — J R Books — in gold. She hazarded a guess that the brown paper parcel contained a map – perhaps two.

Just in case John should spot her, she turned her back on the bookshop. There was a nice shiny shop window in front of her, ideal for reflecting the scene across the road. Undercover cops did things like this all the time. She'd seen it on TV. The trick was to concentrate on the reflection of the bookshop door. The difficulty lay in ignoring the display of chocolate fudge, rum fudge, toffee and Cornish cream fudge, on and on, more mouthwatering favourites . . . Creamy smells filled her head, made her stomach rumble and her mouth water. There was nothing easy about being sneaky.

John finally came out, locked the door and turned instantly away, heading in the direction of Stall Street.

Honey was confident that she knew all there was to know about working undercover. I mean, she thought to herself, how difficult can it be? Those guys on TV do it all the time. She'd watched and learned. That was all there was to it.

First off she counted to ten, took a deep breath then set off in pursuit. The main thing she'd learned from those TV cops was that she had to be quick on her feet. Nipping into a shop doorway or pretending to read a newspaper or study a bus time-table pinned to a lamppost was part of the game. If he should chance to glance over his shoulder, she had to act — and fast!

She analysed what might go through his mind if he did spot her. Would she be instantly recognised? A glance in yet another shop window confirmed it as unlikely. She was just a woman in a headscarf, if he saw her at all. Women in head-scarves are nondescript, she decided, and promised herself never to wear one out of choice. They looked middle-aged. They looked unattractive.

The likely conclusions as to why he would fail to recog-nise her came fast and furious. She only hoped she was right.

There was, of course, an element of guilt in doing this. Despite her suspicions, she had a genuine affection for John Rees. He was the sort of man a woman could openly regard as her closest confidante. OK, yes, he had lover potential writ-ten all over him, and in all honesty she couldn't deny that, if the occasion was right, she might very well be tempted. If he found out she was following him, she'd never figure in any of his sexual fantasies again — not that she knew for sure that she did, but hell, John sometimes figured in hers. In her heart of hearts it would always be Steve Docherty, but it didn't hurt to keep something in reserve. Naughty but nice.

This isn't a mean move, she told herself. You sense that John is holding something back and a pound to a penny it has something to do with Adam Rolfe. He's being secretive. Even deceitful.

She shoved the thought that she was being equally secre-tive and deceitful to the back of her mind. She was Honey Driver, Crime Liaison Officer and superior spook — or were spooks spies? No matter. She could be whatever she wanted to be: Honey Driver, private investigator.

His confident stride took him out of the alley and into the melting melee of shoppers, tourists and people on their way home from work.

John lived in a flat just around the corner from Quiet Street and behind the premises of a magazine publishing company. She supposed that was where he was heading, though it wasn't a dead cert.

Being in disguise was amazingly reassuring. The warmth of the day was gone and her jacket was linen and a little tight around the bust. All the same the two front edges met comfortably enough and kept her warm.

It suddenly occurred to her that if he went straight home she'd have to ring the bell and invite herself in. She practised what she should say, decided that wasn't the only option. The police would do a stakeout and she could do the same.

Easy!

Cobbles were breaking through a thin layer of tarmac in the narrow road where John Rees lived. She dived into the doorway of the Canary Tea Rooms immediately opposite John's front door while he fished for the right key and opened the door.

The Canary Tea Rooms were closed and gloomy within but window glass was a wonderful thing. The old building that housed John's apartment and especially his front door were clearly reflected. Now all she had to do was wait for him to come out — if he came out, that is. She hoped he did. She didn't fancy an overnight stakeout.

The shadow of a passing pedestrian paused behind her. Had she been discovered? Had John spotted her, sneaked out through a secret entrance, and crept up behind her.

Her blood raced. She saw the man's features. It wasn't John. It wasn't anyone she knew.

The man was wearing a khaki sweater, had a thin face, a receding hairline, and a big nose.

'Bit early love, but I'm game if you are. How much you charging?'

Turning round was out of the question just in case John chose that moment to glance out of a window.

'Get lost or you're nicked,' she spat over her shoulder.

'You what?'

He sounded drunk. She had to get rid of him. Mindful that John's window overlooked the street, she only partially turned.

'Get lost or I'll take you down the station and charge you with kerb crawling.'

'A copper? You a copper? You don't look like a copper. You got too big an ass to be a copper.'

'Right,' she said, riled beyond belief. 'I'm nicking you.' She brought a pen and pad from her pocket — her shopping list notebook. 'Name and address. I take it you're married? What would your wife think of you?'

The verbal assault had the effect of making him walk backwards.

'Pig bitch!'

'A female pig is called a sow, you cretin!'

She was angry enough to shout but kept the volume down. It came out as a hiss. Nasty but not loud. It had the desired effect. Her would-be punter for sexual services sloped off. Honey slunk further into the depths of the doorway.

Although it was only just past six o'clock, her stomach began to rumble. The sugary scent of the fudge shop had followed her from the alley. Vanilla, Cornish cream, chocolate, caramel, and almond; it was all there whirling in an afterhours miasma through the twisting alleyways.

Think about something else, she said to herself. But thinking about something other than fudge allowed doubts to creep in.

For a start it wasn't a dead cert that John would re-emerge. What if he stayed indoors till morning? What then?

You'll be the one arrested for lurking in a shop doorway with intent to do something, she thought. Like breaking and entering. Or soliciting.

For various reasons, the pressure to adjourn her stakeout was enormous. Her stomach was the prime mover in this. Real cops doing real stakeouts must have the same problems.

Just when the lure of a supper of devilled kidneys threatened to drag her back to the Green River Hotel, something happened. The dark blue door to John's apartment block opened. John was coming out, carrying a brown paper parcel, one similar to that carried by the two men she'd seen leaving his shop.

John kept up a good pace all the way through the Guildhall Market and out the other side winding his way through the chairs and tables of pavement cafés, skirting billboards and swinging towards Pulteney Bridge — towards the Green River.

The small café immediately overlooking the bridge was shut. By day its customers had the best view possible, its arched windows overlooking the foaming waters of the weir.

John Rees passed the shops and headed down Manvers Street.

With just a teeny pang of jealousy, it occurred to her that he might have a girlfriend. At one time that could have been her, but she'd made her choice. Steve Doherty had been more determined; John more relaxed and casual in his approach. *It's there if you want it*, kind of approach. Still, it didn't hurt to have a spare male interest. Or a spare career prospect. How much did private investigators get paid?

Pacing her steps with his was something of a challenge. There was a definite skill in maintaining the distance between them and she was pleased at her prowess.

Like a panther.

My, oh my, she relished that description. She was so low-key, so stealthy in her approach, and nobody, nobody had recognised her . . .

'Hannah! Hannah! Is that you? What are you doing in that get-up? It doesn't suit you.'

Honey dived beneath the ebullient umbrella of a café table, head hidden between the spokes, body still clearly visible. Nobody who'd ever met her mother could fail to recognise her shrill voice.

Her mother too dived beneath the umbrella, her expression puzzled.

She sniffed. 'What's that smell? Where did you get that scarf? What are you doing going around dressed like a train-spotter's grandmother?'

Honey rolled her eyes. 'It's fancy dress.'

Her mother pulled her down into a chair, one eye narrowed in an expression of disbelief. 'I didn't bring you up to be a liar, Hannah. You look shifty. Are you meeting someone?'

'Of course not.'

'Would you tell me if you were? Is he rich or famous? I do hope he is. Never mind, you don't have to tell me. As long as he's rich, I don't care what he is.'

'Mother, I do not have a new man in my life. I'm perfectly satisfied with the old one.'

Her mother sniffed. 'Is that cats I can smell? Where did you buy that dreadful scarf?'

'Charity shop,' Honey mumbled.

For a moment, her mother stared at her open-mouthed. 'Are things that bad you have to buy second-hand clothes? It smells as though somebody wrapped their cat up in it. It probably had fleas. Cats are very prone to fleas.'

'It belonged to an old lady.'

'Old ladies are famous for keeping cats. It's something they do in their old age. And they talk to them. That's why they got burned as witches, you know. Lindsey told me all about it.'

'You're an old lady, mother.'

Her mother looked seriously affronted. 'I'm not old enough to keep cats. So why are you wearing it?'

'I told you. It's a fancy dress party. I'm on my way there now.'

It was fine to lie. Private investigators did it all the time.

Her mother reappraised the scarf. 'What's the theme of this party? Smelly street people?'

162

'*No*. A scarf party. It's a scarf party.'

'Hmm!' That was it for the moment, purely because Gloria had sighted a waiter going begging for a bar order.

Up shot her hand and click went her fingers. '*Garçon*, get me two schooners of sherry.'

'I don't like sherry,' said Honey.

Gloria Cross ignored her. Gritting her teeth above and beyond the pain threshold, Honey looked away.

'Now,' said her mother, her look intent and her fingers interlocked. This made the rings on each of her fingers bristle like the back of a bejewelled turtle. 'I've been thinking about the fixtures and furnishings of this country hotel — once it's suitably renovated and refurbished, of course. Chintz would be nice. All country houses have chintz. And Chinese carpets. White marble table lamps with pink silk lampshades . . .'

Her mother droned on and on. She had it all planned out. 'I've done drawings — not technical ones, but artistic impressions of what the finished room will look like.'

'Mother, a woman was found murdered in that house. It was me that found her.'

'So? Should that really put you off what could be a very good business deal?'

She gave her mother a firm look. 'Yes.'

'Hannah, I have gone to an awful lot of trouble for you. I've had all these designs done, and now you're telling me you're not going through with the deal?'

Honey sighed. Her mother just wasn't getting it and John Rees was getting away from her.

'OK. Great. Have you got them with you?'

'No. They're at home. You'll have to call in and take a look. Jean Paul helped me draw them up. He's very artistic.'

Honey resisted rolling her eyes again and swigged back the sherry. At first it was sweet on her tongue, but burned at the back of her throat before she swallowed it.

'Who's Jean Paul when he's at home?'

It was faint, but Honey detected a pink spot erupting on each of her mother's cheeks.

'He's a very close friend. He's from the Dordogne.'

'He's an interior designer?' she asked, intrigued.

Her mother shook her head. 'No. Not exactly. He's retired from all that kind of thing. But he's French. He's lived in the UK for a number of years.'

A nasty little niggle gnawed at Honey's insides.

'Did you meet him online? Through your dating site?'

Her mother did coy big time. 'Sort of.'

Honey leaned back in her chair. A little distance was needed, not only to rein in the surprise, but just in case her mother caught fire. She'd started fanning herself with a red paper napkin.

'So he's hot. Is that what you're saying?'

Her mother gave a funny little smile and there was a definite twinkle in her eyes, the kind of twinkling that the over-seventies are not frequently prone to.

'Well, yes. Why pass round the best dishes to one and all? I thought this particular dish I'd keep to myself.'

Honey was amused. 'You know, just because he's French doesn't make him an interior designer.'

'Well Jean Paul is just that.'

Honey wasn't about to argue. When her mother made up her mind about someone or something — especially a man — there was no reasoning with her. In the meantime, John Rees had got lost in the crowds.

The waiter came back. He had white teeth, tanned skin, and blue-black hair slicked back with oily gel.

'Another sherry, ladies?' His smile almost split his face in half.

'Yes. And make it a large one,' snapped Honey.

'I thought you didn't like sherry!' Her mother eyed her accusingly.

Honey whipped off her headscarf and sunglasses. There was no sign of John Rees so no point in maintaining the disguise. Besides which her head was beginning to itch.

Just as she was debating whether to head for home and wash her hair in a mixture of vinegar and something lethal to fleas — like witch hazel — raised voices sounded from inside the wine bar.

She looked towards the door, glancing an interior of dark wood, waxed floors and features lighting.

The waiter who had served them was escorting a young man from the premises. One hand was on the young man's shoulder, the other wrenching his arm up behind his back.

'You can't do this to me,' he shouted, tossing his head and sending his long hair flying. There was a scowl on the public-school features and he was wearing clothes that looked slept in.

'Leave me alone!' he shouted. 'I want another drink. I demand another drink!'

Keeping a firm grip on shoulder and wrist, the waiter bundled him down the steps.

'You have had enough, sir,' he said with grim politeness.

Her mother tutted. 'It's a fact that people in this country drink far too much.' She took another sip of sherry.

The young man heard her. 'Don't you bloody tut at me, you old cow!'

Honey covered her face with her hands and groaned. It was a bad move on his part. Just because her mother was knocking on in years, didn't mean to say she no longer had a fire in her belly.

In a flash, Gloria Cross, five feet five in kitten heels, sprang to her feet. Whack went her handbag around the young man's head. Once. Twice.

'Apologise before I beat you to a pulp. I've got some heavyweight weapons in this handbag, and don't you forget it. There's more if you want it. Well do you want it, punk? Do you?'

Honey came out from behind her hands. When it came to reading, her mother was a great fan of Mills and Boon romance. When it came to films, Clint Eastwood — the real McCoy complete with gun and skinny trousers — did it every time. So did Sean Bean in the title role of Sharpe, though mostly from the tight-trousered rear.

Two more hits from her mother's weighted handbag and the young guy was on the floor.

'No more,' he shouted, arms wrapped over his head. 'That bag's lethal.'

'It's a Mulberry,' cried her mother after biffing him one last time. 'And it's made from renewable resources. Ostrich skin in fact.'

Fearing headlines of *Elderly lady beats drunken youth to death*, Honey intervened.

'Mother, I think he's had enough.'

Her mother lowered the bag, then exclaimed: 'Oh, my! I must look a mess.' She proceeded to sit back down. Powder, lipstick, and magnifying mirror were drawn from her bag. 'No matter what happens in life, there's no excuse for not looking your best,' she said while pursing her lips and retouching her paintwork.

Honey figured she had plenty of excuses for letting her make-up get smeared and her lipstick smudged. Life was too short to spend painting her face.

The teenage boy sat on the pavement, head on knees, arms folded over his head. Honey bent down at his side. 'Are you OK?'

He seemed to think about it a minute before shaking his head.

'No. I'm not OK. Nothing in my life will ever be OK again. It hasn't been OK for seven years. Seven bloody years!'

Taking an interest in the woes of a teenager wasn't high priority on Honey's to-do list. However, she'd experienced enough teenage angst to consider herself something of an expert.

'Come on,' she said, gently touching his shoulder. 'Tell me where you live and I'll take you home.'

She'd expected him to tell her to get lost, but he didn't. He gave her his address. It seemed vaguely familiar. Come to that, she realised, so did he.

She asked him his name and added, 'If you like you can also tell me what the problem is. I'm a good listener.'

He chewed his bottom lip as he considered. 'My name's Dominic Rolfe, and I think I may have killed my stepmother.'

CHAPTER TWENTY-THREE

In the taxi Honey had hailed to take them both home, Dominic Rolfe unburdened himself. Honey was all ears. It wasn't often somebody confessed to murdering their wicked stepmother.

Holding his head in his hands, Dominic told her all about it.

'I had this row with my father. I stormed out, basically calling him a coward. He just wouldn't stand up to her. She wouldn't let us visit him, our own father. And he wouldn't do anything about it.'

Honey listened attentively as it all poured out; the lunchtime meeting at the Café Rouge, Dominic storming out after telling his father not to bother to visit him at university.

'And then?'

Dominic Rolfe had brandy-brown hair that flopped over his forehead. He regarded her out of the corner of his eye from beneath his heavyweight fringe for a moment.

'I phoned him later. Not to apologise, but to try and get him to wake up to the truth. I was so bloody angry. I told him that Arabella was having an affair. That she'd had more than one affair, but that this one was a big one and soon she would walk out on him and he would be alone. We, his children, would be all he'd have left, so wasn't it time to make amends? Isn't blood thicker than water?'

'Of course it is.' This was all super stuff, Honey thought, grist to the mill as far as the crime was concerned. On the other hand, poor Dominic was having a hard time and Honey felt sorry for him.

He let his head fall into his hands.

'So was it true? Was she really having an affair?'

He shrugged. 'I don't know for sure, but my mother said she was. She said there were rumours.'

And your mother wasn't wrong, thought Honey. Dominic's stepmother had been dressed to kill — and had been killed. There had to be a lover. Everybody said so. Stockings and slinky underwear were not made with comfort in mind. They were the tools of seduction, the mainstay of erotic fantasy. You wore them for a someone else's benefit. A night in by the telly, you wore comfortable clothes. The sexy stuff was for special occasions.

'So you told your father that your stepmother was having a serious affair. Who with?'

Dominic folded his fists beneath his chin. His eyes remained fixed on the taxi floor and his face was red. She might have thought he'd been crying if she hadn't seen the way her own mother had whacked the lad with her handbag.

'The estate agent,' he said quietly.

Honey felt a distinct tightening in her chest and a great temptation to shout, 'Whoopee!' She reined in the temptation and took a deep breath.

'Does this estate agent have a name?'

Dominic nodded. 'A daft name. Glenwood Halley. My mum said he's the sort that women can't resist and that Arabella was the sort that men can't resist. She reckoned the two of them were made for each other.'

Honey kept telling herself that this was all hearsay, but boy, oh boy, did she want it to be true. For a start she didn't much like Glenwood Halley. He deserved to be guilty of something and if it happened to be adultery that could

— just could — lead to murder, well how neat would that be? The likely scenario sprang into her head. The lovers arrange to meet, they argue because Arabella wants a serious commitment and Glenwood, although he adores her, isn't quite ready. Glenwood loses his rag and kills her. There were flaws to this scenario of course; number one, Glenwood had looked as shocked as anyone else when Arabella's body was found in the chimney. Apart from that, she would prefer Glenwood to have done the dirty deed rather than young Dominic's father. The family didn't deserve it. However, the more plausible scenario was that Adam may very well have acted on what his son had told him. On finding out about his wife's infidelity — the wife he had given up an established family for, Adam had finally lost his rag, arranged to meet her there and killed her. Case closed.

'So you think your dad killed her because you told him about Glenwood Halley?'

Dominic looked scared. 'You mustn't blame him. It was my fault. I shouldn't have stirred things up. Arrest me if you like, but not him. It was me that made him do it.'

Honey regarded him with a mixture of pity and disappointment. Pity because she felt genuinely sorry for him; disappointment because Adam wasn't around to defend or incriminate himself. One thing was for sure: Adam Rolfe had put himself in the frame big time. He was their prime suspect, now more so than ever.

'No need for you to come in,' he said when they got there.

'Your mother will ask about that,' said Honey, pointing to his bruised cheek.

He tossed his head sending his hair back from his face before it promptly fell back again.

'I'll tell her I had a skirmish with a couple of lager louts.'

CHAPTER TWENTY-FOUR

By the time she got back to the hotel, the suspected occupants of Honey's scarf had her scratching big time.

'Here,' she said, slipping the taxi driver a £10 note. 'Keep the change.'

The itching worsened. In her haste to exit the taxi the scarf fluttered to the ground. She didn't stop to pick it up. Let somebody else deal with its latent life.

She stalked into reception with her phone pressed tight against her ear. Doherty listened as she told him what had happened.

'It's looking grim for Adam Rolfe, isn't it?'

He agreed that it was, then added. 'Have you ever heard of a Sean Fox?'

She admitted that she had, but only in passing. 'Faith Page mentioned him being close to Arabella. Sean and somebody else. They worked with her on the last programme she presented.'

'Hmm. Well we've just found him hanging from a tree. Apparently he'd committed suicide, though there was no note and nothing, according to friends, to say that he'd been depressed.'

Honey frowned as she tried to think of the name of the girl who'd also worked with Fox. 'The other person was Denise. That was it.'

'That's right, Denise Sullivan. Perhaps you could find her, ask her what she knows. I'm finding it difficult co-ordinating tasks from this bed. It's only sensible that you report to me in person when you can. We can plan a mutual strategy.'

She imagined the salacious twinkle he had in his eyes and the path his strategy was likely to take. He wasn't the sort to let injuries stop him in his tracks. She promised to bear his suggestion in mind and cut the call.

Lindsey was on reception and was looking agitated. 'There's a Sofia Camilleri waiting for you in the lounge. She said it's urgent.'

Honey groaned. 'Damn. I need a shower.' She gave her head a good scratch. 'Did she say what she wanted?'

Lindsey shook her head. 'No, but she looked nervous. And she kept speaking in Italian. I gave her a brandy to calm her down. Apparently she's an opera singer. That's according to Mr Rizzo in room fourteen.'

'Ah!' said Honey. If Mr Rizzo said so, then it had to be so. Honey had been dubious about her credentials — she seemed too much of a cliché — but if anyone would know, it was Mr Rizzo. Other residents had complained about the fallout of sound from his MP3 player at breakfast time. It was always an opera classic and nearly always Italian.

The residents' lounge was at the rear of the hotel overlooking a patio and courtyard. A profusion of tea roses in the flowerbeds screened the area from the coach house, the private accommodation shared by Honey and her daughter.

The lounge had panels of eau de nil set into buttery-cream-coloured walls. Sofas and chairs of comfortable vintage covered in brocade and rose-covered chintz were arranged into small groups. The idea was that gatherings of no more than six could congregate; their beverages safe on the small tables in front of them. A large, gilt-framed mirror dominated the room, sitting above a white marble fireplace reflecting the light from the French doors and the two carefully placed chandeliers.

There was a distinct smell of fuchsia emanating from the woman sitting like a queen in a brocade-covered chair.

Sofia Camilleri was everything an opera singer should be. Obviously Italian and in her late forties, she had chocolate-brown eyes and hair to match. She was small in stature, though her bosom looked as though it belonged to somebody else. No big surprise there, thought Honey; wasn't it common knowledge that opera singers had bigger lungs than ordinary folk? And in the case of Sofia Camilleri, she had the boobs to match.

Sofia Camilleri leaned forward, her face stiff with tension.

'How much did my husband pay you to spy on me?' she said, without first offering a greeting. 'I will pay you twice what he paid you if you agree to say nothing, to tell him I am faithful to him.'

This hadn't been what she'd expected her to say, although Victor Bromwell had sprung to mind. She hadn't thought today could get any crazier.

'Signora Camilleri, I'm not sure what you're talking about. I am not employed by your husband.'

The heart-shaped face, running to fat, lost its tension. The jowls slackened.

'You are not?'

Honey shook her head. 'No. I run a hotel. What made you think that I'm a private investigator?'

'Oh! *Scusa*. I thought that . . .' Sofia's expression changed from concern to puzzlement. She placed an elegant hand, nails painted a deep red, over her mouth to muffle a little gasp that escaped from her equally red-painted lips. 'I'm sorry,' she said, heaving her ample proportions back on to her legs and her impossibly high-heeled shoes. 'I should not have come here. I made a mistake. Somebody told me the wrong thing. Big mistake! Big, big mistake!' She hurried from the room.

Honey stared after her, open-mouthed. What was that all about? The only person who was connected to Sofia Camilleri was Victor Bromwell. But why would he tell her that Honey was a private investigator? It just didn't make sense.

Honey rubbed at her aching head. She was having one of those Alice in Wonderland days when things just seemed to get crazier rather than more curious. She needed a nice, hot shower.

Lindsey was still on reception duty when she went back through. A clutch of residents were sitting around a coffee table helping themselves to cream scones, jam, and cups of tea on a tray. A large pizza box lay open on the reception desk. Lindsey explained that the Ferritos' young son from room sixteen had ordered it without his parents' knowledge. 'And ate it right after he'd eaten his dinner,' she added, pulling down onto the lower desk so that residents couldn't see it. She didn't want people thinking their chef wasn't up to scratch.

'Oh, and somebody dropped this off,' said Lindsey. Honey glanced up to see Lindsey dangling something between her finger and thumb. The scarf had returned.

'It smells of cats,' said Lindsey in a low voice so that those scoffing scones couldn't hear her. She did, however, dare to hold it a bit closer, sniffed and wrinkled her nose. 'Definitely cats. I'm beginning to itch. It's full of fleas.'

Honey grimaced. 'Burn it.'

Lindsey pointed out the obvious. 'Um, Mother, we don't have an open fire? Not at this time of year. Or a garden big enough to accommodate a bonfire.'

'Never mind. I'll deal with it.'

Taking the scarf gingerly between finger and thumb, she stuffed it into the pizza box — being encased in cardboard should stop the little devils from claiming more victims — and headed for the kitchen.

It had occurred to her to remove the lid from the centre of the flat top gas range. The ring was always lit and burned very hot. Both pizza box and, more importantly, rancid scarf, would be ash in no time.

Unfortunately, it was covered in everything from small pots containing portions of Bearnaise, Diane, and peppercorn sauces, to large pans of sizzling lobster, pork loins, and spitting duck breasts.

The air bristled with the aromas of roasting meat and fish. Head chef Smudger was like a whirling dervish, his face red as he dealt with one pot after another.

She knew better than to interrupt him. He was a good chef. He was also good at knife-throwing too.

OK, if she couldn't burn the offending article, then she could store it somewhere — at least for now — and burn it in the morning when things were quieter.

The rubbish bins were out the back. Unfortunately, they were full. From experience she knew that if she left the pizza box perched on top the rubbish, every stray moggy for miles around would come sniffing.

Her gaze happened to land on the door to where the cold room sat in one corner and a range of freezers, both chest and upright types, were ranged along the walls.

The freezers were regularly cleared out of food to be cleaned. She couldn't possibly put the box and its offending contents in with fresh food, but she could put it in an empty one.

The second one she opened was empty. In went the pizza box.

CHAPTER TWENTY-FIVE

Honey lay on the bed next to Doherty. They were sharing a chocolate muffin and the crumbs were falling on his chest.

Honey was chewing thoughtfully, considering the crime, her gaze frequently travelling to the muffin crumbs.

'Are you thinking of licking them up?'

Honey's eyes slid sidelong. 'Maybe.'

Though the thought had occurred to her, she purposely sounded non-committal. The duties of a Crime Liaison Officer could not be ignored.

They discussed Dominic blaming himself for his stepmother's death.

'I think it's purely to protect his father. I take it you haven't found him, or if he has been found, nobody is telling you.'

'They wouldn't dare not tell me, so, no, our absent husband has not been located and we have another murder victim. Sean Fox did not commit suicide. He was murdered.'

Honey swallowed the last piece of chocolate muffin. 'Ah!'

'No fingerprints, but somebody hit Fox on the back of the head before stringing him up. And as our friend Mr Rolfe is still missing, we have to consider he might be the murderer.

175

Despite all our efforts, he hasn't shown up. It's not beyond all probabilities that somebody is hiding him.'

'Do you think so?'

Doherty wriggled a little on the bed. 'Hey. You know, I think my back's getting better.'

'Give it time to heal.' She gave him a stern look. 'Concentrate on your muffin. I wonder why Sofia Camilleri thought I was a private investigator?'

'Beats me. You don't look like one.'

'Don't I?' The comment hurt.

'You're not sneaky enough.' He grinned.

It was hard to keep her mouth zipped. She thought she'd made a pretty good job of being sneaky, following John Rees without being seen. The only real downside had been bumping into her mother — oh, and the scarf. Even thinking about the scarf made her feel itchy.

'So who was the lover? Was it Glenwood Halley, like Dominic asserted it was?'

Doherty exhaled a draft of air down his nostrils, like a dragon left with smoke and no fire. 'More to the point, did Adam find out, confront her before this bloke Halley got there, and stuff his wife up the chimney.'

'Or did the lovers argue? Was it really true that Arabella read more into the relationship than Glenwood did? He's a sucker for celebrity status, you know. He's got photos of famous people whose houses he's sold all over the walls of his office.'

'Or is it just an adolescent boy's way of getting back at what he regards as the desertion of his father? The long shot is that Mr and Mrs Rolfe came over all nostalgic. People do get fond of a house if they've lived there a long time.'

'But she wouldn't dress up just to have a last wander around the place. And who threatened her that night in the ladies' bathroom?'

'Ah yes,' said Doherty. 'The mystery voice overheard in a toilet cubicle.'

Her eyes had just settled on a particularly large muffin crumb nestling in Doherty's chest hair, when the phone rang.

It was Lindsey.

'Come quick. Smudger is threatening to marinate a friend of yours in garlic butter.'

'I'll see you tonight,' she said to Doherty, phone thrown into bag and feet into the shoes she'd discarded earlier.

She turned to see him trying to roll himself out of bed and reminded him that he wasn't supposed to exert himself.

'But I'm going stir crazy and my back's moulded itself to the mattress,' he whined. 'I'm out of here.'

'Not yet. Stick to the house. Take it easy.'

He waved a hand dismissively. 'I'm OK. I'm OK.'

She wasn't too sure that he was, but things seemed to have turned ugly round at the Green River. Who was this friend? She hadn't been told and she hadn't asked. That's the way things were when you owned a hotel. You were never off duty. Still, the Green River Hotel wasn't far, whereas if she moved to the country . . .

A pang of remorse settled on her. She needed time to think. Time to consider. In the meantime, it was post-haste home.

CHAPTER TWENTY-SIX

'I only asked him for a well-done fillet,' said Milly Benton. Milly was a successful lawyer who specialised in the transfer of property from vendor to purchaser.

Milly was short for Camilla. The shorter version of the name suited her better than the more elegant, fully fledged version — or at least, it had done. Honey knew Milly from way back as the epitome of what people expected a lawyer to be: brown hair cut in a no-nonsense bob, pale complexion made more so by the addition of heavily framed spectacles. Honey had always had a strong urge to give the woman a makeover. First off: swap the specs for contact lenses, the brown bob for a blonde crop, and the black business suits for something more trendy and bright.

If Honey had gone ahead with the sale of the Green River and the purchase of Cobden Manor, she would have used Milly Benton to help her. And Milly had been fore-warned of this, at least by phone. They had been saying for years that they should meet up for lunch but somehow they just hadn't got round to it. Therefore this meeting turned out as something of a surprise.

Honey stared at her old friend. There she was, Milly Benton, looking trim and gorgeous in a fitted pink and black checked jacket, her short black skirt showing pins to die for. Her hair was urchin cut, blonde and, surprise, surprise, she was wearing make-up. Honey had never known Milly wear make-up before.

Milly was accompanied by a man. Glenwood Halley.

'Milly. You've changed.' It was hard not to stare; hard not to look surprised.

She blushed and fiddled with her hair self-consciously. Honey had never known her blush before. Never known her be self-conscious either. 'Not really. It's the same old me.'

'Glenwood,' said Honey once she'd got over the shock of the remodelled Milly.

If Glenwood was surprised to see her, he didn't show it. Had he forgotten that she owned this place, or had Milly insisted they come here to eat? She fancied the former might be the case.

'Mrs Driver. I didn't know you two knew each other. Milly and I do a lot of business together.' Glenwood was smooth — she had to give him that.

She made the usual apologies for Smudger's behaviour. It didn't happen that often nowadays, but insensitive people did still exist who knew nothing about the cooking of steaks. Milly, it seemed, was one of them.

Milly and Glenwood had quibbled when the message came out from the kitchen that the chef didn't cook fillet steaks to charcoal. That's what had set Smudger off. He'd come out to confront them.

'I think it's best we go elsewhere,' said Milly. She exchanged a look with Glenwood, one that made Honey think they could be an item. After all, Honey thought, it appeared Glenwood did put himself about a bit.

It occurred to her that snaring Glenwood might have been the reason for Milly changing her image. The old one wouldn't have stood a chance.

'Please. Let me buy you a drink,' Honey said smiling, determined to make some hay from the situation. 'It's the least I can do.'

She gripped Glenwood's arm and steered him to where Emmett would pour large doubles as soon as she gave him a nod. She wanted an unguarded Glenwood. That way she might learn something, if nothing else, the true value of Cobden Manor.

He was reluctant, but she was determined. And smiling. And nice, as though he was in with a chance if he played his cards right.

'Glenwood, we just have to talk property, and Milly,' she said, oozing enthusiasm as she placed them immediately next to the bar. 'We just have to talk about your new look. I wouldn't have recognised you. In fact I would have walked past you in the street.'

Milly snorted exasperation. 'You walked past me only recently, though not in the street. I was at the Roman Baths the other night.'

'Did I really?' Honey felt a little embarrassed. 'Well, it's understandable. Talk about a transformation. My, but I'm so surprised — and envious I have to say. How about you tell me your beauty tips,' Honey whispered. 'In private, of course.'

She made a point of doing most of the talking. With Glenwood she talked property. With Milly she mixed property with flattery about her stunning good looks and choice of clothes. The one thing she didn't do was to ask was why she'd undergone such a drastic change, though she guessed the reason was sitting right there with his thigh brushing against hers.

It occurred to her that Dominic Rolfe and his mother were right. Glenwood Halley was indeed a walking groin.

While Glenwood excused himself and retired to the gents' bathroom, Honey plied Milly with more drink.

'He's quite a catch you know, Milly. Good-looking, successful and pretty well off. So when did the spark become a flame?'

Milly was pretty well-oiled now and rising to the occasion. She looked pleased with herself.

'We finally came together that night at the Roman Baths when you walked straight past me. There were lots of famous people there, and Glenwood positively glows around famous people. We'd brushed past each other a few times, but that evening was . . . well . . . as you said, a spark became a flame. It was a pretty good night.'

There was a new rapport between them, and Honey went all out to make the most of it. Two girls together sharing gossip and secrets.

'My, but did you see Arabella Neville? Every man there was huddled around her.'

Milly made a contemptuous sound — something between 'pah' and a spit.

'She was so immature for her age; all pink and fluffy like a bunny rabbit a little kid might take to bed . . .'

Honey thought somebody of more mature years was likely to take Arabella to bed, but made no comment on that score.

'Arabella Neville got her comeuppance in the end, didn't she?' Milly continued. 'Nobody can say that she didn't deserve it. And do you know what,' she said, her voice suddenly dropping to a whisper. 'I think I know who did it.'

She tapped the side of her nose and winked.

Honey gasped. 'Do you really? How fascinating,' she whispered back. 'Do tell.'

Milly drained her glass, poured herself another and leaned closer.

'I heard somebody threaten to kill her. I was in the loo — lavatory, I should say. Loo is so common, don't you think?'

'Whatever,' said Honey, not caring what she called it as long as she spilled the beans. 'So where were you exactly when you heard this?'

'Sitting down in a cubicle of course.'

Honey was dumbfounded. Why had she thought she was the only one there? Milly had been there too!

'So this person who threatened Arabella, you recognised the voice?'

Milly nodded sagely. 'Her name's Petra Deacon. She's an actress and presenter. Glenwood knows her too, don't you darling?'

Glenwood had just returned. Very much the worse for wear after all the doubles Honey had plied him with. Milly eyed him adoringly. Judging by the look on his face, he'd overheard what had been said. The corners of his mouth were down-turned. His velvet brown eyes had turned hard.

Honey smiled at him. 'Milly thinks she overheard somebody by the name of Petra Deacon threatening Arabella Neville. You know her too. Is that right?'

She noticed a tightening of his already firm jaw. 'I don't think so.'

'Of course you do,' gushed Milly, who was as well-oiled as a deep-fat chip pan. 'He was screwing her. Weren't you, Glenwood darling? You were screwing her and now you're screwing me.'

CHAPTER TWENTY-SEVEN

Before informing Doherty that the mystery voice had been recognised, she went out into the kitchen and warned Smudger not to be quite so hot-tempered. That would have been it, except that Clint was washing up tonight. He was also wearing a silk scarf bandana style around his head. Wait. It was *the* flea-ridden silk scarf of horsy design. It almost covered the huge spider and web tattoo that Clint sported instead of hair. The spider was peering out from beneath a horsy stirrup, looking as though it were wearing it.

Doherty was impressed. She could tell that from his silence.

'Well? What do you think of that?'

'So who is this Petra Deacon?'

'A TV actress and presenter. Apparently, and this is what I myself deduced from the conversation, she and Arabella were bitter rivals.'

'And our friend Glenwood Halley was screwing both of them.'

'Well, we only have a real pissed-off university student to vouch for that — or rather his mother. It was her who put the idea in his head in the first place.'

Doherty had progressed to an armchair, phone, drink and food within easy reach. He had time to think about things and his assessment of the situation was making Honey nervous. Adam Rolfe was still prime suspect. The news from the Glenwood Halley front hadn't changed that fact but did give some indication of why Adam had murdered his wife.

'We've checked with old friends and relatives. Nobody knows where he is, or if they do, they're not saying.'

The last comment made her feel uncomfortable. She should tell him of her suspicions about John Rees, but she couldn't do it.

John Rees owned lots of books. People who owned lots of books were above suspicion.

Doherty demanded she keep in close touch, so she sent him texts and kept in regular phone contact. It didn't matter whether she was at home working in the hotel or out detecting. He wanted reports. He also wanted her to join him in bed.

'It gets pretty boring lying here all by myself.'

'You've strained a muscle. You have to rest until it heals.'

'I think a little exercise would do me good.'

'Not that sort of exercise.'

'Why not? It sure beats jogging.'

* * *

The day had to come when he could stand it no longer and her report regarding Glenwood Halley was the impetus he needed.

'Drive me,' he said when she arrived with yet two more chocolate muffins.

She held up the bag. 'Don't you want a muffin?'

'I hate muffins.'

'So why did you eat them?'

'I like the way you lick up the crumbs.'

And so it was that Doherty folded himself into her car, as stiff as an unwieldy deckchair.

'I want to speak to the first Mrs Rolfe.'

At the other end of the journey, Honey unfolded Doherty from the front passenger seat. It wasn't easy, but she figured that more muffins to re-energise her wouldn't add to her fatty deposits. Doherty, it had to be said, wasn't the best of patients. He winced and made low-key groans through clenched teeth.

'It's no good complaining. You insisted on coming,' she told him.

'It's all part of the healing process.'

The first Mrs Rolfe was dark-haired and trim. She was wearing an open-necked blouse, beige jeans and a butcher-striped apron that was covered in flour. She looked homely but pretty, certainly not in the glamour-puss league of the second Mrs Rolfe. Although the house wasn't a patch on Cobden Manor, it had big windows, a drive and a substantial garden.

It was pretty obvious from Dominic's blank face that he hadn't told his mother about his confession. Neither, Honey guessed, had he told her about the message from his father.

All the same, Susan Rolfe seemed to sense that something was amiss. She frowned at her son. 'Aren't you packed yet?' she said curtly.

'Just sorting the bike, but I think they want to talk to me.'

Doherty confirmed that, yes, they did want to talk to him, and then asked for a chair. 'I've pulled a muscle,' he explained.

Mrs Rolfe went inside and returned manhandling a chair through the door, apparently not wanting to invite them in. Dominic just stood there looking guilty. He had a right to, thought Honey. He'd possibly stirred up a lot of trouble — especially for his stepmother.

Doherty lowered himself onto the chair before forming the number one question.

'Your son told Honey here that he was responsible for killing Arabella Rolfe. We want to clarify exactly why he said that.'

Dominic shoved his hands into the pockets of his low-slung Levis and shuffled his feet. 'Do I have to stay?'

His mother looked shell-shocked. 'That's ridiculous. My son's been in Leicester all this time. Looking at the university.'

'Then he's got nothing to worry about,' said Doherty. 'But he has admitted ringing his father and telling him that his stepmother was having an affair.'

Mrs Rolfe scowled. 'Arabella was a prize tart. Everyone knows that — except my ex-husband.'

'So I understand,' said Doherty, hand on the small of his back as he raised himself from the chair. 'Look, can we come in?'

'I've just got that chair out here for you.'

'I know. But I'm considering your privacy. Do you really want to answer questions out here?'

Her velvet brown eyes, as large as her son's, eyed him speculatively.

'Well . . . I suppose so. You'll have to excuse the mess. I'm cooking.' As if to emphasise the fact, she wiped her hands down her apron. Her movements were quick and jerky. Honey surmised that the divorce had dented her confidence. The responsibility for keeping the home and family together lay heavily on her shoulders.

'Something smells good,' said Doherty, his movements vaguely reminiscent of a robot from *Star Wars*.

'Cottage pie,' said Mrs Rolfe.

She marched swiftly to the kitchen, turned out the oven and bid them sit down. A large pine table and matching chairs sanctioned one end of the room. Dominic stayed standing up, resting his backside on a radiator. Behind him a picture window displayed a panoramic view of the garden.

They declined the tea Mrs Rolfe reluctantly offered them.

Once she'd helped Doherty sit down, Honey asked to use the bathroom.

Susan Rolfe nodded. 'You'll have to use the main bathroom upstairs. The downstairs cloakroom has a leak.'

Honey thanked her. Asking to use the bathroom had been a strategy she and Doherty had decided on beforehand. He interrogated, she investigated. A two-pronged attack.

There were all the signs of a family along the landing — discarded games, one black shoe four feet away from its partner.

There was no sign of the children. Honey presumed the two youngest were both at school.

The bathroom was large, the suite and fittings a bit dated, and the vinyl floor-covering snagged around the edges. She washed her hands with soap moulded from leftover bits, a sure sign of frugal living.

The towel was rough, the colour a little tired. Everything pointed to the fact that Susan Rolfe was struggling. She wondered how much Adam Rolfe had been paying towards the upkeep of his ex-wife and their children. This place wasn't obviously not cheap to run. Neither were three kids.

One bedroom door was slightly ajar. Pretty sure that she was right about the kids being at school, she gently pushed the door open.

Stencilled fairies danced on lilac-painted walls. Curtains and bedspread matched and a large dolls' house took up one corner. Everything was pristine, far more so than the rest of the house.

Judging by the poster of a teenage pop star on one wall, this room belonged to the older daughter. Honey tried to think of the pop star's name, but couldn't. They came young; they went young. The fans got older, married and had kids. The next generation went on to the next craze.

It was easy to identify the next room as belonging to Dominic. The young man who was on his way to university, had an iPod, a computer, a TV and a mobile phone. The phone screen lit up with a message. Deciding she had nothing to lose, Honey read it before it disappeared. Naughty, but needs must.

If you feel like coming to stay again, just give me a ring. But don't worry. Everything will be all right. Get going to Uni. Love you, son.

It was from a contact saved as 'Nanna'. It looked like a grandmother's message to her grandson; loving, to the point and full of concern. 'Nanna' could mean grandmother, or it could mean a professional nanny. At some point this family had been wealthy enough to provide for a nanny.

There was a second message below that which she just managed to read:

I'm just messaging to say, take care of your mother. None of this is her fault. It's mine. All mine. Love you.

The message was from an unknown number.

Taking the phone to trace the message was illegal. She knew that. But all the same, she eyed it sitting there, tempting her to pocket it.

She weighed up the pros and cons, gave the phone a stern look, put it in her pocket then took it out again. No, it had to be done right. And it could be done right.

Back downstairs, she found Doherty wearing a grim expression and Susan Rolfe voicing exactly what she felt about Arabella.

'You won't catch me crying for that woman. Arabella ruined my husband, my life and my family. I'm glad that she's dead, but I do not believe Adam did it. Neither do I believe that anything my son said to his father made any difference to Adam's foolishness. He was obsessed with the woman.'

'Have you heard anything from your father?' Honey asked. At the same time she threw Doherty a telling glance. If they were really in tune with each other — and she believed that they were — he'd pick up on the line of questioning and take it further.

Dominic shook his head, but there was no doubting the furtive look that briefly crossed his face.

Doherty addressed him. 'Do you have a mobile phone?'

Dominic's pale complexion turned paler. 'Yes.'

'Please fetch it for me.'

'Look, my phone calls are private . . .'

'Do I have to issue a summons?'

Seeing the pointlessness of arguing with a grim-faced policeman, Dominic went to fetch his phone.

'Now look here!' Mrs Rolfe looked angry. 'I can't believe you're doing this. Dominic is just a boy. He's innocent.'

'We're not arresting him.' Doherty said to her. 'Please just keep calm.'

'Calm! How can I be calm? That bloody woman wrecked our lives!'

'Tell me about that,' said Doherty, recognising that Mrs Rolfe would do anything and say anything to protect her son.

'She was a bitch! A she-wolf.' She said plenty of other things, things that Doherty already suspected but made a mental note of.

Doherty decided to involve Honey in getting the ball rolling.

'Mrs Rolfe assures me that the rumours regarding Arabella are correct. She has also stated that her son had nothing to do with the death and that she knew nothing of him phoning his father to tell him of his wife's —Mrs Arabella Rolfe's — secret lovers.'

Susan Rolfe butted in. 'Only they weren't that secret. Everyone knew. Take Glenwood Halley. He is such a toady for famous people. He collects trophies, you know. Records when and where he met them, bedded them, or escorted them to some showbiz event. I bet he gives them a mark out of ten.'

Honey looked at Doherty. He didn't look up, but she was pretty certain he was thinking the same as she was.

'Does he bed all his clients, Mrs Rolfe?'

Her arms were folded in front of her, her fingers tapping on her elbows, breasts heaving.

'I'm sure he does.'

'How do you know?'

She coloured up. 'I just do,' she said huffily.

'Did you and your ex-husband sell your house through him?'

Her colour increased. 'Yes. So what?' she snapped.

'And this house? Did you purchase this through him?'

'No. My husband did. I wouldn't have anything to do with him.'

'Because of your past experience?' asked Doherty. 'Did he try to bed you, Mrs Rolfe?'

'No,' she said, too hastily to be fully believed. 'I wasn't famous enough by then. Or rich enough; not like when we . . .'

'. . . Purchased your house? You and your husband?'

Susan Rolfe crumpled. 'He can be quite a charmer.'

Honey had to agree with her, though he hadn't tried his charm on her. Such was the price of fame — or in her case not being famous. Or rich. Glenwood Halley, she decided, had moved on up the pecking order.

Dominic came back down from his bedroom, swinging through the door in a couldn't-care-less fashion. He had a pout on his full lips, Mick Jagger-style. The corners of his mouth were turned down, his whole demeanour typically teenage. He handed Doherty his phone.

'Thank you. Is there any message on this phone that you'd like to declare to us?' Doherty asked him.

Dominic shook his head. 'No.'

Doherty asked Dominic to unlock the phone and then scrolled through the messages.

'Is this the only phone you have?' Doherty asked.

'Yes.'

It wasn't always easy to pick up if somebody was lying. But in this case it was. She'd read those messages. They'd been there and now they were not.

'Is there anything else you'd like to tell me, Dominic?'

'No. So if you've finished with me, I'd like to go, please.'

Doherty nodded. 'I've finished. For now.'

Honey was fully aware that even deleted calls could be picked up and traced. Nothing ever really got deleted. Lindsey had told her that. On the other hand, was Dominic telling the truth or had she guessed right? That he had two phones.

190

Doherty had returned to serious police interrogation without much effort. Having a bad back didn't affect his mind. He was right in there, assessing, delving, and adding up the probabilities.

'Then I need to finish my packing,' said Dominic and left them.

'No,' said Doherty when Honey attempted to help him rise. 'I can do this for myself.'

He got as far as the front door before he groaned and rubbed at the base of his spine.

Determined to get Dominic to himself, Honey began delving in her bag.

'Drat! I've left my purse up in the bathroom. Had to take it up with me,' she said to Susan Rolfe. 'Time of the month.' Actually she never kept tampons in her purse, but seeing as she still had her handbag with her, it seemed as good an excuse as any for going back upstairs.

When she got back upstairs, Dominic was doing exactly what she'd expected him to be doing; he was looking at the messages on his phone.

'You shouldn't have done that,' she said to him.

He looked startled.

'This is private,' he said to her, angry now, no longer feeling sorry for himself.

'Your father's been in touch, hasn't he? Let me guess, he sent you a message. Where is he, Dominic?'

Dominic stared at her, his eyes as round as billiard balls. 'I don't know. It was from an unknown number.'

Honey held out her hand. 'Give me the phone, Dominic. The police can try and trace the message.'

'But he'll be caught.'

He needs to be caught, she thought to herself, but didn't couch her statement in quite those terms.

'Dominic, we need to find your father so he can clear his name.'

'Look, I told you. I told him about Arabella having an affair with that bloke. It must have got to him. It must have.'

'You're laying too much at his door, Dominic. You're surmising. Think about it. Do you regard your father as being a violent man? Was he prone to fits of temper? Did he beat you or your mother?'

He shook his head. 'No. My dad wasn't — isn't — like that. He's soft. That's his trouble.'

Hand still outstretched, Honey wriggled her fingers. 'Give me the phone.'

Doherty had managed to crank himself into the car. Honey leaned through the open window and placed the phone onto his lap.

'He had two phones of the same type. I think you'll find this is the one with the messages on. Hope you can trace it.'

'Will do.'

Honey slid into the passenger seat. Something suddenly hit her.

'I wonder why she lied about the cooking?'

Doherty shook his head. 'My nose never lies. She was cooking.'

'But not cottage pie . . . She was covered in flour. Cottage pie is meat with a mashed potato topping. No pastry.'

He shrugged. 'I can't see the relevance in the naming of a pie but this is obviously leading somewhere, so go on.'

'The kids' rooms are immaculate and they lack for nothing. But she cuts corners in other ways.'

'Like cottage pie?'

'That's just one thing. There's also the soap.'

She explained about leftover bits being melded together, the torn vinyl flooring, and the faded towel.

'And the toiletries were all Tesco own-brands.'

'Does that matter?'

'To someone who used to afford Dior it would. There was just a single bottle of upmarket lotion there with about half an inch of lotion at the bottom. All that's left of her former wealth I suppose. Adam Rolfe used to be a millionaire. He was able to afford to keep two homes in luxury for a while, but then it all went belly up. Once that happened his ex-wife's income must have nosedived. She's struggling — and it shows.'

'Is it enough for her to want to kill him though?'

'Possibly.'

'I get your point,' said Doherty. 'That's a big house to keep going all by herself.'

'But she is resourceful and determined to make things good for her kids. Stuff like that can move mountains.'

Steering Doherty's car with one hand, Honey ran her fingers through her windblown hair with the other.

'I bet she used to have her own cook, if not she ate out most of the time. I bet she also had a woman who came in to clean two or three days a week. I'm betting she's not exactly grieving that her blonde bimbo replacement is dead, but I'm not sure how she feels about her ex-husband. Does she still love him, and if so, would she hide him?'

'You sound jealous.'

'Of Mrs Rolfe?'

'No. Of the cleaner.'

'Never mind. Let's leave the woman in peace — for now.'

'She's got good reason to feel aggrieved.'

'Good enough to commit murder? If he can, Adam is bound to be more generous now Arabella's not on the scene.' She paused as the obvious thought came to her. 'Do you think she might have done it?'

'I don't know that she would be strong enough to get Arabella up that chimney.'

'Unless she had help from somebody bigger and stronger than her; so the money is still on Adam — or his son.'

CHAPTER TWENTY-EIGHT

'*Scusa*, Mrs Driver, but was that Sofia Camilleri I saw here the other day?'

Honey recognised Gabriella Rizzo from number fourteen, her with the opera buff husband. Mrs Rizzo was slim, with classic good looks and streaked blonde hair.

Honey said that indeed it was and added, as if she didn't already know, 'Are you a fan of hers?'

Mrs Rizzo tossed her head from side to side. 'So, so. She has a great voice, but a terrible reputation. Hot-blooded, you see. Easily angered. My sister used to work for her. Sofia threw things at her when she was in a bad mood. She threw a bowl of pasta at my sister once. Luckily it was cold or she would have been burned.'

* * *

Successful surveillance, Honey decided, depended a lot on luck. Franco Rizzo was off playing golf for the day. Mrs Rizzo stated her intention to go shopping.

'We will meet for tea at four?' she said hopefully.

Honey said she would be very pleased to meet her for coffee rather than tea.

'You have coffee. I will have tea. I will also have more scones and jam and cream. Or perhaps butter. We will have to have butter too. I think Mary Jane prefers butter. She is coming too.' Gabriella tossed her luxuriant mane of hair. 'She will read the tea leaves for me. She is very good at things like that.'

Honey said she was looking forward to it, but that was purely out of politeness. She had a hotel to run and rooms to fill. The log for advance winter bookings was looking bleak. The carpet along one of the landings needed to be replaced before next summer. Mary Jane had caught her foot in it and fallen headlong. A rug had been placed over it for now. It would have to suffice until she got a new one; not everyone would dismiss falling down as Mary Jane had. Money for the new carpet was needed. Those rooms had to be filled.

Just when Anna had brought her the news that the mattress in room twenty was wet through and somebody had upset coffee over a bedspread in room twenty, Casper phoned to ask how the case was going. Mind only half on the job, she gave him the details and said she was hopeful.

'Incidentally,' she said. 'The terms of me accepting the job of Crime Liaison Officer were that my rooms would be filled during the winter. Due to the lightness of my business account, my bank manager has suggested I convert from hotel to bail hostel. He reckons on there being more felons than tourists around in February.'

She detected a sharp intake of breath from Casper.

'I'll phone you back.'

Her eyes stayed fixed on the phone. She badly needed Casper to come up with the goods.

Mary Jane caught her staring at the phone.

'Has that phone done something to you?'

She glanced at Mary Jane, bemused. 'It's a phone. It can't do anything.'

'Even inanimate objects have spirits,' Mary Jane said ominously. 'Did you see *Most Haunted* last night?'

Honey admitted that she hadn't seen it last night. In fact she'd never watched the TV programme which, from what she had heard, consisted of a team of psychics dashing around in a dark house hunting for ghosts. Why they didn't bother to turn the lights on she didn't know. But then, it was probably all about getting the viewing public nicely scared. Darkness was always scary because you couldn't see anything including the sound technician, the camera man and the catering people serving tea and buns in the background.

'Neither did I,' said Mary Jane which seemed to make her asking the question a bit pointless. 'I've applied for tickets to that new show that's being made. I took the opportunity of taking a note of that woman's address in Tintern. You did mention to her that I was a professional, didn't you?'

Honey told her that she had. She would like to have added that Faith Page wasn't likely to respond. But Mary Jane looked so enthused Honey didn't have the energy to burst her bubble.

'Can you check my mail?'

Honey did as asked. 'Nothing for you today.'

Mary Jane looked disappointed. 'Drat. I was hoping the agent had got something for me. I know I'd be great on TV. If they'd answered I was going to buy myself a new outfit. I thought something with sequins, though sticking to my favourite primary colours.'

Honey balked at the idea of bright pink, blue or lime green sequins sparkling on screen.

'Perhaps you should check with them first. I think they have guidelines on that score.'

'You're probably right,' said Mary Jane, her eyes glittering as she tapped her chin thoughtfully. 'I'll check which colour they'd prefer me to wear and how they feel about sequins.'

Left to herself and a catalogue of carpet samples was kind of soothing, Honey reflected. Hotel stuff instead of crime stuff. She found herself coveting one hundred per cent Berber wool, and creamy Fleur de Lys scattered over an old gold background.

The fitted carpet she was particularly attracted to was made to measure, only available by special order, and thus crushingly expensive.

The money she would have made from the sale of the Green River would have paid off all her debts and left enough to buy Cobden Manor, renovations to be achieved over two years. Still, all that was definitely out of the window. There was no way she was moving now, so instead she'd splash out a little on the Green River. A new carpet on the second-floor landing was just one of those upgrades. A Jacuzzi might be nice. And perhaps a sauna? A gym?

'How about we invest in a gym?' Honey said to Lindsey who had just come on duty.

'You don't like physical exercise, Mother. Well not that kind anyway.'

'I meant for the guests. We could even hire a professional trainer for, say, two days a week.'

'You have your own personal trainer. His name's Steve Doherty.' She grinned. 'Speaking of, has he found the missing husband yet?'

'No.'

She was close to sharing her suspicions about John Rees, but the phone rang. It was Casper.

'There's a party coming over from Sweden in mid-February,' he said to her. 'They're yours. Fifteen rooms. Six couples who want double beds. Three twin-bedded rooms and six singles. Can you oblige?'

Of course she could.

'Are they here for any specific reason?'

'A conference on European defence logistics at the Ministry of Defence.'

'Fifteen rooms in February,' she exclaimed. Excitedly she conveyed the details of the rooming arrangements.

'And they all work for the MOD?' Lindsey said quizzically.

Honey caught the raising of Lindsey's eyebrow. 'I don't care. They can sleep with whoever they want — as long as it's not with me.'

CHAPTER TWENTY-NINE

Taking her list of clues, suspects and a shopping list, Honey traipsed around to the sausage shop in Green Street close to closing time. Once that was done her head was clear for considering the crime, the suicide and the missing husband.

A cup of tea and a piece of cake would help her concentration. She was sitting at the same pavement table where she'd met Dominic Rolfe but before she could fully apply herself to the job in hand, she spotted John Rees hurrying along in the direction of Bathwick.

It was six o'clock at night. Yet again he was carrying a brown paper parcel under his arm. Supplies for a fugitive? Quite possibly.

On account of the fact that he had very long legs, it wasn't too long before he was almost out of sight. Quickly paying, she was off in pursuit. This case was personal. She had to hang in there.

Luckily a taxi appeared on cue, the driver totally unfazed when she asked to be let out just a few hundred yards down the road. The fare was still pretty stiff, but Honey didn't care. With luck she might relocate John and resume her pursuit. Nothing was certain. She could but try.

Here she was, alighted from the taxi, standing on the pavement but she couldn't see John anywhere. There was no sign of the familiar figure striding head high above the crowds, just customers puffing clouds of nicotine outside The Curfew pub and juggernauts puffing out diesel fumes on Cleveland Bridge.

There were a number of directions he could have gone in, some of them more attractive than others. She certainly didn't fancy trudging along the London Road with all that traffic travelling nose to tail. It may have been judgement; it may have been instinct but she opted for the prettier route.

Professional tails wouldn't choose the more scenic or intriguing route, but as an amateur, she could afford to be different. Accordingly she considered her options and what might have happened.

Get inside John's mind.

As she marched along, various possible scenarios scampered through her mind like frightened rabbits. Number one: John was hiding Adam, perhaps in the rear of his shop? Some of those cardboard boxes the books came in were pretty big. A full-grown man could hide in one. Homeless people lived in them. But if John was hiding Adam, did that mean Adam was guilty or too scared to come forward? Or was he guilty? Was John his accomplice?

She shivered at the thought of it. I mean, she said to herself, did he actually *look* guilty?

A vision of how he'd been dressed flashed through her mind. Dark cords, dark sweater, dark shoes. No change there. Again, a brown paper package tucked beneath his arm. Frowning, she concentrated her mind on what it might contain. Too thin to be a book. It had to be a map. Or a picture.

Bath was an old city of old buildings, old alleys and old shadows that at certain times of day fell blackly and densely on rumpled pavements.

There were distinct possibilities. He could have been delivering that package somewhere. To a client? Possibly. Suddenly she had a Mary Jane moment.

When all else fails, let your instinct take over.

Sometimes Mary Jane talked rubbish, but sometimes, just sometimes, her well-worn sayings resurfaced, sounding far wiser than when first heard. The times when this happened were usually when there was no other alternative.

Instinct, Honey thought, half closing her eyes to minimise the distractions.

Her feet headed down St John's Road. Ivy-covered walls separated St John's churchyard from the road. At one point the old rectory had been turned into a hotel but it had closed, possibly because the diocese had refused to allow it to have a drinks licence. Most tourists were pretty thirsty people.

She eyed the dark trees surrounding the old place. Part of the grounds had been developed into senior citizens accommodation, but the churchyard still existed. Not that she wanted to go nosing around down there. It was getting dark and she had no intention of entering a graveyard after sunset. The fear was a leftover from her youth when she'd gone to the pictures with a boyfriend. At that time, she'd liked horror movies and had become engrossed in the film, so much so that she'd forgotten she wasn't alone.

Her companion had not been concentrating on the film; his attention had wandered. So had his hands, or at least one of them. Just as Dracula sank his fangs into a female neck on screen, a hand landed on Honey's breast. She'd screamed, jumped three feet out of her seat, and scattered a tub of popcorn on to the people in front. Her boyfriend had gone off muttering about the price he'd paid for the popcorn should have been enough to allow for a few little liberties. Honey hadn't agreed with him. Neither had the people in the row in front.

She'd never gone to a horror movie again. Or gone out with the boyfriend again. Neither had she read any Gothic novels, the experience of a cold hand at a chilly moment was embedded in her bones — or more correctly on her bosom.

'Options, options, options.'

Exasperated, she left the road and took the steps down to the river just below the Old Dispensary. The water looked cool and she was feeling hot.

Slumping onto a wooden bench she took a deep breath. Off came her shoes. The shoes had heels and were smart but weren't made for walking great distances. Trailing someone called for sensible footwear. She made a mental note to remember that in future.

The A4 London Road was full of traffic leaving the city. Most pedestrians stuck to the city's heart where cafés, restaurants and individual shops jostled for business and the air smelled of coffee and full-cream fudge.

But John was on foot and was striking an outward trail.

Once her feet were rested, she made her way back up the steps to road level and headed across Cleveland Bridge past the fire station.

There was always traffic on the A36, the city planners doing their best to get it around and out of the city as quickly as possible. Those involved in the tourist trade preferred it to hang around — more business that way. Between the two of them they'd created abject gridlock.

Another Bath pub, The Crown, sat beside the main A36 just before the turning into Forester Road. Built in the early twentieth century with a stone facade and mock mullion windows, it was a cross between a late Georgian house and the type of house that shouts Home Counties wealth.

Two elderly people were manhandling a suitcase across the pavement to a waiting taxi. In the process they were holding up whoever else was trying to exit the pub. One person had no option but to assist them. It was John Rees.

Honey held back. She hadn't expected this but guessed that at some stage John had spotted her, led her on a marathon of a walk around the city, and then dived into the pub for a quick pint. She missed her scarf, though not the fleas.

Still, she thought, my persistence has paid off. He thought he'd lost me, and it turns out he hasn't.

Now she had him and was pretty sure he hadn't seen her. Once the taxi door had closed, John was off, still carrying the brown paper parcel under his arm.

It looked like the parcel might be a picture; perhaps a map that he'd sold and was off to deliver.

A dark green sign pointed to Bathwick Boating Station. John shot down Forester Road. The road was lined with solid houses, mostly dating from the Edwardian era with big roofs covered in little red Rosemary tiles and carved weatherboards. Square panes in bay windows glistened with cleanliness. Kerbside parking was usually readily available, though not tonight, and the end of the street seemed more crowded than usual. A few of the houses were given over to Bed and Breakfast. Some had been turned into flats, but that wouldn't be enough to warrant the road being this packed with parked cars. It had to be overspill from the boating station. Something was going on here. Honey was curious.

At the end of the road a wrought iron arch curved over the entrance to Bathwick Boating Station. The road formed a U-shape so it was no big deal to wander past the boating station and circle back to the main road.

Something seemed to be going on at the boat house; the lovely old riverside restaurant and self-contained letting accommodation. A sign outside referred to it being something to do with art. People funnelling like lemmings along the narrow path to the restaurant entrance.

First rule of tailing someone was to fit in. At first she was one of the crowd; just before the entrance, she took a detour making her way off to the right and down around the front of the building between it and the river.

Lawns of soft green grass curved salaciously to the river where weeping willows sighed over the dark green water. There were flowers everywhere, tumbling from huge hanging baskets and festooned in windows boxes on the letting accommodation next door. The boating station took in guests, people who wanted to dip into the city's delights, but also get a good night's sleep.

The crowds that had been funnelling in remained inside the boating station, networking around the restaurant on the first floor. A hum of conversation and light laughter sounded from the wide balcony above her head. The air smelled of warm garlic and tinkled with the sound of wine glasses. She craned her neck looking for John.

Damn. She was just too low down. The balcony was too high, the big windows behind it set too far back. She had no option but to go back round to the main entrance and hope she could blag her way in.

Nipping up the steps on the other side, she found herself back in the car park. She backed away from the entrance, eyeing the parked cars, searching just in case John had spotted her and gone back outside.

No one was hiding between the cars, or if they were, she wasn't seeing them.

Just as she made her way to the entrance, a sleek and very classic Austin Healey drew up, almost running over her foot. She froze. There was only one car of such salubrious quality in Bath.

Casper St John Gervais, chairman of the Bath Hotels Association, had arrived, and he'd seen her. There was no escape.

After easing himself out from the leather driver's seat, Casper flicked his trousers into their already well-defined creases and straightened. He was wearing a mustard jacket over light lemon slacks. A dark red-and-mustard cravat erupted like a turkey's gizzard at his throat.

'I didn't expect to see you here,' Honey said. She made it sound as though she had an official invite. Casper certainly would be in possession of one. He considered himself quite an art aficionado. Ditto acting, chamber music, and sacred arias performed by beefy Italian tenors.

He looked at her a little oddly.

'Did you walk here?'

'Yes,' she said brightly. 'How did you know?'

'You look sweaty. Well, come on. We'd better go in.'

203

Casper's comment stung. It made her wonder whether she smelled as sweaty as she looked.

'I am informed that we are privileged to inspect tonight's showing,' he said. 'There are people exhibiting here who show great potential for future investment. Now do be careful what you buy, and if you're not sure about the artistic merit of any particular piece, I would be pleased indeed to advise you.'

'That's very kind of you,' Honey blustered, though investing in art was the furthest thing from her mind.

So that was it. Artists were showcasing their work.

The restaurant consisted of one large room and a wide balcony overlooking the river where punts snuggled against a mossy green bank. There was even a duck alighting on the roof of an adjacent building, though on taking a second look she realised it wasn't real.

On entry a tray of something white and sparkling was offered. They helped themselves.

Casper took a sip and pulled a face.

'The things I do for art,' he groaned. 'This isn't even proper Champagne.'

Honey didn't have a clue whether the paintings were good or bad, but hey, she could play the part couldn't she? Of course she could.

Adopting a serious expression she took a look around, lingering over the artwork that seemed different or unusual. Would Casper buy this kind of thing? Possibly those that were 'different' might be considered 'skilled'. The more con-servative — the scenes of French cafés on a wet street or a red-roofed Tuscan farmhouse were the ones that she really liked. At least she could see what they were.

'So what do you think of this?' asked Casper.

'Well . . .' she was about to comment on what looked like a piece of cooked liver entitled *Heart of the Matter*.

Casper had his own ideas and laid them out without waiting for her response.

'I prefer that which I can recognise — Old Masters rather than old mattress. Do you recall the Emperor's New Clothes,

204

so fine that they were invisible to all and sundry unless you were a fool? Nobody wanted to be thought a fool so nobody pointed out that the poor old chap was totally naked. Well, that's how I feel about art. A dead cow is a dead cow. It's not art. Art requires skill. A dead cow requires a butcher with a good set of sharp knives. Which brings Arabella Rolfe to mind. Do we know yet who had the good sense to do away with the wretched woman?'

Casper had a resonant voice. He didn't shout, but he spoke as though he were addressing a meeting. Heads turned.

'Not yet,' said Honey, feeling slightly embarrassed. 'Though we do have leads.'

'The husband. It has to be the husband. A husband is always prime suspect.'

'He's missing.'

'Well there you are, then.' Casper looked triumphant. 'A sign of guilt if ever there was one. My, my, Honey, but one does get variety in murder. I wonder if this is a reflection of our modern society, influenced as it is by cheap drama and gory thrillers. Strangled and shoved up the chimney!' He tutted loudly. 'Still, thank heaven for small mercies. At least there wasn't any blood dripping into the grate. It's a very nice grate. It was decorated with Minton tiles if my memory serves me correctly.'

'You know the place?' This was the first time she'd had any inkling that he did.

'I thought about buying it at one time in partnership with an old flame of mine. Then he jumped ship. Literally. He was in the Royal Navy. Got involved with a gaucho in Argentina from whence he sent me a dear John letter.' He shrugged. 'Still, everything works out for the best. Culture versus cows, so to speak.'

Honey muttered an agreement, but she'd just spotted John Rees. He was out on the balcony, in urgent conversation with the same man she'd seen in the shop. She tried to recall his name . . .

Occasionally John or his companion, or both of them, glanced to where a number of people were gathered around one particular piece of artwork. A piece of brown paper together with string was tucked under a nearby woman's arm; the woman seemed to be in charge.

Honey frowned. 'Casper, did Arabella Rolfe paint?'

Casper snorted. 'I believe she did daub a little.'

His tone was contemptuous. He hadn't extended her the courtesy of being a painter, just a dauber.

'Am I right in thinking that one of her paintings is being exhibited here?' She checked the programme she'd been given on the way in. 'Yep. There it is.'

He raised his eyebrows. They were beautifully arched, plucked by a visiting beautician who also removed excess hair from places she'd rather not think about. Rumours of the most intimate variety travelled fast in Bath.

'I'm intrigued,' he said loftily, inspecting the rim of his wine glass before allowing it to reach his mouth. 'Lead me to it.'

Contempt colouring his judgement, he led her to a picture of white daisies set in a vase. It was ordinary. Honey was no connoisseur but even she had to agree with him.

'Flowers,' he said.

Honey's attention was drawn to the painting next to it — it was of the tumbledown stable block that the dead woman had been found in.

'The outbuilding at Cobden Manor,' she whispered. It had a desolate, haunted look about it.

Honey peered closer, narrowing her eyes so she could more easily take in the details.

Casper read out the title. '*Intruder*. Hmmm. An intriguing title. Not a bad painting. Acceptable in a suburban kind of way.'

His voice was sour with condemnation. Although the painting would look very good in a modern living room, it wouldn't suit Casper's taste. Anyway, he had the money for better.

Intrigued as much as anything else, Honey forgot she was in the company of local experts — everyone was an expert if they had money to spend — and she gave her opinion.

'I don't think it's that bad. Odd title though — or perhaps not,' she added thoughtfully. She narrowed her eyes again as she studied a small square window next to the stable door. There was a face there, a face she recognised. The man she'd seen talking to John at J R Books.

The same man he was with now.

Casper's attention was elsewhere. He had been asked for his opinion on an ink drawing with painted red inserts. He wouldn't miss her.

She headed for the balcony determined to just ask John about his relationship with Arabella Rolfe and the whereabouts of her husband, Adam. She took a deep breath. This wouldn't be easy. John was a good friend. But she had to.

As she approached, John straightened as though readying himself for some kind of onslaught, watching as she tripped in his direction.

'John.'

'Honey.'

'I need to ask you some questions. Hope you don't mind.'

'What if I've no wish to answer them?'

She got out her phone, holding it aloft so he could see what it was. 'Then I have to tell the police that I believe you're harbouring Adam Rolfe.'

CHAPTER THIRTY

They made their way out on to the riverbank. John walked thoughtfully, head bowed, hands jammed into trouser pockets. The grass was damp, the earth beneath it soft and spongy. The spindly-heeled shoes had done their worst and Honey had had enough of them. She walked barefoot, one shoe in each hand.

'I promised Adam,' John said at last. 'He needs the money.'

'So where is he?'

John sighed. 'I don't know. He's got a riverboat somewhere — on the Thames, I think. He phones me daily.'

'John, you really have to get him to give himself up.'

'I know, I know.' He shook his head. 'But he didn't kill Arabella. I can't believe that he did. I *won't* believe that he did.'

'Where does he say he was that night?'

'Well. He likes opera . . . and he's got this friend. They're very close. A friend who's married to an opera singer gave him a ticket.'

'Don't tell me he's friend with the husband of Sofia Camilleri.'

He nodded. 'She's quite a firebrand.'

'Her husband thinks so too. She thinks he's having her followed by a private detective. She thought it was me. She's also being squired by a sexpot in Spandex. Funny how that brings out the lust in middle-aged ladies.'

'Husband and wife are apart a lot, but it isn't quite . . .'

Honey wasn't listening. 'I can see where things might lead.'

'You've got it wrong,' he said to her.

They came to a stop on the riverbank. Honey threw him a direct look. 'I knew Adam had money worries, but I didn't realise he was having an affair.'

John looked at her. 'They weren't. It's purely about painting. Sofia is into watercolours. Adam let her have the run of Cobden Manor.'

'The picture,' said Honey, pointing back over her shoulder.

'That's it, but you were right about Adam's investments. He'd done pretty well investing in property. Made a fortune in fact. But then he invested in a Spanish development, a really big one, too big for him to raise the finance on himself. So a consortium was arranged and other people were brought on board. Unfortunately, it all went wrong. The land they'd started building on turned out not to have permission and to not actually to belong to them. On top of that, when the losses began to mount, he found that he'd laid his personal possessions on the line. Everything collapsed like a pack of cards.'

'I suppose Arabella didn't help.'

His wry smile went with a sidelong look that hinted at chastisement. 'Arabella was not quite the bad bitch everyone makes her out to be. She gave him her own money. Apparently she had quite a nest egg. Family money.'

Certain alarm bells began to ring in Honey's head. 'From her father?'

He shrugged and slid his hands into the pockets of his cords. 'I suppose so. I don't rightly know.'

'Did you know she used to be called Tracey Casey?'

'Really?' His eyebrows rose high and an amused smile lightened his features. 'Her parents should have been shot.'

'Then she became Mrs Dwyer.'

'She was married before? I didn't know that either.'

'So you didn't know she'd been married before, so consequently you never heard of her having any children.'

He stopped in his tracks, the willows across the river forming a backdrop to his lean frame. There was no doubting his surprise.

'I don't know if she had any children — I thought she hated them.'

Honey was thoughtful. If she did have children, where were they? Perhaps she had no access to them. She might have been banned from seeing them, taken away from her long ago. By her father-in-law perhaps? Was that it?

'Dominic thinks his father did it. The boy's pretty het up about it.'

John sucked in his bottom lip, looked at her then looked away. Some spot on the other side of the river seemed to have caught his attention. Then he shrugged. 'Adam sounds like he's a bad way. He's worried and I don't think it is just about his son.' John frowned. 'I think there's more going on here, but I don't know what. He loves his kids. You know that, don't you?'

Honey frowned. 'Of course he does, but where is he? He's the prime suspect and because of that, you could be held as an accessory to murder. You do know that, don't you?'

A whole host of emotions crossed his face before he nodded. 'He's got a new phone. I've got the number. I don't think anyone else has.'

'Get him to turn himself in. It's the only way to prove his innocence and the only way you're going to avoid not being charged too. Your phone can be confiscated and the number traced. You know that.'

The shadows of overhanging trees obscured the light from the restaurant, flickering in a disconsolate fashion over his features. She held her breath. Then she saw him nod.

'Leave it with me. I'll see what I can do. But he didn't do it, Honey. He hasn't got the guts to do something like that. And he's scared. I don't know what of, but trust me. He's scared.'

Honey shook her head, wisps of hair blown around her face by the water-driven breeze. She thought she knew who he was scared of, although he might not know the reason why. It had to be something to do with Arabella's past.

She looked at John. 'That's for the law to decide, John. It's not infallible, but it's all we have. You've got until tomorrow morning.' She turned abruptly and walked away.

'I'll walk you home,' he called after her.

She waved at him over her shoulder. 'Not tonight,' she called back. She swallowed the lump in her throat.

* * *

Steve Doherty was up and about, refusing to admit that he wasn't fully mended.

Honey called and told him that she had a good lead regarding the whereabouts of Adam Rolfe.

'Did you know that Arabella painted?' she went on. 'I saw her painting at a gallery last night.'

'Was it any good?'

Honey frowned. 'No. Anyway, I was drawn to the one next to it. It was of the outbuilding where we found her. The artist was that mad opera singer that came to see me. It was spooky.'

'Arabella's could be valuable now she's dead,' he mused.

She shook her head. 'I don't think so.'

'That bad?'

She nodded. 'That bad.'

Doherty groaned.

'Be careful with that back,' Honey warned. 'It needs a lot of TLC.'

'I'll count on you to give it that. See you tonight.'

She phoned Casper to apologise for shooting off from the boating station without saying goodbye.

211

'But I'm glad I attended,' she said to him. 'It resulted in a very important lead in this murder case.'

'Spare me the details, my dear girl! Suffice to say that I look forward to the regaining of our self-respect.'

It occurred to her that he sounded like a second-rate actress who'd been caught doing topless glamour.

For her part, Honey was less than happy, but the promise of meeting Doherty later at the Zodiac Club helped lift her mood.

'I'll tell you how it goes,' she promised.

Things were buzzing back at the Green River where the Newbourne Nannies were holding their annual conference.

'According to Mary Jane, they're not a patch on Mary Poppins,' Lindsey observed, watching them from her post on reception, 'though personally I think they are.'

Fresh-faced young women, impeccably dressed and full of energy, poured out of the conference room. Trained to look after the children of the very wealthy, the nannies were in great demand all over the world. The Newbourne Nannies had been established way back when anyone who could afford it left their babies to young women and a strictly followed routine.

On catching sight of her, Adelaide Newbourne, grand-daughter of the agency's founder, Matthias Newbourne, beamed broadly and marched over. A big-framed woman, she positively glowed with efficiency.

'Mrs Driver. Newbourne Nannies salute you. Impeccable presentation. Nothing overlooked. Though Earl Grey would have been preferred. Or Darjeeling. My girls are used to rather select beverages, as are their employers.'

Honey thanked her for the compliment about everything. She also promised to ensure that the preferred tea was available at future 'nanny' events.

Adelaide Newbourne grunted her satisfaction. 'Praise where praise is due. To this young lady too,' she said, aiming a curt nod in Lindsey's direction. 'Very commendable. If ever you consider a career change, young lady, do give me a call.'

To anyone else the sudden tightening of Lindsey's features might have passed unnoticed, but Honey picked up on it.

'So how do you like children?' Ms Newbourne asked cheerily, her rustic cheeks as shiny as polished apples.

Lindsey smiled. 'Preferably at a great distance.'

CHAPTER THIRTY-ONE

The Zodiac Club was a hive of activity, though bees from a hive would have had trouble breathing or flying in the smoky blue atmosphere. Steaks, sausages, and garlic-smothered prawns were sizzling on the grill. Waitresses were skirting tables, a platter of food carried aloft in each hand.

Honey and Doherty were discussing the pros and cons of the case, starting with Adam Rolfe's first wife, Susan.

'Funny that she lives in Bradford-on-Avon,' said Doherty. 'In my opinion, it's too close for a woman scorned. I would have thought she'd have wanted to get away. Start a new life and all that.'

'I thought that too. But then they do share three children. The husband has access rights. Not that he was allowed to exercise those rights by his second wife — according to John Rees she hated the children and he didn't know anything about her first marriage or that she might have had children herself.'

Doherty's eyes darkened. 'I would have thought he would have made the effort, though. I would, I do.'

Doherty and his own wife had over a hundred miles between them. His teenage daughter appeared occasionally, though only when she'd had a fallout with her mother and wanted his support — and his money — to keep her going.

Honey was unrelenting. 'She still carries a candle for him. Bet you a tenner.'

'Bet's on.'

'I'm not sure Adam did it though, Steve. I mean, he was a bit of a mouse. She was much stronger than him. And he isn't a big man — broad in the shoulders, though.'

Doherty pursed his lips. 'Her ex Dwyer was big all over. So were his brothers.'

* * *

It came as a big though pleasant surprise to Steve Doherty when Adam Rolfe presented himself at Manvers Street the following day. Not that he let the grass grow under his feet as regards interrogation.

The atmosphere in the interview room felt electric; Doherty put it down to foregone conclusion. As it turned out he wasn't far wrong, though the feeling didn't last that long.

Adam Rolfe sat there with his knees clamped tightly against his clasped hands. His face was gaunt, his gaze fixed firmly on the floor.

'I did it. I killed Arabella.' He said it firmly enough, though Doherty didn't set much store by that. On the contrary, he hadn't even started the interrogation. Confessing before he'd even asked a question was not just off-putting, it didn't feel right. A little cut and thrust had to be done before anybody confessed — really confessed — as though they meant it.

Doherty folded his arms.

'Why?'

Adam Rolfe raised his eyes, eyelids flickering nervously. 'Why? Well, um, because she deserved it.'

'*Why?*'

In Doherty's opinion, Adam Rolfe was lying. Doherty could see all the signs: the fidgeting fingers, the legs tightly clasped as though he were riding a horse. Maybe Rolfe thought he was doing the right thing and that his confession would be taken at face value. He gave all the signs that he was protecting someone else. But who and why?

Doherty needed to delve deeper, ask for confirmation that Adam really had killed his wife.

'I just did,' he blurted.

Doherty rubbed his fingers over his bristled chin. 'We all want to kill our wives and partners at some point. But something has to trigger it. What was this one last almighty row where you finally snapped. Tell me when you finally snapped, Mr Rolfe. Tell me when you finally decided you could take no more, clobbered your wife, and stuffed her up the chimney.'

Rolfe stared at him round-eyed. Doherty could almost smell his fear but knew instinctively it was not for himself that Adam feared. Mr Rolfe was protecting someone.

'Your son didn't do it either, Mr Rolfe. So no need to protect him either. We know he was at his grandmother's on the night in question.'

There was a strange moment when Adam Rolfe seemed to freeze then swell up. His head fell forward into his hands. Doherty knew he was crying.

'On another score, Mr Rolfe,' he said above the sound of sobbing. 'Do you know a man named Sean Fox?'

A tear-stained face appeared from behind the white trembling hands. 'What?'

Doherty glanced at the list supplied by Glenwood.

'Sean Fox. Do you know him?'

He shrugged in an offhand manner. 'Not really. He was just somebody my wife used to work with.'

'Were they close?'

He shook his head. 'I couldn't really say. I tried not to have anything to do with television people. I didn't like them very much.'

If that was the case, why the hell had he married Arabella?

The million-dollar question was next. 'Did your wife ever mention having been married before?' Doherty asked.

Adam's face was as white as unbaked dough. He looked lost. He looked frightened.

'Or the fact that she had children?'

He paused, before exclaiming, 'What? No!'

His voice echoed around the interview room. There was something about that echo that didn't ring true.

'Where were you on the night of her murder?'

He sighed. 'I was with Susan. We met at a pub. She wanted to discuss a few things.'

'Did you often meet up to discuss things?'

He nodded.

'Without telling Arabella?'

He nodded again. 'It was best not to. She was so jealous of anything I did with the kids.'

'Jealous? Of Susan or the kids?'

'She didn't like kids.'

Doherty pursed his lips and steepled his fingers. 'OK. We'll check this with Susan.'

Doherty couldn't put his finger on it, but he felt sure there was more to be had from Adam Rolfe. Keeping to the obvious questions based on facts he knew was not going to work.

He took a stab in the dark.

'Did she have children by her first marriage?'

Adam's eyes seemed to sink into their hollows, yet at the same time stand proud of his face.

'None of my business.'

Docherty felt a surge of triumph. He had to know more. 'Their names, Mr Rolfe. What were their names and where might we find them?'

He shook his head. 'I don't know what you're talking about. She just worked with someone called Sean Fox. That's all I know.'

Doherty eyed him silently.

'So you knew nothing about your wife's former marriage or the whereabouts of her two children by that marriage?'

'No.'

Adam was not meeting his look; that was when he knew, he absolutely knew, that Adam Rolfe was lying. Unfortunately he had no evidence.

'I let him go,' he said later to Honey. 'I'm confused as to who was married to who and was having an affair with X, Y or Z. I always thought Bath was supposed to be gentrified.'

Honey laughed. 'I don't know much about how the Romans carried on, but I do know Bath in the eighteenth century was a hotbed of affairs. The Prince Regent used to come down from London with his entourage. The wives stayed with them up at the Royal Crescent and Circus. The mistresses, and there were carriages full of them and professional women, were housed down in Green Park.' She shook her head and poured him a glass of wine. 'Things ain't changed that much, that's for sure.'

CHAPTER THIRTY-TWO

Susan Rolfe confirmed that her husband had been with her. 'We needed to discuss things regarding the children.'

So the husband was off the hook. The barman at the pub, the Crooked Oak near Farrington Gurney, was certain that he remembered them.

'Pint of lager and an amaretto and cranberry juice for the lady.'

Doherty had no good reason to hold on to Adam Rolfe as a suspect. The alibi checked out. There was no evidence to attest that he'd been at Cobden Manor that night.

Exasperated, he caught up with Honey just after lunch.

As usual she was in a dizzy spin of busyness. Clint had gone to the natural childbirth classes with Anna and the dishwasher had broken down. Honey had suggested to Smudger that he help her do the dishes by hand. The stony look he'd given her was all the answer needed. So Doherty was washing while she wiped. At the same time, he was giving her the details and washing up as swiftly as he could.

'And Petra Deacon?'

'Ah yes. The woman in the ladies' loo. My officers have already spoken to her. She denied saying any such thing

— which means that you and I need to pay her a visit. You were there. You heard her.'

Frowning, he helped himself to coffee and continued: 'Adam appeared unsettled when I mentioned Arabella having been married before, but he didn't seem surprised. Sure, he pretended to be but something didn't seem right. It's like he already knew.'

* * *

Petra Deacon lived in the wing of an old country house. Once upon a time Haverton Hall had been home to a nine-teenth-century wool merchant. Already comfortably off, Cecil Haverton had become mega rich following the inven-tion of a new system for combing the lanolin out of fleece. The method and resultant benefits to the chemical as well as the wool industry, had earned him a fortune. Thus he'd found a nice hill some miles west of Bath with a lovely view of Clevedon Bay.

The house was built in a mix of styles; Tudor, Gothic, and a touch of fairy-tale Hollywood at a time before Walt Disney was even born.

Long gone were the days when anyone of wealth could or would want such a sprawling place. Thus it was now divided into a dozen luxurious apartments which all shared the tennis courts, the residents' lounge and concierge services.

Petra's apartment was accessed via a lift to the second floor and took up two floors of a corner tower of Strawberry Hillesque Gothic design.

The lift doors opened on to a landing of shiny brightness.

Someone came out of a door some way ahead of them. Honey glimpsed a tall man smartly dressed and quick on his feet, so quick that with one glance in their direction he was off down the stairs.

Honey frowned. 'It might be my imagination, but I think I've seen him somewhere before.'

Doherty regarded her seriously. 'Anywhere special?'

She knew he meant with regard to the murder.

She shrugged. 'No idea. But it'll come to me.'

Petra Deacon was one of the coolest women Honey had ever met. She was tall, lean of body, and had the kind of flawless complexion usually only seen on airbrushed photos. Her hair was a veil of reddish brown tumbling down her back. Her eyes were that wonderful shade of green only found on heroines of romantic fiction. She was wearing a cream off-the-shoulder sweater that clung to her waist and her trousers were a speckled mix of cream and tan. Her feet were bare, her toenails painted in alternate shades of pink and purple.

'Yes?' she said, white teeth flashing between glossy apricot lips.

Doherty flashed his warrant card and explained why they were there.

'You do recall attending the event at the Roman Baths?' he asked her.

She could hardly deny it. Her name had been on the list supplied by Glenwood Halley. Until recently her name had not attracted any interest — until Milly had admitted to seeing her and recognising her voice.

She looked loath to let them in despite Doherty's warrant card.

'What's this about?'

Her voice was husky. If she hadn't been a television presenter, she could have made a good living selling online smut. She'd have had them drooling.

Doherty explained about the death of Arabella Rolfe. 'You may have known her better as Arabella Neville. She was a TV presenter.'

The perfectly poised expression froze. The soft lips seemed to adhere more tightly to her teeth.

'I knew her. I heard she was dead. What's that got to do with me?'

'You were seen, and overheard, threatening to kill her.'

'Who says so?'

Honey spoke up. 'I do.'

221

Her mouth opened slightly and her eyes hardened.

'Now,' said Doherty, taking one step inside the door. 'Do you mind if we come in?'

Silently, she let them in.

'Right,' she said, folding her arms, her stance defensive and hostile all at the same time. 'What am I supposed to have said?'

The hostility was directed at Honey.

'Your threat to kill Arabella Neville; did you carry it out?'

She rolled her eyes. 'Of course not. I'm not an aggressive person.'

'You said you knew people who could carry out the job,' said Honey.

'Get lost!'

'Do you know the right people?' Doherty asked her. His tone was firm and without emotion.

'I just said. I didn't actually do it, for God's sake. Neither did I pay anyone to do it. We hated each other. I got the job she was after. Anyway, it was her own fault. She flounced off the set.'

'She argued with someone?'

'Arabella was argumentative, full stop! Especially if she didn't get her own way.'

'So we hear. Who did she argue with?'

'Beats me.'

'Was there anyone in particular she didn't get on with?'

'Everybody.'

'Oh, come on, Ms Deacon. Somebody had to like her.'

She snorted. 'A needle in a haystack! I certainly didn't like her! That bitch ran off the set, then phoned me later that same night accusing me of stealing her handbag.'

'Come on,' persisted Doherty. 'You must have some idea of what the argument was about?'

'I don't know. Someone phoned her, she shouted at them and then she stormed off.'

'And her handbag. Did you take it?'

222

'Why the hell would I? We didn't share the same taste in fashion. She was so much *older* than me.'

'Who else would want to murder her?'

'A lot of people.'

'Who was the phone call from? Do you know?'

'I've already told you, I don't know. Husband? Boyfriend?' When she shrugged her sweatshirt slid further down her arm exposing yet more sultry shoulder, more of her silky upper arm.

People willingly invited the likes of Petra Deacon into their homes via their television sets thinking her a really lovely person. If only they knew, thought Honey. Petra Deacon was a celebrity, hero-worshipped by those who knew no better.

Doherty continued to probe. 'Did you know much of her past life?'

Petra burst into mocking laughter. 'What do you think I am? A bloody psychic? Arabella kept her private life private — except when it was likely to benefit her financially then it was all over the tabloids. Anyone who would pay for her story — and I mean *story* — could have it.'

Just titbits, thought Honey, and then suddenly it came to her. Nobody had known anything about her background. Was it possible that someone had made it their business to find out more than was publicly available?

Doherty was fixing the TV presenter with a questioning eye.

'I take it you knew Sean Fox.'

'Yes.'

'He was found hanging from a tree.'

'I'd heard he committed suicide.'

'He didn't commit suicide. He was murdered.'

Petra's defensive stance shattered. Honey judged that the moment would only be short-lived and jumped in.

'Excuse me,' she said, 'but who was that gentleman who left here just before we arrived?'

'A friend,' Petra stuttered. 'Just a friend.'

Seeing where this was going, Doherty picked up the baton. 'How about a name?'

She tossed her head nonchalantly, back in control, defensive stance firmly in place. Her eyes blazing in an attempt to stare him down. 'He was just a friend.'

Doherty was persistent. 'Then perhaps you would give me his name.'

Her jaw moved. She was grinding her teeth.

'Gabriel Forbes. He's been asking questions too. The man's obsessed. Thinks his wife is having affairs. The bloody woman should have one. More than one. She can't even go off to paint a watercolour without him having her followed.'

CHAPTER THIRTY-THREE

On the drive back Honey tried to work through the puzzle of how all these people were interlinked. She remained thoughtful for too long.

Their sudden braking heralded an abrupt standstill in a handy lay-by.

'OK. What gives?'

The engine was off. The hood was down. She felt the questioning look in his eyes even before she turned to face him.

'That man. Gabriel Forbes. Sofia's husband. I've seen him before. He was in JR's Bookshop.'

'Your friend's place. John, isn't it?'

The fact that he'd referred to John as her friend came as something of a surprise. She'd always played it so cool on that front.

She nodded. 'I saw him there.'

'Does he have any bearing on the case?'

She chewed her bottom lip a little. 'Only with regard to John and Adam Rolfe being old friends. That's the only connection. But that doesn't matter now, does it? Adam is off the hook.'

Doherty reached a hand around her neck and stroked it. 'Honey. There's something important that we have to do.'

Convinced he was going to ask her about her relationship with John, her heart went racing, leaping over five-foot fences.

'What's that?' she said after a good swallow.

'We have to find Arabella's phone. Whoever phoned her knows who murdered her.'

'Or did murder her?'

'Correct.'

'And Sean Fox?'

He frowned. 'I'm not sure how he fits in with things, but I'm certain he does.'

* * *

The tickets for a live recording of the programme, *Past Lives and Prophesies*, came as a complete surprise. The compliment slip was from Faith Page.

'I think you will find the production extremely enlightening.'

Two tickets. Honey flicked them against her chin. Steve Doherty needed to be told this. She rang but was told by a female officer that he was unavailable.

'He's been called out to an incident.'

'What sort of incident?'

The female officer at the other end of the phone was far from forthcoming.

'A very serious incident. That's all the information I'm prepared to give you.'

Raising her gaze from the tickets brought her into eye contact with Mary Jane.

'Care to see a paranormal television programme being made?'

'Is it in Chinese?'

Honey frowned. A straight yes or no would have been preferable. She gave the tickets the once-over. Nowhere did it say anything about the programme being in Chinese.

'No . . .' she said, shaking her head. 'Not according to the tickets.'

'Great. I had this dream last night, and some details of it have stayed with me. This Chinese guy in particular. He wore a green silk jacket with a lot of embroidery and a little black hat. And he had a long pigtail. Old-fashioned I know. Pigtail hairdos went out with the death of the last Chinese emperor. Say, do we need to take a bite to eat?'

'It doesn't say so.'

Mary Jane closed one eye, the other one squinting thoughtfully. 'I'll take some rice cakes and a tub of humus just in case. Can't have the spirits coming through and finding me with an empty stomach. My stomach makes angry noises when I'm hungry and it upsets my concentration.'

Honey gave the production company a ring. 'I'm working with the police on the murder of Arabella Rolfe, or Neville to use her professional name. I understand that quite a few of the production team had worked with her on the first programme of the series. Would it be OK if I talked to them?'

The person she was speaking to asked her to wait while she checked. 'Greensleeves' played as she waited — the tune made her eyelids turn heavy.

The response was snappy. 'Yes. You may ask questions.'

'Great.'

The spokesperson went on, 'Though only about Arabella Rolfe of the people who knew her, NOT, repeat, NOT about the private lives of any of the psychics taking part.'

Honey made a promise that she would stick to the point.

Mary Jane was bubbling with excitement. 'So where's the party? The programme's always made outside. Where is it?'

Again, Honey reviewed the card. 'Bulwark Castle. Can't say I know it.'

'Wow!' exclaimed Mary Jane, her face pink with enthusiasm. 'Wow and wow again. Bulwark Castle! It's only the most haunted castle in the country. I'll wear my best for that one. Sure as hell I will.'

* * *

227

'You'll love it,' said Lindsey when her mother told her about the two tickets. 'Who's going with you?'

'Mary Jane.'

Lindsey sniggered. 'Oh dear.'

'Lindsey . . .'

Her daughter's grin was wide enough to crack her face. She made an attempt to be serious.

'You'll love it. Of course you'll love it.'

Honey pointed an accusing finger. 'One of these days I'll come back and haunt you.'

Heaven knows where the notion came from, but Honey couldn't help thinking that Mary Jane's car ran on autopilot like an aircraft or a boat. Mary Jane drove her car as though it had eyes and could think for itself. On the whole, Honey hoped that it did. It made her feel safer thinking that.

Honey hung on, knuckles white and totally unable to take her eyes from the road figuring she might as well face her fate head-on. What will be will be — especially when Mary Jane was in the driving seat.

Her only consolation was that she was a passenger rather than a pedestrian. Bunches of innocent tourists dived for cover. The elderly found a greater spring in their step than they'd had for years, and persistent jaywalkers gained the kerb in double quick time once they realised the pink Cadillac Coupe was as brazen as they were.

Mary Jane was talking excitedly about being on the set of *Past Lives and Prophesies*.

'I hope it's good. None of this pseudo mumbo-jumbo. It has to be the real thing.'

She went on to describe the downfalls of some programme she'd watched on TV the night before.

'I'm going to give that cable TV station a ring and give them a piece of my mind. Hell, some facts were just not true. There is no such thing as death. Any medium worth their salt knows that.'

'Good to know,' said Honey.

Mary Jane's pronouncement was reassuring seeing as they were diving into gaps in the traffic too small for a Mini, let alone a Cadillac Coupe. Luckily the tyres screeched at their approach so nobody got killed, not today anyway.

But something was bound to give.

'I need a coffee,' said Honey. 'How about we have a coffee break? We're not far from the Mall. We can go there.'

Mary Jane was all for it. 'Sure. A little comfort break wouldn't hurt before we get to the shoot.'

They had to be there on the set at four; there was just enough time.

As they swerved into the Mall's copious car park, Honey squeezed her eyes shut, half opening them as they finally screeched into a parking place, where something dull red in colour caught her eye.

'You've run over a carpet,' she said.

Mary Jane was instantly impressed. 'Gee! Isn't that the height of luxury? Carpeting a parking spot!'

Honey looked around them. All the other parking spots were plain concrete, not a carpet in sight.

'Only this one, I think,' she said feeling distinctly uneasy, after all, nobody placed a carpet on the ground for no reason.

Out of the corner of her eye, she spotted a man wearing a long white robe. He was jumping up and down, waving his arms and shouting in.

'Look what you have done, you stupid woman! My prayer rug! You've run over my prayer rug!'

Glad for the respite from Mary Jane's driving, Honey was willing to face anything.

'I'm not the driver.' She pointed at Mary Jane. 'She is.'

Mary Jane towered over the man. He looked up at her.

'Well that's a pretty stupid place to put a prayer rug,' said the septuagenarian Californian. 'Isn't there somewhere else you could take it?'

The man's eyes were blazing. 'I am at work!'

'So why not pray indoors? What if it rains?'

Mary Jane was nothing if not persistent when it came to matters of religious or spiritual trivia.

'I cannot pray indoors. When I face east indoors in the staff canteen I am facing the men's lavatories. That would be disrespectful to Allah. When it rains, I use an umbrella, *and* I have a plastic rain mac,' he added. 'Look.'

They looked. The clearness of the plastic was scattered with bright pink sunflowers with impossibly lime green leaves.

'Nice mac,' said Mary Jane, instantly smitten by her favourite colour combination. 'Did you buy it at John Lewis?'

More calmly now though somewhat surprised at her interest in his mac, he shook his head. 'No. My brother-in-law owns an import/export warehouse. He gives me a very good discount. Can I get one for you? Orders taken.' He got out a small notepad and stubby pencil. 'I have many satisfied customers.' He held up his hand as a woman wearing the navy-blue uniform of a famous chain store beneath a see-through plastic raincoat covered in multi-coloured butterflies hurried past.

They declined his offer but said they would no doubt run into him again.

'I know her,' said Mary Jane, her eyes following the lady. 'I've seen her somewhere before, though I'm jiggered if I can remember where it was.'

Mary Jane had a habit of making the acquaintance of people in passing, so Honey took little notice. Besides, she needed a coffee fix.

'Let's give the man his carpet back.'

CHAPTER THIRTY-FOUR

Doherty's call came through just as they were crossing the Severn Bridge.

She explained where they were going and asked him what he wanted.

'I've got something for you,' he said. 'An update. We've fished Arabella's phone out of the river. It was a massive stroke of luck. The weir was being cleaned. The cleaners use nets on the end of poles — like kids who are looking for tadpoles. In their case, amongst other things they came up with Arabella's phone. It was in its own case and had her name inside.'

'Correct me if I'm wrong, but will it need drying out before you have the last number that called her?'

'I will not correct you. You're not wrong!'

'So where are you right now?' she asked him.

'Not far from you,' he said grimly. 'I'll be in touch.'

* * *

A dead man had been found in a truck belonging to the Welsh National Opera. His wallet had revealed his identify. It was Adam Rolfe.

The truck was parked in a lay-by close to Chepstow, a border town, respectable and long colonised from just over the border by upmarket English.

'Once the scenery has been unloaded, we leave the back of the trailer open to advertise the fact.'

Doherty nodded. Leaving the back doors open was common practice. It saved the thieves wasting their time and big repair bills as a result of forced entry.

'Glad we've got a confirmed identification,' said Detective Inspector Emlyn Morgan, who had come up from Cardiff. Doherty himself had identified the body. He did this after he'd arranged for someone from Manvers Street to call in and inform the first Mrs Rolfe that her ex-husband was dead.

'Ask her about her alibi. Ask her if she was telling the truth.'

Now he was there, near Chepstow, taking a look at the scene of the crime.

Apparently, it was a regular occurrence for two of the Welsh National Opera trucks to park in the lay-by overnight on their way back from London.

'Glad you sent for me.'

'No problem. The driver is pretty sure that the body wasn't there before he went to sleep. They were late leaving London last night and too tired to go on. He found the victim at around eight this morning. Gave the poor man quite a fright.'

'Cause of death?'

'Multiple lesions and bruises, plus one big lump on the back of the head. It looks as though he was knocked unconscious first, then run over a few times. Not here though on the main road. From the looks of it, it was done up in the forest somewhere. There's plenty of forest round here.'

* * *

The fine afternoon was turning into evening. It began to rain.

Not good. Driving in the dry with Mary Jane was bad enough. Driving in the wet was much worse.

Just before leaving the Mall, she'd phoned Lindsey.

'If I'm not back by midnight, my last will and testament is in the safe underneath the *I Love Chocolate* annual.'

Lindsey informed her that Alistair from the auction rooms had popped in and asked that she gave him a call.

'Auction of ladies' personal items on the twentieth. I thought you might be interested.'

Alistair sometimes excited the female bidders at auction by appearing in his kilt, so much so that the firm he worked for actually encouraged him to wear it. Not so much on aesthetic grounds, but it seemed that bids — from the female clientele — went twenty per cent higher when he did. They put this down to them losing their concentration, allowing themselves to get carried away in the bidding due to the sight of Alistair's muscular calves.

Honey took on board what he told her. There was a very nice flapper corset from the twenties. It had a flat front and straps at the back, designed to flatten the bust. Added to that was a single lot of nylon pants from the late fifties and early sixties. Luminous, was how the auction house described the colours. It occurred to Honey that Mary Jane would probably have worn the same colours in her youth.

'Not for me,' said Honey with regard to the multi-coloured panties.

'How about the Brigitte Bardot pink gingham bikini and the generously proportioned brassiere, à la Jane Russell,' asked Alistair? 'Or the rubber roll-on from the fifties?'

'My mother used to wear a thing like that. She reckoned that putting it on was like giving birth, and taking it off was like peeling a superglued banana. Terrible things.'

'Talcum powder. That's what she should have used. Talcum powder,' said Alistair wisely.

Honey opened her mouth, about to ask how come he knew that. Then she thought of his kilt and decided not to go there.

CHAPTER THIRTY-FIVE

Bulwark Castle dominated a cliff overlooking the river. It only took forty minutes to get there, though it seemed like a lot longer.

Honey spotted someone she knew from the Bath Film and Television unit. She waved.

Crispin was in his mid-twenties, had patrician good looks, and spoke with languid confidence as though everything in the world was his for the asking. With his money it possibly was.

'Honey! Darling!' She got the air sucked from around each ear and his goatee beard — no more than a thin line on his chin — tickled.

'How's Lindsey?'

'Fine.' She gave him a big hug. 'If she'd known you were here, she might have come too.'

'Never mind, Honey darling. Give her my love. Just for the record I'm now in a steady relationship. His name's Cecil.'

He did a little finger wave to a black guy with an ear piercing standing nearby.

Shame, she thought. She'd had hopes for him and Lindsey at one time. Crispin had a title. Her mother would have been well pleased, strutting around the Senior Citizens Club like a dowager duchess.

Honey explained to him why she was there.

'Crime Liaison Officer! Well, holy cheesecakes. Lindsey's mum is a private detective.'

'Well, not exactly . . .'

'Oh come on. Don't be bashful. And let me help you in this. I'll fix things up with the team with regards to your asking them questions.'

'Only those who were there that night.'

'Absolutely, dahling. In the meantime, you must come to the front. You'll be able to see and hear better what's going on. Your friend can come too.'

'Everyone to the castle,' shouted one of the TV team. 'Be warned, the rain is likely to get heavier. Umbrellas would be useful.'

In a wafer-thin crocodile, they wound out of the hall in which they'd been gathered, and across the road into the car park of Bulwark Castle.

The old battlements were silhouetted black against the lead-grey sky.

'That old place has got a host of stories to tell,' muttered Mary Jane. 'Did I tell you that it's the most haunted castle in the country?'

'You did.'

Was she hallucinating or were the VIPs taking part — the Very Irritating Psychics — all wearing plastic raincoats with brightly coloured motifs?

She nudged Mary Jane. 'Look at what they're wearing. I bet they were all at the Mall before driving here and all bought raincoats. I bet that guy keeps a secret stash there.'

Mary Jane was struggling to get her umbrella up but managed to cast a glance in their direction.

'Darn it. We should have bought some, though he might have charged us over the rate seeing as I ran over his carpet.'

Honey asked Crispin. 'How come the psychic team are all wearing the same raincoats?'

'Honey, darling, there's nothing sinister in that. The production company probably sent somebody to the Mall to buy wet-weather gear.'

'And met the same guy we did,' said Mary Jane.

'But didn't run over his prayer mat.'

A person with blue-black hair sidled over from out of the crowd.

'I saw you at the Mall. You were talking to Ahmed.'

Honey recognised the woman who had hurried past them in the carpark.

'You are interested in the occult?' she addressed Mary Jane.

Obviously she can tell that I'm a trifle on the sceptical side, thought Honey.

'Of course,' said Mary Jane, 'though I prefer to think of it as communication.'

'We *have* met before,' she heard the girl say. 'At the ghost tour.'

Nobody could fail to forget someone who dressed like Mary Jane.

Snapping her umbrella into up mode, Mary Jane narrowed her eyes and took a good look at the psychics who would be appearing on programme.

'Well,' she said. 'Will you just look at that! Four of a kind, and I don't mean a good hand in poker. They're all members of the Midas Circle. Why am I not surprised that they're all appearing on the same programme at the same time?'

Honey shook her head. 'What, when it's at home, is the Midas Circle?'

While production staff shepherded them into position — ghost hunters beneath the postern gate, audience corralled in the open — Mary Jane explained.

'Haven't you ever watched *Ghost in the Pantry*? *Come Haunt with Me*? Or read *Arm Yourself to Ghost Hunt*?'

Honey shook her head to each one. 'You're telling me this Midas Circle is about ghost hunting?'

Mary Jane's eyes usually sparkled when she smiled. On this occasion they did not. Her smile had meaning, mostly disapproval.

'From what I hear, the Midas Circle are not professionals. They've gone commercial; their aim is to further their careers. There are about eight of them in all. When a TV programme on haunting or other paranormal stuff is scheduled, the Midas Circle is in there. One gets offered a role and if more psychics are needed, that one recommends another member of the circle. They keep the goodies in the family so to speak.'

'Ah! I see,' said Honey, nodding as the idea took hold. She managed to waylay a member of the production team. 'Excuse me. Who is actually presenting this programme?'

'Arthur King,' said the gum-chewing girl. 'He stepped in at the last minute after Arabella Rolfe died.'

'How sad.' Honey adopted a suitably sad expression.

The girl's face seemed to freeze. 'For some it was.'

'Are you Denise Sullivan?'

The girl had been about to move on but stalled when asked the question.

'Yes. I am. How did you know?'

'I understand you got on with her pretty well, that you were close in fact.'

The girl hesitated to answer. 'You're with the police, aren't you?'

'Yes. Liaison Officer.'

Honey was purposely oblique, not wanting any probing as to her official capacity.

There was just a beat of hesitation before she answered. 'I did for a time, but then, you find people out don't you.'

When Denise looked at her straight on in a good light, the truth hit her.

She recalled the perfect features looking out from photographs of the dead diva. The resemblance was too striking to ignore.

'Would I be right in guessing that Arabella was your mother?'

The girl's face froze beneath her rain-soaked hood. 'Who told you that?'

'Arabella — in a manner of speaking. Your real name's Dwyer, isn't it?'

'None of your business.' Even beneath the shadow of her rain hood, Honey could see the sudden taut expression.

'I understand she insisted you keep it a secret from everyone.'

'She insisted on keeping it a big secret even after we found out from our grandmother.'

'Your grandparents kept it from you?'

She nodded. 'Arabella tried to make amends by getting us a job with this production company. Both of us had a degree in media studies and both of us had worked in production before, so it was no big deal.'

'So she did you some good. I mean, she did care.'

'Hmph! Not enough to let it affect her career or how people perceived her. She'd done enough damage herself in that direction. That's what she told me.'

'Well, she had,' said Honey. 'There was a lot of bad publicity over her affair and marriage to Adam Rolfe.'

'Of course there was. Sad Sam, he was. Never knew the truth until I told him who our mother really was.'

'*You* told him?' This was news.

'After I heard that Sean had killed himself, yes.'

'So despite the different names, Sean was your brother.'

'Fox was his professional name. Sullivan was mine. Arabella thought it best that we didn't disclose that we were brother and sister.'

A chill fear was creeping from the base of Honey's spine, slowly meandering like a snake climbing a tree.

'So what did Adam say?'

'I didn't tell him then and there. A while back I left a message to meet him on the day we started setting up for filming here. There's a little spot in the forest I know called Whitestone. I said I would meet him there, but . . .' she shrugged. 'He never turned up.'

'Denise, darling! We're waiting for you.' Someone on the other side of the lighting equipment was waving her over.

Denise called back that she would be just a minute. She turned back to Honey.

'And before you ask, I won't miss my mother, purely because I never really knew her.'

Denise moved off through those assembled to form an audience toward the gateway and the stars of the show. One man stood out from the others. He was not just tall, he was imposing. Wearing a rain-soaked Barbour jacket with corduroy collar and cuffs, he had what those in the world of showbiz called presence. Even his peers, those he was appearing with, seemed to give way to his superiority, hovering around him like sparrows around a peacock.

'Who is that?' she whispered to Mary Jane.

'Arthur King,' said her companion and narrowed her eyes. 'He's got charisma, but I'm not sure he's got the gift,' she added, shaking her head.

Lifting her collar against the pouring rain, Honey fixed her attention on what was happening beneath the arched gateway. The four psychics were going through their spiel as avidly as actors in a Victorian melodrama.

Each one commented on what they were feeling, though none sounded so believable as Arthur King. Honey found herself spellbound at the sound of his voice, the hypnotic eyes. The man was mesmerising, so scary, she got to the point of being scared to look round — just in case the ghouls and ghosties were erupting like ragwort from the crevices, the lopsided doorways, the eerily dark battlements.

He was now reaching his crescendo. 'I feel, I see the evil that happened here, the killings, the betrayals, the passion of lovers, the jealousy of those rejected . . .'

Mary Jane broke the spell. 'Rubbish. All that was here was lukewarm soup!'

Soup? Honey was jerked out of her inertia. Where had that comment come from?

'Soup. I can smell it,' said Mary Jane. 'Lukewarm soup. Gruel more like; made of barley with bits of cabbage stalk floating round in it. And a bit of rabbit. The innards mostly. That's all that's here. That's all that went on around this gate; cooking. Just cooking.'

'I should have known,' Honey murmured under her breath. 'If you want a genuine psychic to give you a reading, bring one with you.'

'Cut!'

There were plenty of cuts and breaks to allow the cameras to be reset, the sound man to get his equipment in order, and the psychics to re-energise their batteries. It was during one of these that Honey approached Crispin.

'I believe Arabella was scheduled to present this programme before she was killed?'

He nodded. 'True. And Petra couldn't make it either. She's having an operation on an ingrown toenail, of all things. We were lucky to get Arthur offering to stand in at such late notice.'

The inverted toenail thing came as something of a surprise. Petra had been barefooted when she'd seen her last and her painted toenails had looked quite — well — stunning.

Her eyes went back to Arthur King. At first sight the name seemed incongruous — too old for the man standing there, holding the attention of every woman in the audience. Until she considered. *King Arthur!* Got it.

'And I'm Guinevere,' she muttered before asking Crispin another question.

'Can I ask you, did they know each other very well — Arthur and Arabella?'

'Arabella knew them all. She was into that sort of thing, supernatural stuff, that's why she suited the show. She didn't fake her responses. She was well up for it. I think Arthur might have had something to do with that. She followed his predictions and conclusions with great gusto. I think he was the only one she truly believed was gifted.'

In more ways than one, thought Honey. So there it was, staring her in the face. Arabella had gone storming off the set following a partial shoot and a phone call.

'I hear she stormed off the set just before she was murdered,' she said.

Crispin acknowledged that that had indeed been the case. 'She'd had her own facilities at the Greyhound Inn, the haunted hostelry we were using that night.'

Honey's eyes were on Arthur King when she asked the next question.

'Did she and Arthur have rooms next to each other?'

Crispin frowned. 'I believe so. I think she'd insisted that they did. Hang on. I'll check with Cecil.'

He waved a come-over signal to his partner.

It seemed to take the long-legged man only six strides to be with them, though in reality it had to be more. Crispin asked him to confirm what he'd just said.

'Absolutely,' said Cecil, in a deep calm voice. 'Arabella insisted, though I must admit Arthur was taken back a little. I think Arabella had the hots for him.'

Honey was straight in there. 'And did he have the hots for her?'

Cecil placed one elegant hand on an equally elegant hip and shook his head.

'Not one iota. Arthur likes them young. The younger the better, though he's not a cradle snatcher, mark you. He just doesn't go for women closer to his own age. Denise was about as old as it gets.'

Honey could feel herself going cold, her teeth on edge as a hideous truth presented itself. Arabella Neville had been dressed to the nines because she'd made a play for Arthur King. King had rejected her. Not only that he'd probably put it plain; she was too old for him. She was married.

As Mary Jane had intimated, Arthur's supernatural pronouncements were total tosh. He was concocting a story, telling lies as easily as some tell the truth. At the same time, he had done his homework, researched into some of the old legends surrounding the place. Later on in the programme he would select a member of the audience and give them some facts about their own lives, their own ancestors. This would take the form of somebody local. The truth was that previous to the programme he'd been given a list of names and addresses. From that list he'd selected a few likely options, gone online, phoned neighbours, family and friends, and listed the bits of information in a believable order. Arthur King was thorough. He was now also her main interest regarding the death of Arabella Neville.

She looked up at Crispin. 'I have to speak to that man. Now.'

Without waiting for his response, she pushed her way through the crowd, Crispin and Mary Jane following close behind. Mary Jane was muttering the word charlatan under her breath.

Honey tapped Arthur King on the shoulder. 'Excuse me.'

He looked down at her. She couldn't help the butterflies in her stomach. He was the sort who can make your toes curl up with one flash of his eyes. His eyes, she noticed, were dark blue; deep pools of intensity.

His smile and the smooth, gentlemanly way he took her hand were designed to make her go weak at the knees. 'Let me see. Are you Angharad Jones?'

Honey gathered herself in, stopped the toe-curling and concentrated.

'No. I'm Honey Driver and I work with the police. We're currently investigating the murder of Arabella Neville. Can you tell me what happened on the night Arabella stormed off the set?'

To his credit, Arthur King didn't bat an eyelid. Neither did his face freeze as most folks do when they're being asked a leading question.

'I understand you had rooms next to each other.'

His smile went from oily to wet cement in the process of setting.

'We did. Both had stout locks on the doors. Arabella was a married woman. And before you ask, nothing untoward was going on between us. We worked together. That's all.'

Out of the corner of her eye, she saw someone move. Denise Sullivan had thrown her hood back. Her eyes were on Arthur at first, then they switched to Honey, though only briefly. That look said everything. Crispin had said that Arthur liked them younger.

'My mother was out of order,' Denise cut in. 'But she couldn't help it. She didn't know about Artie and me.'

'Denise, Denise! You don't need to say anything.' Arthur rolled his eyes skywards.

'Yes, I do, Artie.' Her eyes swept back to Honey. 'Artie . . . Arthur had nothing to do with it.'

'Denise! There's no need to go on. There's a good girl.' Arthur King's smooth veneer had faltered a little, but his voice was still like molasses.

To Honey's ears, he sounded like a loving father chastising his beloved daughter. Despite that, it was pretty obvious that Arthur didn't like what Denise was saying. He turned to Crispin who was looking totally dumbfounded. 'Crispin. My audience is close at hand. A little privacy wouldn't come amiss.'

It seemed to Honey that even Crispin was not immune to Arthur King's charm. On the other hand that was part of his job — keeping the stars happy.

Crispin was all waving arms and avid attention. 'Certainly! Certainly!'

He ushered them to a stone-clad alcove that at some time might have been a guardroom beside the turnstile where the paying public entered. Behind it was a shop with a counter which had a huge mirror behind it. Their reflections were mainly wet and soggy with the exception of Arthur King's, as he had been furnished with a golfing umbrella, courtesy of Marriott Hotels.

Limp with apologies, Crispin attempted to make amends. 'Arthur, I am so . . .'

'Of course you are. That's your job.' The timbre of Arthur King's voice had a voluptuous resonance. Crispin was positively grovelling but knew when he'd been dismissed.

Mary Jane left too. 'I can't abide the company,' she growled. The mean look was for Arthur King.

Denise Sullivan, on the other hand, looked up at him adoringly. 'He told my mother how it was. That she wasn't in with a chance. That Artie and I . . .'

'Are very good friends,' said Arthur, his eyes deeply penetrating, almost as though he were willing Honey to believe anything and everything he said. 'I told Arabella that my relationship with her could only ever be professional. I'm afraid she'd arranged for a romantic dinner to be delivered for the two of us in one of our rooms. I told her how it was. Denise overheard and confirmed the relationship between us. Arabella was like a latter-day Queen Victoria, I'm afraid. She was most definitely not amused.'

The truth had finally been laid bare. Honey felt for the girl; felt for the mother too. This case was not so simple as husband kills wife. That's how it was in families. Nothing was ever straightforward or happy ever after.

'So she stormed off, upset that her daughter had upstaged her — or that as a mother she disapproved of her daughter's choice of man,' stated Honey as the truth was finally laid bare.

Arthur tossed his head dramatically. 'Before you ask why we didn't report any of this to the police, we didn't think it had any bearing on the case.'

'Besides, we didn't want to get involved,' said Denise.

'And the handbag?'

Denise frowned. 'What you mean?'

'Your mother had details of her contacts and possible contracts in a notebook. She left it here when she stormed off. Whoever kept it phoned the production company, got in touch with the right people. You had that book, Arthur, and when it became obvious they wanted a female presenter, you put Petra Deacon forward for the job knowing you'd get to be the numero uno psychic star . . . Right?'

'Yes. I did.'

Denise gasped and looked up at him. There was surprise on her face, but as yet she was still enamoured, though not, thought Honey, for long.

'I don't believe it,' she said coldly.

Arthur looked down at her, one eyebrow slightly raised.

'One must grasp opportunity when opportunity raises its head. My timing was perfect. Arabella had a reputation for throwing tantrums. She'd thrown one too many. So I saw my chance and took it.'

'Ah,' said Honey. 'Isn't that just what the Midas Club is all about?'

Arthur nodded, his smile triumphant now.

A small frown had appeared on Denise's forehead.

'How did you find out that Arabella was your mother?' Honey asked Denise.

Denise hugged herself and her voice went quiet. 'We've always known. We used to watch her on television when we were children. Our grandmother wouldn't allow us to visit her.'

'Your grandmother Dwyer brought you up?'

Denise nodded, her eyes alternating between being downcast and gazing at Arthur King.

'She blamed her for our father's death. She took us away from our mother. It was supposed to be punishment for what she'd done. It never occurred to our grandmother that we were the ones being punished. We lost touch with her.'

There was no point in asking what the hold was that Grandmother Dwyer had had over the girl who used to be Tracey Casey. Rumour had it that Arabella's father had done the dirty deed. The grandparents had had their reasons. If Tracey — Arabella — had fought to get her children back, her father would have ended up in prison where he would likely have died.

Arthur King scrutinised his watch. 'Right. We're due to restart. Do excuse us.'

Denise, the director's assistant, trailed out behind Arthur King, the star of the show. Honey wondered just how long the relationship would last. How long would it be before Denise saw through his handsome persona to what lay beneath?

Having been a hotelier for a number of years, Honey had met plenty of liars, including people who could tell lies as if they were the truth. Up close and personal, Arthur King was one of those people.

'The police will be in touch,' Honey called after them.

* * *

She looked around the shop. There was the usual stuff you might find in a tourist store, though being a castle some were a little different than others. Even though they were plastic, daggers, swords and maces were safely ensconced in glass cabinets. Not that she was really taking them in. Her mind was with Arabella's chaotic family history.

Once outside she filtered through the audience who were still milling around, waiting for the action to recommence.

Mary Jane was still conversing with the woman they'd met at the Mall.

Honey grabbed her attention. 'I'm going outside. I need some air and I need to phone Doherty.'

CHAPTER THIRTY-SIX

Cold air blew through the archway where an iron portcullis had once secured the keep against the enemy. The rain was coming down in sheets, the light flooding out from behind her turning it silver.

Halfway through the archway she tried her phone. Nothing happened. On reaching the other side, the tried again. The screen stayed blank. The battery had gone flat. She swore under her breath.

On the other side outside the dark archway, the cobbled driveway shone like molten blobs of metal. A few technicians were huddled around their vans, disappearing into the open doors at the back of the vehicles when they'd done what had to be done.

'I wanted to speak to you.'

The sudden voice made her start. To her right a large woman in a billowing raincoat stood with one hand in her pocket, the other holding a lit cigarette.

Honey recognised Faith Page, Arabella's agent.

Faith looked at her through eyes narrowed against the rain.

Honey pretended she hadn't been startled and said, 'I guessed there had to be some reason for sending me those tickets.' She sounded brave even if she didn't feel it.

Faith's expression stayed stony and wet, rain trickling from her bare head and down her face.

'Stupid cow,' she spat. 'She thought she could do better by herself. New agent. New man in her life. It didn't work out. She really blew it.'

Faith turned abruptly away.

'Blew it? Why do you say that, Faith? Why do you say that she blew it?'

Flicking the still lighted cigarette into the grass, Faith strode away into the rain and the darkness.

Honey followed.

The path was slippery and ran high above grass-covered embankments. The rain was relentless. Eventually the path terminated against a flying buttress. It was a case of go back, stop or slide, down the slippery grass of the embankment. Faith Page stopped where she was and watched as Honey approached.

'Cigarette?' She offered an opened packet.

Honey declined. 'I don't smoke.'

Faith lit herself a cigarette, cupping the lighter's flame against the driving rain.

'Nasty day,' she said, blowing out a plume of smoke.

'What is it you want to tell me?'

Water dripped from around the brim of Faith's hat. It was leather — Australian drover style. The collar of her coat was turned up around her face.

'What makes you think I have something to tell you?'

Somehow Honey knew that Faith had never quite believed her bullshit story about having a script to sell. If Faith was worth her salt as an agent, she would have done a little background check. Alternatively, being used to working with creative people should have made her more instinctive. In her game it was a definite plus.

Faith looked up from beneath the dripping brim.

'Arabella was a right cow, but there's something going on here that I'm not getting.'

Honey frowned. Droplets of water ran into her eyes. She brushed them aside, swiping at them with the back of her hand.

'In what way?'

'If I knew that, I wouldn't be asking you to help out here, now would I,' snapped Faith.

She flicked her half-smoked cigarette into the wet grass where it fizzed red then died, a single string of smoke trailing into nothing.

Rain had found its way around Honey's collar and was slowing trickling down her back. She wanted to hear what Faith had to say but would have preferred to be in the dry.

'You're leaving me guessing,' she said. 'Let's put it another way. What do *you* think it's about? What's your gut instinct?'

Faith's eyes bored into her. They were piercing eyes, bleary when under the influence, but totally the opposite when she was sober. And she was sober now.

Faith sniffed, then shook the brim of her hat.

'One thing you have to understand about Arabella, she loved fame. Loved her job. OK, she was ambitious and difficult, but she did a good job. She was ideal for presenting this programme and landed it with ease, but . . . she had baggage. She had problems.'

'Did you know she'd set her cap at Arthur King?'

Faith's laugh was hollow. 'She set her aim high, did our Arabella. The silly cow was going to sue her old man for divorce. Thought she could have everything she wanted — her kids, and another man. Arthur is a born charmer and strung her along as long as it suited him. As if Arthur was interested in her! No chance. It came as one hell of a shock when she found out it was her daughter he was interested in, not her.'

'It must have done.'

The whole scenario was looking sadder than ever. Arabella had given the impression that she hated kids. The truth, it seemed, was that having Adam's kids visit must have hit a nerve. She'd ditched her past and everything in it, trying to forge out a new life without her children. She'd had success, but not what she'd really wanted.

Everything suddenly seemed clearer, as if the rain had stopped. On reflection Honey could see it hadn't — it still poured down, the grass was slick and shiny, and both she and Faith Page were soaked through. Yet something had happened here. Something had erupted into the light.

'So she didn't exactly leave the agency?' Honey suggested.

Faith snorted. 'Oh, yes. She did that all right. She told me this was all about new beginnings.'

'She phoned you that night didn't she.'

Faith nodded. 'Yes. I was over in Wales. I lost my phone for a few days. Gordon's fault.'

Honey didn't bother to ask who Gordon was. Gin was Gordon's, wasn't it?

So the phone call Arabella had received was from her husband. The sexy underwear hadn't been for him but in the hope of seducing Arthur King. Arthur had spurned her, so when Adam had asked to meet her, she was still dressed to the nines. Though unplanned, she'd asked him for a divorce. She'd left a message on her agent's lost phone saying as much. At the same time, she'd told him everything there was to tell about her real name, her background, her first husband and her children and then what? Taunted him that, despite everything, her kids were desperate to see her and his son couldn't care less?

'She told him,' she said suddenly. 'Adam. She told him everything and then Denise had told him. He must have been devastated.'

Faith Page stared at her at first, but then her face crumpled and she looked sadder, older than she really was.

'And he killed her. That's what you're surmising. Yes?'

Honey nodded. 'Yes. Imagine how it must have felt. She'd kept him apart from his children and now she was telling him that she'd never told him the truth about herself. What with the affairs as well, it was the last straw. Adam broke.' She turned away, meaning to leave, when a thought came to her.

'Can I borrow your phone?'

Doherty answered almost immediately. 'Where are you?'

She explained about Arabella, that their first guess had been the right one.

The silence on Doherty's part was disturbing.

'What is it? What's happened?'

'Adam Rolfe has been found murdered. We understand from John Rees that he was on his way to where you are.'

'. . . To kill Arthur King.'

'Sounds that way. Seems he was the victim of a hit and run. The driver didn't want him found too quickly, so he left him in the back of an open truck belonging to the Welsh National Opera. We think it happened in the early hours of this morning. Nobody saw anything.'

'The opera singer! The one who thought her husband had hired me to spy on her?'

'What?'

'No,' she said abruptly, shaking her head. 'It had to be a pure hit and run.'

'You're being swayed by the fact that the body was found in the back of a truck belonging to the opera company.'

* * *

Suddenly the phone went dead. Just after it disconnected, it rang again at Doherty's end.

'Honey?'

'No. Sorry to disappoint you. It's Emlyn Morgan. Thought I'd let you know that there's more to Adam Rolfe's murder. My boys found something in the truck that the driver said wasn't there before. We think it may have come off when whoever knocked your boy down heaved him up into the truck. It's a gold bracelet. Judging by the weight and the size it looks to be a man's bracelet. Not something I would wear, but there, takes all sorts though.'

CHAPTER THIRTY-SEVEN

Honey strayed around the castle precincts, the view from the battlements attracting her attention far more than what was happening below in the courtyard.

From the battlements she could see the whole town rising up behind her. Looking directly down she could see the river, meandering past, the tide out now leaving small boats marooned in the mud. By the time she got back down, the programme was over. The audience had long since drifted out of the castle and back to where they'd parked their cars.

Desperate to fill Doherty in on the details, Honey wanted to do the same. Unfortunately, Mary Jane had wandered off.

'Wait a minute. I'm sure the director is still here. I want to ask him what the chances are for a REAL psychic on this production.'

Although there seemed to be few people left, Mary Jane had collared the man inside the gift shop next to the main gate.

She tried looking at her watch, but it was too dark. Mary Jane was not likely to rush things.

Honey shivered. The weather was bad enough; then there was the journey back and Mary Jane's driving. In the hope of warming herself up, she went back into the portcullis arch out of the wind and rain. Mary Jane would have to walk in this direction. Then it was whizzing back to Bath in the car, eyes shut and a few prayers rendered to the gods of reckless driving.

At present her eyes were wide open. Two of the psychics had already passed her without noticing her presence. She thought that odd seeing as they were supposed to be hypersensitive to spirits. Surely that also went for living people too?

Only a few people remained in the castle courtyard. The programme editing crew were already running through the rushes, setting them up for the following day when the serious editing would be done.

Surrounded by darkness, she saw all but nobody saw her. She might as well have been a shadow herself.

Suddenly the beam of car headlights flashed swiftly over the lower half of a ruined turret. There was the soft thudding of a car door.

Fed up with waiting, she headed into the inner courtyard, wondering where the hell Mary Jane had got to. The yard was uncommonly quiet. Everything was dark and nothing was moving. The only place still showing a light was the gift shop and ticket office.

She was within ten yards of the shop door when two hands caught hold of her shoulders.

Her eyes opened wide, though the darkness was so absolute that she couldn't see his face. Not that she needed to.

His voice was instantly recognisable and she felt instantly safe.

'You were right about Adam Rolfe,' said Doherty in a low voice. 'He killed his wife. It must have been one taunt too many from a woman he'd come to hate. Rolfe *was* lying — but only about not knowing about Denise and Sean. I've got to say, it was a great double bluff, confessing like that.

'Susan Rolfe admitted that she'd been deliberately vague about the timings — despite all that happened, she still loved him enough to want to protect him. There was enough time for Adam to have killed Arabella and still got to the bar to meet Susan. She said that "he'd finally come to his senses" and she didn't want to deprive Dominic of his father anymore, so was willing to lie for him.

'And we questioned the barman again — he's only been in the job five minutes and although he remembered serving them, he had no idea what time that was. We also know who killed Adam's stepson, Sean Fox.'

'So if it's all wrapped up, what are you doing here? Wait, who did kill Sean Fox?'

'Adam Rolfe was the victim of a hit and run — or so we thought — until the Gwent police found a large contusion at the back of his neck and a man's gold bracelet beneath his body. It was very distinctive…'

Honey gasped. 'You don't mean? I'll never trust an estate agent again.'

'I didn't think anybody did anyway.' Doherty sounded genuinely surprised.

Honey looked towards the shop. 'He must be in there. It's the only place still lit up. So he's after Arthur King.'

'I think so.'

'Am I right in thinking . . .'

'Sean Fox had to have told him that Arabella had received a phone call that night and suggested it was from her husband.'

'I think Sean also told him about some psychic that Arabella was lusting after . . . so, I assume he killed Sean because he didn't want him telling anyone that he was after Arthur King. Right?'

'We can only assume! His mind was pretty troubled.'

Honey nodded towards the gatehouse shop. 'He's in there. He's got to be still in there. Trouble is, so is Mary Jane. So's the director.'

'Ah-uh.'

'A resume would help put my surmising into some kind of order.'

'OK. Gabriel Forbes warned Glenwood to stop pestering his wife, Sofia Camilleri, the opera singer. We interviewed

Forbes, who also happens to collect rare maps, by the way. He admitted to warning Glenwood off. We have also to assume that our estate agent friend wasn't nearly so obsessed with the diva Camilleri as he was with Arabella.'

'So Glenwood's in there and now we go in and get him.'

'No. I go in and get him. You stay here.'

'No.'

Doherty was a man most women wanted and a lot of men would have liked to be like him. Her mother was a notable exception to this rule, but, boy oh boy, if she could just see him now. There was no hesitation; in he went looking as though he meant business. Honey followed. No way was she going to miss this. If she did, how could she boast of his prowess and spin a long and heroic tale? Or discuss his actions in intimate detail with him while being intimate?

Glenwood Halley was as tall as Arthur King. If Arthur had possessed the same colouring as Glenwood, they would have resembled a pair of bookends.

Arthur was looking unnerved, verging on scared stiff. Their stance was reflected in the mirrored door behind them, the one Honey had noticed earlier. The door was edged with a frame of stained glass depicting medieval figures — the kind you might find in an ancient abbey or church.

Mary Jane was not there. Neither was the director. Honey swallowed. Please, God, don't let her be lying dead behind that shop counter. I'll accept the director being dead, but not Mary Jane.

Glenwood was holding a dagger to Arthur's throat. She guessed it hadn't come out of one of the glass cabinets. And it looked too lethal to be plastic.

There was a wildness in Glenwood's eyes. His skin was slick with sweat. Gone was the Savile Row suit; he was dressed in a black cashmere sweater, chinos and thick-soled deck shoes.

Doherty placed himself in front of her, shielding her without impairing the view.

'Glenwood. What are you doing with that knife?'

'I'm going to kill him. It was his fault. He led her on. She was the star and he destroyed her. He got her killed.'

Doherty spoke firmly and calmly. 'Mr Halley. Glenwood. You don't want to do this. Think now. Think about it carefully.'

His voice made her toes curl but had no effect on Glenwood Halley, who was quite possibly mad.

She thought of the photos of showbiz people on Glenwood's wall. The warning signs had been there, though she'd never really thought them through. How many of them had he become obsessed with? How many had he stalked and been warned off by the likes of Gabriel Forbes?

Doherty was cool, pulling up a chair and placing it between her and the two men who stood as if frozen in action.

He addressed Glenwood. 'So now what? You're going to kill King Arthur here, is that a good idea?'

Glenwood gave a short harsh laugh. 'King Arthur. That's a good one.'

'Bad if he ends up dead.'

'Arabella's death has to be avenged.'

'I thought you'd already done that. You killed her husband, Adam. You arranged to meet him, knocked him to the ground, then ran over him in your car. Then you attempted to hide his body. Were you trying to lay the blame on Sofia Camilleri, aka Forbes, by using the opera van? The opera singer. You stalked her for a while.'

Glenwood was completely unmoved. 'He killed her. It was his fault.'

Doherty sighed heavily. 'Does it really matter?'

Glenwood rounded on him, eyes staring and round. 'To her it does. She counted on me to sort things out for her. I lent her the money for the apartment, the one she'd bought without her husband knowing. I thought it was going to be for us. But it wasn't. It was supposed to be for him and her! Would you credit it? *Him*. That bastard. And Arthur. He just played with her.'

256

Honey thought about Denise. Arthur was a man who liked to play games. She'd seen Denise leaving. She'd been in floods of tears. Had she too been cast aside?

'What about Sean Fox, Glenwood? Why did he have to die?'

Glenwood sneered. 'I knew Sean was her confidante. I knew he'd know all the details. Once I knew them, too, then he had to go. He just had to.'

'Arabella wouldn't thank you for that,' said Honey. 'Sean was her son.'

Doherty had risen to his feet. She felt his hand brush hers and knew he was about to go into action. Someone was going to get hurt. Glenwood Halley was the most likely candidate, Arthur King a close second.

Mention of Sean Fox being Arabella's son seemed to have no effect on Glenwood. Honey guessed that he'd given up listening and was lost in his own little world, one hand gripping the hilt of the dagger, the palm of the other poised over the end of the hilt and about to hit it home.

Suddenly the mirrored door behind them burst open. Glenwood was knocked sideways.

As Glenwood and Doherty grappled, Arthur King — the man who styled himself as a medieval king of wide renown — cowered in the corner.

Seemingly energised by madness, Glenwood was on top of Doherty, trying his best to bring down the top half of a pair of stocks over the policeman's head.

In her search for a weapon, Honey tried undoing the glass cabinets, just in case one of those maces, or a dagger or a sword, wasn't made of plastic. No luck. She looked around for something else.

There was no mace to twirl, though she'd quite hoped there was, it seemed like a fun thing to do. A keen weight hanging on a length of something. She pounced on the credit card machine, pulled it from its socket, wound the wire round her fist, and swung the rest of it above her head.

Thwack! It made a reassuringly crunching sound against Glenwood's head.

Clunk! Then rattle, rattle! The dagger hit the floor.

Doherty pounced, looked in his pocket for handcuffs but found none.

'Drat!'

Honey pointed. 'It's only plastic, but . . .'

Glenwood Halley was fitted into the stocks. Doherty straightened, looking well satisfied despite the intense pain in his back. 'That should keep him until Gwent Police arrive.'

Mary Jane stepped out from the darkness on the other side of the open door.

'Hey! How about that for timing. Good, huh? It's a two-way mirror, you know,' she said, jerking her thumb at the wide-open door. 'Bet that wasn't there in medieval times.'

'It's for shoplifters when staff are out the back,' said Arthur King, his voice shaky but his pride intact. 'They didn't have them back then.'

'True,' said Mary Jane. 'They did disfigurement instead. Chopped bits off so everyone would know a felon when they saw one. Not that they'd have done that to this guy. Hung, drawn and quartered. Which reminds me, I'm hungry. Anyone fancy stopping for a Big Mac on the way home?'

CHAPTER THIRTY-EIGHT

'So I pulled on my fishnet stockings, shoved my feet into my killer heels, and I was ready for action. Can you believe I've already snagged them? Brand new too. You don't suppose I could borrow yours, could I? Plus some sexy underwear to go with it? I favour black but at a push I'll consider scarlet.'

Steve Doherty was a good detective with a reputation for getting results. Tonight he was trying to engage Honey over a good meal and fine wine. He could tell she hadn't heard a word he'd said.

'Honey, what's bugging you?'

Honey was staring over the top of her wine glass which, like the seafood thermidor on the plate in front of her, was barely touched.

Doherty reached across, took the glass from her hand and put it down on the table.

Tonight, he was wearing a black open-necked shirt, black trousers, and black shoes. Black was the colour he favoured. When she'd pointed it out to him he said that wearing one colour meant he didn't have to make big wardrobe choices. Black matched black, though he also favoured navy blue.

'Arabella Rolfe left her estate to her children and Adam's children. Did I tell you that?'

259

She shook her head. 'No.' Her attention was still elsewhere.

'Happy families. Is there any such thing? I mean, we really don't know what happens behind closed doors, do we?'

'Grandparents, parents, and kids; we don't choose any of them.'

Doherty frowned and wondered what the hell she was talking about. His eyes flickered between her face and the scene beyond her left shoulder.

'Am I seeing what I think I'm seeing?'

Honey nodded. Her mother was also dining out tonight.

'So who's the man?' Doherty asked.

'Wilbur Williams, and he's looking for a bride.'

Doherty peered beyond her shoulder, ducking down before her mother could see him. 'Has she seen us?'

'No. Her attention is on Wilbur.'

'Have you told her about us?'

'Until I'm blue in the face. I've told you before, my mother has her own views as to who's the man for me.' She patted his arm. 'Leave it with me, darling. It'll all come out in the wash!'

Doherty caught hold of her left hand, examining it closely, especially her ring finger and the sapphire and diamonds of the ring he'd bought her.

He sighed. 'I hope it's enough for you.'

'Enough? Why shouldn't it be enough?' She eyed him quizzically, a slight smile curving her lips.

He shrugged. 'You could have bought a country hotel. You could have acted like lady of the manor. Have you definitely changed your mind?'

'Yes,' she said, nodding emphatically. 'I knew you wouldn't be keen to leave your job right away. I worked out how many nights we'd sleep together — even when we were married — you working in the city and me in the country. I didn't like the sums.'

'How many?'

'Three times.'

'A week? That's not so bad.'

She shook her head. 'A month.'

260

Doherty shook himself. 'No way! So what's going to happen to Cobden Manor?'

'I've no idea. Rumours abound. A school, a hotel, health spa or even an old peoples' home.'

Doherty glanced past her again. Gloria Cross was in deep conversation with the man sitting opposite her.

'No,' said Honey reading his mind. 'My mother won't be going there. Though there is the chance that she might get married long before we do.'

THE END

ALSO BY JEAN G. GOODHIND

HONEY DRIVER MYSTERY SERIES
Book 1: MURDER, BED & BREAKFAST
Book 2: MENU FOR MURDER
Book 3: WALKING WITH MURDER
Book 4: THE JANE AUSTEN MURDERS
Book 5: MURDER BY LAMPSHADE
Book 6: MURDER BY MUDPACK
Book 7: MURDER AT THE ROMAN BATHS
Book 8: MURDER FOR CHRISTMAS
Book 9: MURDER AT THE MANOR HOUSE

Thank you for reading this book.

If you enjoyed it please leave feedback on Amazon or Goodreads, and if there is anything we missed or you have a question about, then please get in touch. We appreciate you choosing our book.

Founded in 2014 in Shoreditch, London, we at Joffe Books pride ourselves on our history of innovative publishing. We were thrilled to be shortlisted for Independent Publisher of the Year at the British Book Awards.

www.joffebooks.com

We're very grateful to eagle-eyed readers who take the time to contact us. Please send any errors you find to corrections@joffebooks.com. We'll get them fixed ASAP.

Printed in the USA
CPSIA information can be obtained
at www.ICGtesting.com
LVHW091636140923
758243LV00027B/239

9 781804 055984